REBELLION

DRAGONBORN, BOOK 4

BRETT HUMPHREY

Print ISBN13: 978-1-73411-767-7
eBook ISBN13: 978-1-73411-766-0

Published by Brett Humphrey
2487 S. Gilbert Rd.
Ste. 106-105
Gilbert, AZ 85295

To Jennifer, my biggest fan and supporter.
Thank you for being on the adventure with me.

To those who love to read, we can change the world if we choose to
positively impact people we come into
contact with each day.

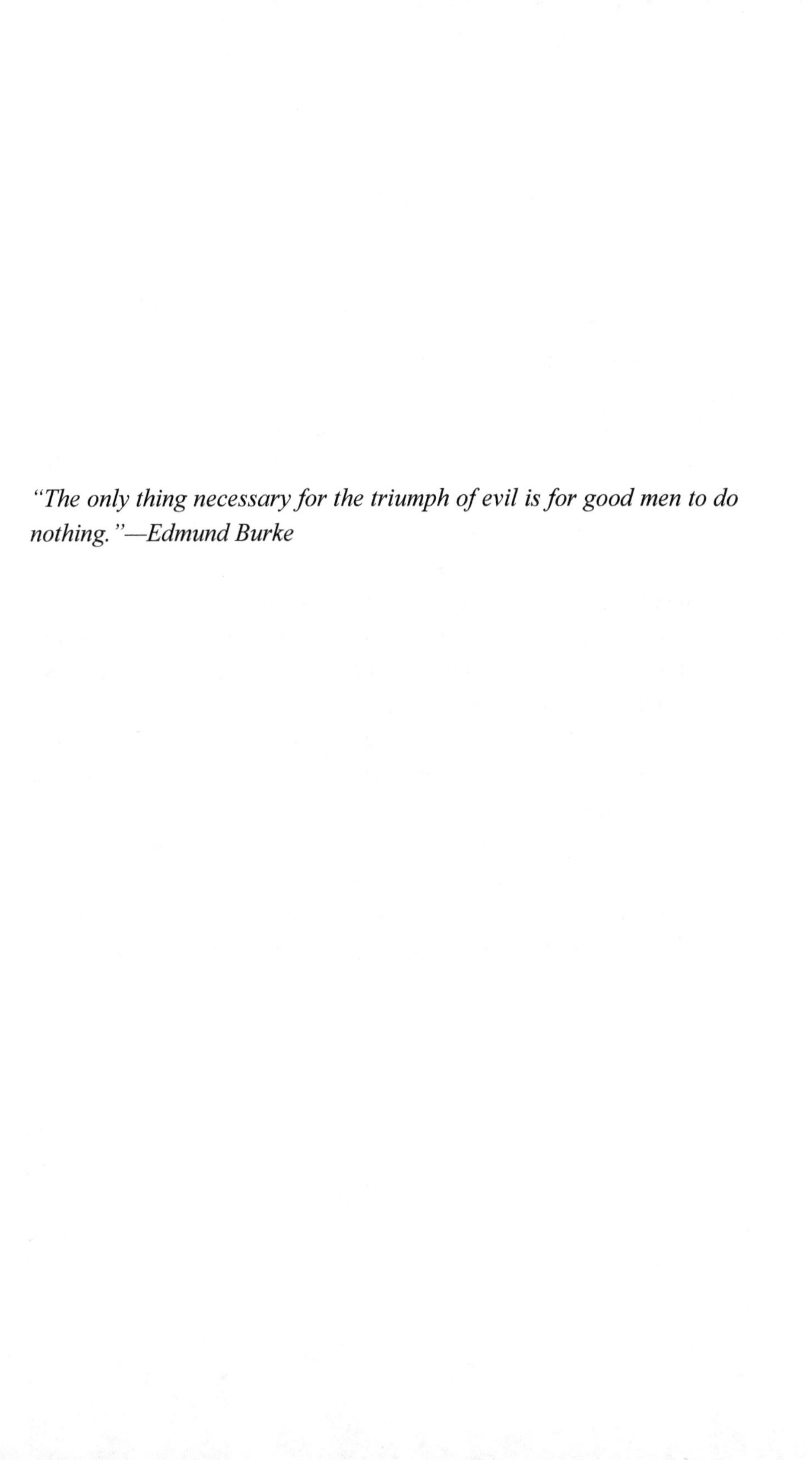

"The only thing necessary for the triumph of evil is for good men to do nothing."—Edmund Burke

ACKNOWLEDGMENTS

My amazing family—Jennifer, Kenny, Sarah, Josh, Chelsea, Sofie and Avery. You help make me a better husband, father and papa. You are supportive of me and these stories I write.

Sister Cyndi and Brother Erich—you know why.

Amazing Beta Readers: Brian, Dianne, Hans, Joe, Joshua, Kelly, Kim and Mark.

Brian "Release the Kraken" Tedeschi-I love you brother and couldn't imagine a better friend.

High Fantasy/Magic Group on Instagram.

Fellow authors—Skye Horn, Susan Perry, Katie Dunn, Karen Crawford, Vashti Quiroz-Vega, Ginger Li—you've all been so amazingly supportive and encouraging.

Every fan who bought my earlier books, *Awakening, Return* and *Reunite*. Your feedback on how much you enjoy my stories keeps me writing; thank you.

And finally, my editor and friend, Joe Scholes, who has helped me become a better storyteller and continues to push me to get better.

A heartfelt ***thank you*** to everyone. Your support, inspiration and participation have all contributed to my happiness and success.

Brett Humphrey
August 2020

ABOUT THE AUTHOR

Brett Humphrey is the author of the Dragonborn Series as well as various comedic sketches, plays and many other stories he hasn't written—yet.

He has worked with children and families for thirty years and has taught in the United States and countries around the world. His passion for reading started when he was a young child and he is still an avid reader of both fiction and non-fiction. His greatest desire as an author is to create books parents will want to read to their children, hopefully using different voices for the characters.

Brett lives in Arizona with his patient and supportive wife, who encouraged him to finally sit down and write one of the stories that lives in his head.

ALSO BY BRETT HUMPHREY

Dragonborn Series:

Awakening

Return

Reunite

Rebellion

Winter *

Therian Shapeshifter Academy Series:

Fierce Protector *

Tionchar Tales Series:

Scales of Justice *

** Forthcoming*

PROLOGUE

$\mathcal{I}$ knelt amidst the carnage on the field of battle, weeping over the bodies of my two best friends. Bernie and Shelley had died back to back and even in death, they still held hands. They were surrounded by the bodies of enemy shifters—their attackers paid with their lives. However, it didn't matter in the end; everyone was dead.

Hearing a noise behind me, I turned to see a shadowy figure in a hooded cloak holding a golden goblet. I couldn't see the face of the figure but I knew it wanted me to take the cup and drink. The menacing specter compelled me to move toward it.

My outstretched hand, covered with the blood of my friends, trembled with the effort to fight the compulsion. Helplessly overcome, I took the cup and drained the bittersweet contents. My mouth and throat burned and I could feel the liquid travel into my stomach. The fiery pain was replaced by freezing cold and my limbs became numb. I heard a roar and saw Aileene streaking toward me as I fell to my knees, my vision darkening at the edges.

My eyes were fixed on my mate as a shaft streaked from the ground and struck her in the chest. Even from my position, I could see the life drain from her eyes before she crashed to the ground and lay still. My limbs turned to rubber and I also fell face-first onto the bloody earth. I was roughly flipped onto my back and once again confronted by my faceless enemy, my body void of feeling or strength. My heartbeat faltered and stilled in my chest while my sight faded.

The last thing I heard before slipping into oblivion was one word.

"Soon."

CHAPTER ONE

Síocháin 8, 10,257

  Alister, wake up, Aileene shouted in my mind, waking me from my nightmare.

"Ugh, I hate dreams," I muttered and rubbed the sleep from my eyes. *I'm okay,* I sent but was startled when the door to my bedroom burst open and Aileene barged in. She made her way over to my bed and I scooted over so she could sit beside me.

"That was different," Aileene said as she smoothed the hair away from my sweaty forehead. "Do you want to tell me what the dream was about?"

Shelley stumbled into my room. "Why do you have to have these dreams in the middle of the night?" he grumbled. "I was having a good dream." When he noticed I was still in bed, his face turned serious and he stood beside Aileene. "That bad, huh?"

I nodded, still unable to speak due to the lump in my throat. Even though Shelley was alive and standing in front of me, I couldn't shake the image of his dead face from my dream.

"I'll call the others, you should probably get dressed," Aileene said gently and I nodded in agreement.

Twenty minutes later we were gathered in the living room of my suite and I could feel the gentle rocking of the HMS Beatrice as we sailed towards Cetacea. We'd spent a month and a half preparing for the journey after returning from Earth. We left Theria on the first day of Síocháin, and were now a week into our sixteen-day journey. We were as prepared as we could be for our diplomatic mission. Ostensibly we were on an around-the-world tour to present Aileene and me as the future Queen and King of Theria; I knew we were really on this journey to prevent a war.

"Thank you for coming. I'm sorry to interrupt your sleep." I apologized to everyone gathered in the room.

"No worries, Sire, as long as you have coffee, you can wake me anytime you want." Brarth smiled as he wheeled the cart laden with food and containers of coffee. He raised his mug of coffee in salute as he stepped out of the room and shut the door. Brarth and his brother Gekur, both ogre shifters, were part of the contingent of palace guards sent by my father. Brarth always volunteered to guard my door and now I knew why; it was for the coffee.

Also in the room were the members of my Inner Circle, including Hillaes, and they helped themselves to food and drinks. My mom and dad stayed behind to aid my Father and Mother in ruling the kingdom as my regents.

"I've had another one of my dreams and I want to discuss it with all of you." I must have looked troubled because Aileene took my hand in hers and squeezed it, giving me the strength to continue. I described the dream to everyone in the room and we sat in silence once I concluded.

"So—in this version of the dream not only do all of us perish, you and Aileene die as well?" Bernie finally asked.

"It seems that way," I began. "Aileene was killed by a projectile fired from the ground and it appears that I died from some sort of poison."

"We will not let that happen," Shelley ground out in anger. "I will not allow anyone else to die on my watch."

Before I could respond, Stavros put his hand on his son's shoulder and spoke softly, "Gustav's death was not your fault."

Shelley's eyes welled and he quickly turned his face away so we wouldn't see his pain. Bernie sat next to him and grabbed his hand.

My heart broke for my friend, but I had to keep the discussion moving forward. "Wu, please correct me if I'm wrong but the only thing that can penetrate the scales of a Royal Dragon is another Royal Dragon or a weapon made from the bones of one, correct?"

"I suppose a weapon from one of the other dimensions could also cause that kind of damage, but after your recent encounter with the attack helicopter on Earth, I would say that isn't likely."

"Wu, how are you adjusting to your new role as The Historian?" Aileene asked.

Gustav had chosen Wu to be his replacement because he had planned on stepping down from that role when he and Seraset were married. However, those plans were altered when Gustav was murdered on Earth. The mantle of The Historian fell to Wu upon Gustav's death and now Wu carried all the knowledge that went with his new position.

"It has been difficult until now because I receive new information each day. It feels like thousands of years of history has been downloaded directly into my brain. I'm still trying to sort it all out," Wu answered.

"Well, I'm glad you were finally well enough to make the journey with us," Aileene comforted.

"Yeah, me, too," Shelley grumbled. "Now, what do we do about the poison and protecting our King and future Queen?"

I looked at Shelley in surprise as his usually good-natured expression had been replaced by a scowl. In fact, the last time I remember him joking around was when we were in Cyndi's house right before we left Earth. I made a mental note to talk to him about this later.

"Shelley, the only known instance of poison being used against a Royal Dragon is when Dimitri tried to kill King Phillip and Queen Beatrice fourteen years ago. And even then, the poison only affected them in their human forms and put them to sleep rather than kill them," Wu answered.

"We will have to assume that Dimitri was able to get a message out about the poison he created, after his death," Stavros added.

"That could be possible, but we questioned every shifter in Dimitri's army as well as those trapped in his fortress," Frieda answered.

Those who had been threatened or coerced by Dimitri have been reintegrated into our society as they recovered from their injuries. Those who had willingly supported and taken part in Dimitri's evil were either imprisoned or executed.

"I'm not sure how the poison Dimitri created was transported to other kingdoms," Frieda said.

After a moment of thoughtful silence, Miriam spoke up. "What if we're looking at this the wrong way? What if Dimitri didn't create the poison but rather received it from another kingdom?"

"That would make things worse," Fritz muttered, "but it's a credible theory."

"If this is true, then Dimitri was only part of a wider rebellion and we'll be facing greater danger on this journey than we have before. Does that sum things up?" I asked.

"Don't forget about the unknown enemy having weapons and poison that can kill you and Aileene and if you aren't successful then we're all dead," Bernie quipped.

"Yeah, we don't want to forget about that," Aileene smiled.

"What's wrong with you two?" Shelley fumed, "this isn't something to joke about."

We were all stunned into silence because Shelley was always the first to make a joke when things looked dire. Before anyone could respond, he huffed in frustration and stormed out of the suite slamming the door as he left.

"He's been on edge since returning from Earth," Miriam apologized.

"He's blaming himself for Gustav's death and nothing we say can help him get past this," Bernie said sadly. "I hate seeing him in so much pain, but I don't know what to do."

"I'll talk to him," I said, "and if his mood doesn't improve, I'll toss him overboard," I finished with a smile to let the others know I was kidding—mostly.

"What do we do about the poison and the weapons that can harm you and Aileene?" Mkali asked quietly.

"Those could be easier to deal with than helping Shelley with his problems," Bernie grumped.

I didn't want to say it aloud, but I almost agreed with her.

Planet Theria

Unknown Location

The great beast stirred in its slumber. The cavernous chamber echoed with the dry, rasping sound of its scales rubbing against one another as the beast settled into a more comfortable position. A new scent wafted along the air current in the inky darkness. The beast opened one eye lazily and the cat-like pupil expanded to engulf the faint light that had suddenly appeared above the chamber.

The beast came fully awake at the harsh clanging of the chains as they rapidly raised the metal portcullis and locked it open, revealing a huddle of frightened animals. The quick movement of the beast belied its size as it stood on its four limbs and roared in challenge. The terrified bleating of animals bounced off the walls as the beast rustled its wings to settle them against its back. It stretched its long, sinuous neck towards the quaking animals. Its gaping maw exposed rows of dagger-like teeth, dripping with saliva in anticipation. With another roar, it spat a gout of flame at the cowering prey which were immediately immolated by the blast.

As it settled down to eat, words drifted from the observation chamber above, "Soon my pet, soon you will feast on other flesh. Eat and rest," followed by an evil chuckle.

Alister

HMS Beatrice

I waited until dawn had broken over the horizon before I looked for Shelley. I paused on the deck to appreciate the simple beauty of the sunrise. The green, blue and orange streaks painted against the slowly lightening sky brought a smile to my face. The briny scent of the ocean assailed my nostrils and I inhaled deeply, enjoying the crisp morning air. The rhythmic lapping of the ocean waves against the side of the ship as we sailed was hypnotic. It was so peaceful I was tempted to stay rooted in place to enjoy the moment a bit longer. But I had a friend in pain and I needed to find him.

It was easy enough for me to follow our connection to the aft deck of the ship where he was leaning against the rails looking back the way we'd come. The trail of white foam amidst the blue-green water was the only evidence marking the passing of the ship as we sailed along, and Shelley was staring at the trail as though he was focused on the past.

The HMS Beatrice was a beautiful ship and, like many things on Theria, was a blend of old and new technology. The ship was made from the wood of the dragon tree, which resembled the redwoods of California, but was twice as large. When milled, the grain resembled interlocking dragon scales and after being treated by dragon fire, was harder than steel. The ship was over six-hundred feet long and eighty-feet wide. It was powered by electric motors that used solar energy during the day and high-capacity batteries at night. Captain Jormis told us the batteries held enough charge to power the engines for a month if there wasn't enough sun.

The main part of the ship was four stories tall and had twenty-five individual cabins as well as four large cabins that served as berthing compartments. The fore and aft decks were large enough for Aileene and me to take off and land as dragons. The entire ship was painted green and scarlet and the royal flag, a scarlet dragon in flight against a green background, flew from the mast. There was a figurehead of a scarlet dragon with wings stretched in flight and a terrifying expression on its face; I was sure it was modeled after my Mother.

As I walked towards Shelley, I noticed the dejected slump of his shoulders. As I stepped up to the rail to join him, he wiped tears from his face.

"Everyone tells me that it's not my fault Gustav died but if I hadn't told Alex we were going to Hero Con, Paterson wouldn't have been there," Shelley said quietly.

After taking a deep breath, I answered my hurting friend. "I don't agree." I held up my hand to stop his response. "Okay, Paterson wouldn't have known we would be there the first day, but I don't think we could have kept our presence a secret. How many pictures did we pose for? How many people posted those pictures on social media? Somehow the pictures of us with The Rock were broadcast, too. Paterson would have known we were there at some point. You may have let Alex know where we were going but Alex was the one who betrayed us to Paterson. Alex and Paterson killed Gustav, not you," I said with finality.

Shelley eventually responded. "So much has changed, and not all of it's good. Don't get me wrong, I love knowing I'm a Therian shifter, but there are times I feel like part of our childhood was stolen from us. I know we're technically nineteen, but one day I was twelve and on my thirteenth birthday I fell asleep and gained an extra five years of memories and awoke an adult. I was really hoping we would be able to act like kids while we were on Earth, but we had people trying to kill us and Gustav died."

"If I remember correctly, you did wear that horrible outfit to breakfast. If that's not kid-like, I don't know what is." I grinned as I nudged Shelley with my elbow.

He smiled at that. "It was pretty awesome seeing Bernie's face when I walked into the restaurant." After a moment, his face fell again, and he was somber once more. "But then we went to Hero Con and everything fell apart." He took another deep breath and let it out slowly. "I can't help thinking if I had been more alert, doing what I was supposed to do as one of your Knights instead of playing like a silly kid, I could have stopped Paterson."

"Dude, I know Aileene already told you this but Paterson was watching each of us and if we'd moved, he would have opened fire earlier. Gustav was the only one he didn't know. If you hadn't given Gustav the VIP pass, he couldn't have saved those people. Gustav died a hero. None of us could ask for more than that."

"I know, but I'm having trouble processing all this. We've been in danger since finding out who we really are and now it seems like we're heading into a situation where we could all die. I don't know what I'd do if anything happened to you, Bernie or Aileene."

"Then we'll just have to figure out a way to take out our enemies without getting ourselves killed," I said as I punched Shelley in the arm.

"Watch it Stretch," Shelley smiled, "you may be King and all, but I can still take you down."

"You wish," I grinned. "Shelley, I need you to be you and stop being so serious all the time. Your humor is part of who you are and it's one of your greatest strengths. You, Bernie and I all feel the same about losing years of our lives, but we'll get through this if we stick together."

"Yeah, you're probably right. What are we going to do about the poison and the weapon?" Shelley asked.

"The other rulers of Theria don't know how proficient I am with magic. I'll work with Hillaes to figure out how to create a spell to detect and neutralize poisons, and that will help us in the long run."

"It's a good thing you brought her with us then," Shelley said suspiciously.

I laughed, "I can't take credit for bringing Hillaes and Jeffrey with us, An'Ceann suggested they might come in handy on the journey."

"What can Jeffrey do to help us?" Shelley wondered.

"He was deep in Dimitri's counsel. He might know if Dimitri had contact with any of the other kingdoms before the shield covered the Kingdom of Theria."

"Good thinking. I always knew you were more than just a pretty face—" Shelley trailed off when he realized what he said.

"I'm not sure how I feel about you thinking I have a pretty face. Whatever will we tell Bernie?" I teased.

"Shut up," Shelley growled and punched me in the arm.

I slung the same arm around his shoulder and gave him a one-armed hug. "You're my best friend, Shelley. It's good to have you back. I told the others I would toss you overboard if I couldn't talk sense into you."

"Hmmm," Shelley grunted as he looked out at the water. "How far do you think you could throw me if you really tried?"

"I'm not sure, but I'm willing to experiment if you are," I grinned.

His stomach rumbled and he answered, "Maybe after breakfast." After a few moments of silence, he continued. "Thanks Alister, you are a good friend, I appreciate you coming to talk with me."

"My pleasure. Although, it would be a good idea for you to talk to your parents as well. I'm sure they've had similar experiences in their long lives that we could benefit from."

Shelley nodded and turned away from the railing. "You're right. If you don't mind, I think I'll have breakfast with them."

"Sounds good, see you later," I said as Shelley walked away.

I turned back to the railing and watched the water for a bit.

"That was well done, young dragon," a deep voice rumbled next to me.

I turned and laughed at the sight of An'Ceann in his lion form with his paws resting on the top rails. "I'd ask how you got on board, but you can do pretty much whatever you want, can't you?"

"Pretty much," An'Ceann grinned at me. "You helped your friend begin to work through his distress, and that is a good thing."

I nodded silently. "Will there ever be a day when we won't have to fight all the time?"

"I know it may feel like you've been constantly fighting but you've only known your true nature for a little more than a year. There are many things that need to be put right before true peace is restored to Theria."

"How could so much change in the thirteen years my parents were comatose?"

"The decay was already in place before they were attacked; it just took this long to fully manifest," An'Ceann answered.

"Can't you just tell me who I need to take care of so I can avoid the danger?" I asked hopefully.

"What a great idea, why didn't I think of that?" An'Ceann asked sarcastically and looked at me.

"Yeah, I know," I grumped, "if you gave me all the answers, I wouldn't grow the way you think I should."

He leaned down and kissed my forehead, "It may be a small consolation, but I really do think you can handle whatever comes your way. However, there are two things I want you to remember—don't hesitate to act when you know what you're supposed to do and rely on the strengths of those around you."

"Wow, could you be more enigmatic?" I asked then held up my hand to stop his answer and laughed, "of course you could."

"You have no idea," An'Ceann grinned again and faded away.

I was grinning as I turned back to watch the waves. Even though I knew danger was looming over the horizon, I felt better after my talks with Shelley and An'Ceann. Today was going to be a good day.

Earth

Cyndi

I made my way down the stairs from my house to the sand of my private beach, being careful not to fall. As I neared the bottom my excitement got the better of me and I missed the last step, falling headlong into the sand.

"How can I be so graceful in the water yet so clumsy on land?" I muttered and took off my robe and threw it on the back of the lounge chair sitting there. The sky was still dark and clouds obscured the stars, but the sound of the crashing waves beckoned me as I walked towards the water. Jason was going to be away for two weeks and I didn't have any events planned so I decided to spend a couple weeks in the ocean. I'd been having dreams about the Therian equipment I found near the ruins of Atlantis and I wanted to investigate it.

I double-checked to make sure the thought-medallion was around my neck. King Alister had created one for me before he left for Theria and had also included a pocket dimension where I stored my clothes. Even though the thought-medallion could keep me clothed when I transformed it was pointless for me to wear them before shifting into my mermaid form because they would be wet when I transformed back into human.

When I thought about all the movies and cartoons showing mermaids wearing shell bikinis I had to laugh, they would just get ripped off when I swam full speed underwater. I'm not sure how fast I can go but I know I can make the twenty-six miles to Catalina Island in about five minutes. King Alister assured me that the medallion would survive. I believed him because somehow, he was able to transform into an enormous dragon and keep his medallion intact.

Once I was sure I had everything I would need for my adventure I walked into the surf and dove under the first wave. I'm sure the water was cold, but I didn't feel it due to my mermaid physiology. I swam underwater in my human form until my lungs started to ache from the lack of oxygen and then transformed into my true form.

The change was instantaneous, but I could feel my legs fuse together and form my beautiful tail. The iridescent vermillion-green, deep purple and cobalt blue scales start at my flukes and match the other fins on my body. These fins help with movement but are also extremely sensitive to vibrations in the water and are another part of my superior senses. Underwater I'm able to see light-waves beyond the range of my human sight, including ultraviolet and infrared, and can use the streaks of phosphorus in the water to see clearly, even in the deepest parts of the ocean.

I breathe through the gills on my neck and sides but can pull water through my nose and mouth to scent prey in the water. It always takes me a few moments to adjust from my limited human senses and engage all my other senses to read the ocean water around me. I smiled in delight and began to swim towards my treasure cache. Even though I was headed to Atlantis to explore the Therian machinery, it wouldn't hurt to grab some gold in case I had the opportunity to do some shopping. After all, with my new pocket dimension, I could pick up a few things and carry them with me without having to worry about keeping my hands free.

A yellowtail darted in front of me, so I extended the razor-sharp claws from my webbed right hand and speared the fish, distended my jaw to open my mouth wide and popped the whole thing in my mouth as I continued swimming. My first stop after visiting my underwater bank was Hawaii and if I hurried, I might be able to get there in time for a late dinner.

Alister

HMS Beatrice

Shelley felt much better after the day with his parents. I'm glad I suggested spending time with them during our conversation this morning. Shelley and Bernie walked up arm-in-arm, with Mkali in tow, and joined Aileene and me where we were lounging on the deck chairs. Shelley settled in his chair to my left and Bernie sat next to him. Mkali sat on the other side of Aileene.

"We're not disturbing you, are we?" Shelley smirked as he put his hands behind his head.

"As a matter of fact—," Aileene began.

"Too bad," Bernie added with a laugh, "we have important things to talk about."

Mkali giggled so Aileene pounced on her and started tickling her side, "Oh, so you think that's funny young squire? Don't listen to these two reprobates, they'll corrupt you." Aileene smiled fondly at the younger girl who lay back on the lounge chair, exhausted from laughing.

"Now, what do you want to talk about?" I asked my friends.

"We talked to our parents over lunch about the best way to protect you both," Bernie answered. "We needed their wisdom because they've been part of your parents' Inner Circle for centuries."

"Should Wu be part of this discussion?" I asked.

"I've already sent thought-speak to him and asked him to bring Hillaes—here they are now," Shelley finished as they walked up.

Wu grabbed two more deck chairs and set them up, so they faced our group.

"Okay, now that everyone's here, what's on your mind?" I asked leaning forward to look at Shelley and Bernie. Shelley nodded to Bernie, so she explained.

"We know there's not really much we can do to protect either you or Aileene because you're Royal Dragons, but we want to figure out how to help you anyway. Over lunch we asked our parents the most difficult thing for them as members of your parents' Inner Circle and they all agreed it's trying to do their jobs to keep the King and Queen safe," Bernie said.

"Yeah, for some reason Royal Dragons tend to think they're indestructible and have a hard time letting other people do their jobs," Shelley commented dryly.

"But we are, for the most part," Aileene answered.

"Yes, and it's the 'for the most part' we want to talk to you about," Bernie agreed. "Shelley, Mkali and I understand there were things going on while we were on Earth you two can't talk about. We don't like it, but we get it. However, Alister, you left us behind too many times, and we don't think that's wise."

"But—," I began, and Bernie held out her hand to stop me.

"Please, hear us out first," she pleaded. After I nodded, she continued. "We realize we are more vulnerable than you are and can be injured easier than you two ever could, but we do have strengths you don't have. My parents told me they argued with King Phillip and Queen Beatrice about going with them to Dimitri's fortress. If they had been there, they would have been able to tell that Dimitri was lying and they never would have sat down to dinner with him."

"And, if my parents would have been with them, they might've been able to detect the poison before your parents drank it," Shelley added.

"Historically, whenever a High King or Queen either ignored their

Inner Circle or tried to 'shelter them from harm,' there were tragic results." Wu gently added.

Hillaes must have seen the conflict on my face because she spoke up. "Alister, you wield a greater amount of magic than I ever could. Why do you come to me for training?"

"Because you have more experience with magic than I do," I answered.

"But among everyone here," she pointed to my friends sitting on their chairs, "I'm the most vulnerable since I'm human and unable to change forms."

"That's true, but you've proven you can take care of yourself," I added lamely.

"But so have we," Mkali said softly. "I know I'm the youngest one here, but I've been training to be a warrior my whole life. Let us help you by using the strengths we have so you can use the strengths that only you and Aileene have."

They're right, you know, Aileene sent to me with a smile.

I nodded at her words, *They are, but it doesn't mean we have to like it.*

No, but we must recognize the wisdom they've shared with us about how to do the right thing. Now we need the courage to do it, Aileene finished.

"You all make valid points," I admitted. "I can't promise I'll always get it right, but I will do my best."

"Me, too," Aileene added. "We've already learned that we are better together. We'll face this latest challenge the same way. Thank you, friends."

"See Bernie, you can teach an old dragon new tricks," Shelley smiled as he leaned back on his chair to relax.

Before I could respond, there was a sound of a huge splash on the port side of the ship followed by an explosive concussion, a flume of water and the rocking of the ship. Alarm bells split the air and Captain Jormis' thoughts were broadcast throughout the ship, *All hands to battle stations, we are under attack.*

CHAPTER TWO

We jumped from our chairs and searched the seas for any signs of our attackers. The HMS Beatrice crew poured from the hatch and took positions along the forward railing. As I looked around me, I saw crew members doing the same thing on each deck.

Keep your eyes peeled, we're lucky that first shot missed, we won't be as lucky next time, the Captain warned.

Since we were on the starboard side of the ship we couldn't see where the attacks came from. I expanded my senses to find any shifters in the area who weren't already on the ship.

They're above us, I shouted mentally to everyone aboard.

All flyers into the air, Captain Jormis commanded and shifters surrounding us began to shed their clothing to shift. In moments, the air was filled with griffins, harpies, rocs, gargoyles, phoenixes and even a thunderbird.

Captain, our people are outnumbered two to one and there are another thirty flyers on their way, I announced to the Captain and my Inner Circle.

After some creative cursing Captain Jormis responded, *Sire, can you and Lady Aileene help us?*

Aye, aye Captain, I sent, *we're on it.*

Shelley snickered and slapped me on the back, "Aye, aye Captain?"

I shrugged. "I always wanted to say that. Hillaes, can you lay down some cover fire to aid our people? If possible, I want these shifters alive."

She nodded and began to fire bolts of lightning at the enemy combatants.

Stavros, you and Miriam organize the defenses in case the enemy makes it on board. "Wu, you guard Mkali's back while she engages the enemy with her bow."

Wu shifted and Mkali started firing arrows selectively to wound the enemy rather than kill, and to avoid our flyers. She had expected my request and had pulled her bow and quiver from her pocket dimension as she shifted to her centaur form.

"Shelley and Bernie—" I started

"You're not leaving us behind," Bernie said with her hands on her hips.

"Of course not," I said, "I heard what you said earlier. You two are with Aileene and me. We'll even the odds a bit then go searching for the enemy vessel."

"Have fun," Aileene called to me as she and Bernie ran to the other side of the ship so she could transform.

"Ready?" I asked Shelley as I also ran away to transform. When I was far enough away that I wouldn't crush my best friend, I shifted. Even though I am also perfectly comfortable in my human skin I feel like I'm fully alive when I transform into my dragon. I settled down on the deck of the ship and Shelley ran towards me, jumped onto my foreleg and settled at the base of my neck like we had practiced.

He locked himself into the harness we had added to our gear and I heaved myself into the air. I had figured out that just like the thought-medallion can hold the clothes we have on when we're human, it can also hold anything we wear when we're in our natural form. The harness was a great addition for aerial maneuvers.

If you want to live, surrender now, I shouted in thought-speak to the fighting shifters. While some faltered, no one gave up the attack.

Alister, there's a speed boat at five-o'clock rapidly approaching our ship, Shelley warned me.

Recommendations? I asked as I banked hard to the right and dove toward the approaching vessel.

Plasma-torch, Shelley answered quickly.

We had spent a rather productive afternoon categorizing the different types of flame I could produce, and we named them based on their destructive capabilities. They ranged from gentle-breeze, which was a twenty-foot wide swath of flame that lit everything in its path on fire, to inferno, which could melt granite within thirty seconds. Plasma-torch was a highly concentrated beam of fire that I could use to precisely cut through almost anything.

Incoming, I shouted as projectile weapons fire bounced off my scales. I activated the *Spheara* spell to cover Shelley and drew closer to the boat. I breathed out the flame and the small beam cut across the bow of the boat, neatly shearing it off. The boat began to sink, and enemy shifters dove off the sides into the water. I roared my displeasure at those surrounding the sinking vessel and climbed back into the sky to rejoin the aerial battle.

I was met with the magnificent sight of Aileene's green dragon flying next to a much smaller ice-blue dragon. Aileene was rapidly spitting fire at flying enemies and the blue dragon was spitting ice in the same way. Ice dragons were so rare I would have enjoyed seeing him in action, but I had my own battle to fight.

It looks like you're having fun, I sent to Aileene and I could feel her amusement through our bond as mates.

I am, but I don't understand this enemy. We are trying our best not to kill any of them, but they seem to prefer death to capture.

Opening my connection to all the shifters around me, I could feel the life force of the enemy combatants wink out of existence the moment one of them was captured. At once, the life of every shifter I had just left in the water was snuffed like a candle flame.

There is no need to end your lives, if you surrender, we will treat you fairly, I mentally shouted to those fighting us, but it had no effect. If anything, they fought more fiercely.

Enough of this, let's find where they're coming from, I mentally shouted and started flying along the line of shifters that kept coming to battle my people. I roared and began to ram into the enemy as we flew. They kept trying to attack but nothing they did hurt me. As I flew into a large cluster of shifters coming at me, I did a barrel roll and knocked them out of the air with my wings. I must have knocked down fifty enemy shifters with my body, my forelegs and even slammed a couple with my head. None of the damage I did to them was lethal but for each one I hit their life force winked out before they hit the water.

This doesn't make any sense, I sent to Shelley, *every shifter we've met dies shortly after we make contact.*

How about we work on the mystery after we find the ship? Shelley mentally grumbled, *I'm still a bit dizzy from the aerobatics.*

I spotted the ship about a mile away and dove towards it. It reminded me of a cargo ship but instead of containers I could see the remnants of blankets and bedding on the deck which showed that was where those shifters had been sleeping.

It's time for me to get my paws dirty, Shelley sent, *I don't see anyone on deck, do you?*

The deck looks clear; I'll drop you there. Watch your back, they could be lying in wait.

Will do, Shelley answered as I slowed my descent so I could drop him on board. When I was ten feet off the deck Shelley shouted, "I'm away," and landed on board as a grizzly bear.

I watched him land then turned my attention forward again so I could look at the ship as I passed over it. However, I was met with a blinding flash of light, the sight of something flying towards me and then the feeling of being wrapped in a net. I tried to flex the netting off but instead of making progress I felt hundreds of pinpricks along my body and my wings became hopelessly entangled in the clinging material.

I crashed onto the deck and could feel the wood give way under the weight of my body. My forward momentum was such that I smashed through the deck and into the water. The last thing I heard before sinking beneath the waves was the sound of the ship exploding around me. Since I'd taken a deep breath before hitting the water, I wasn't sinking but I was so tightly bound by the constricting net I couldn't swim. I wasn't worried by the debris falling past me, but I was worried about my best friend who had been on the ship.

Shelley, can you hear me? I sent my panicked thoughts out to my best friend.

After an agonizingly long time he finally answered me, *I can hear you, what happened?*

Nothing much—I'm just trapped in a net, the ship exploded, and I thought you might be dead. Oh, and, I'm currently underwater and unable to get to the surface. I responded dryly.

So basically, a Tuesday? He asked sarcastically.

I laughed mentally, *Are you injured?*

Just singed a bit. It's a good thing bears can swim. How long can you stay underwater?

I've never experimented with my limit but I'm fine for at least twenty minutes. I keep trying to break this net but whenever I do, it feels like something is digging into my scales and I'm being flayed alive.

Can you change back to human?

Probably, but I'm worried what may happen if the net clings to me the same way. I can't hold my breath as long in that form. Can you see me at all?

Hold on a sec, Shelley responded. After about a minute he re-established our mental connection. *Okay, I updated Aileene. She and Bernie are on their way. I can't see you from my position so I hope Aileene will be able to see you from the air.*

Thanks, I was kind of hoping you would be able to get to me without telling her about this. It's embarrassing to be brought down by a net.

Yeah, sucks to be you, Shelley sent. *I guess you're not so indestructible after all.*

Before I could agree with him, Aileene broke into my thoughts. *Alister, are you okay?*

Fine so far, I just can't seem to get free from this netting. Somehow, it's biting into my scales.

Hang on, I can see you and I've brought some help. She sent and I heard three bodies dropping into the water.

I must have been deeper than I thought because it took a few moments before three cecaelia swam into view. They looked like mermaids but instead of having a tail, they had the tentacles of an octopus. This was the first time I had seen this type of shifter, and I was grateful they were here.

Hello, Sire, I am Commander Chelsea, said the blonde cecaelia in the middle, *and this is Lieutenant Davis and Ensign Gibbs,* she pointed to the cecaelia with red hair on her right and the one with purple hair on her left. *Okay ladies let's get the King to the surface then we can figure out how to get this net off him.*

Thank you for your assistance, I sent as they got into position and started pushing me upwards. After a few minutes I broke the surface and was able to take a deep breath.

I'm going to shift into my human form to see if I can get untangled from this net. I was relieved to see Aileene hovering over the water with both Bernie and Shelley on her back.

Alister, you're bleeding, and the net is being held in place by barbed hooks, Aileene's concerned voice sounded in my head.

That explains why it hurts to move, I agreed. *I'm going to get free from this net.* I sent to those surrounding me.

We won't let you sink, Commander Chelsea sent. *Whenever you're ready, Sire.*

Here goes, I sent, and screamed as I shifted. I was overwhelmed as each of the barbed hooks were ripped out of my scales and dragged across my human skin when the net tightened on my smaller body. Even though everything happened quickly I could feel each slice on my body and the agonizing shock as my wounds were drenched by saltwater. My nervous system overloaded with the excruciating pain, but I heard Aileene roaring in agony as I mercifully blacked out.

The first thing I noticed was my tongue was thick and sticking to the roof of my mouth. When I swallowed it felt like there was broken glass in my throat. I tried to open my eyes to see what the pressure on my chest was, but it felt like there were weights holding my eyelids down. My aching body confirmed that I wasn't dead but the way my head was pounding with each heartbeat, I couldn't decide if that was a good or bad thing. The last thing I remembered was having my flesh ripped open by the net, then passing out.

I tried opening my eyes again and managed to crack my left eye open and saw auburn hair and understood the pressure on my chest came from Aileene laying her head on me while she slept. I smiled when I heard her gently snore and moved my hand to stroke her hair from her face.

"I'm sorry," I whispered hoarsely, "it seems as though I've gotten myself injured again."

"Alister, it was so much worse than that, I was sure I was going to lose you this time," Aileene said as she sat up and looked at me intently. Her sapphire-blue eyes bored into mine and I could tell she was frightened. "You've never been this bad before. I thought you were close to death after you saved your parents but that was nothing compared to this. Your poor body was torn to shreds and there was so much blood." She started to sob and buried her face in my chest again.

I embraced her, although it was awkward from my position on the bed. "Hey, I survived," I croaked. As Aileene released her pent up emotions, I did an inventory of my limbs and wiggled my fingers and toes to prove to myself that I could.

Can you help me sit up and get me something to drink? I sent because it was too difficult to speak.

Aileene quickly sat up, wiped her face with the back of her hand and after helping me sit up, handed me a cup. I tried to take a drink while she propped pillows behind my back, but I was too weak. She looked at me with pity and gently kissed my forehead. I was exhausted and fell back against the pillows, but my throat did feel better.

"What happened after I transformed?" I breathed.

Aileene's face reflected her stormy thoughts. My heart warmed because she was so angry on my behalf and I reached out and grasped her hand in mine.

"The netting was made of a special material that contracted when you turned human. It was designed to kill you, Alister," she responded.

"How were the hooks able to pierce my scales?" I asked.

"It seems they were made of Royal Dragon bone and were razor-sharp on all sides. Once the hooks imbedded themselves into your scales they dragged through your flesh when you shifted. If I hadn't been there to immediately pour healing energy into your body, you would have bled out. I had enough power to heal your shredded skin, but it's taken me the last three days to get you healthy enough to wake up. Since I can't open a gate to Middle Earth to get an infusion of magical energy, I had to wait until my magic reservoir filled up enough each day before I could use the *Sanos* spell. I was so worried."

Her eyes brimmed with tears and I reached up and wiped away the single tear that had escaped with my thumb. "I'm sorry," I said, "I didn't mean to get hurt."

She blew out a frustrated breath, "It's not your fault. You did what we were talking about the other day. You took Shelley with you and if you hadn't it could have been worse."

"Did we lose any of our people and do we know who did this?"

"None of ours died, but we had a lot of people injured. The healers were able to get everyone back on their feet. The Einhorns and Hillaes have been amazing, I just wish their healing magic worked on Royal Dragons. We don't know who attacked us because there weren't any survivors to question."

"Our people killed them all?" I asked.

"No, but the enemy combatants dropped dead the same time the enemy ship blew up. Alister, the purpose of that attack was to kill either you or me. Whoever planned this knew one of us would fly to that ship where the net was waiting. This was a trap and we don't even know who set it."

I breathed deeply and a wave of dizziness passed over me. I knew I needed sleep but wanted to get Aileene the magical energy she needed before I did. "I'm going to open a pinhole gate to Middle Earth for you, but we need Captain Jormis to drop anchor since I don't know what will happen if I leave a gate open in the middle of the ocean."

"Do you think that's wise?" Aileene asked me and then got that faraway look that let me know she was mentally communicating with the Captain.

"I don't know if it's wise, but you need the magic if you're going to heal me completely. I know I'll eventually heal but if I've been out of it for three days, we're getting closer to our first destination and it would be a bad idea to show any weakness on our part."

Aileene nodded and for a few minutes she filled me in on the rest of the rescue and how the three cecaelia women protected me from ocean predators until the HMS Beatrice arrived. There was a lot of blood in the water and I was rather vulnerable. Aileene was impressed with the fighting skills of the three oceanic shifters.

"Captain Jormis says we are at full stop and he will do his best to keep us in this spot until you give the all clear," Aileene informed me.

"Ok, here goes," I said and concentrated on the wardrobe near the bed. It's easier to make a pinhole gate if I can connect it with a physical object. Normally I only have to think about creating a gate and one opens. This time it took more energy than it should. I felt sweat break out all over my body and I could feel myself slipping into unconsciousness as I created the gate. I felt the rush of magical energy as the gate opened but also felt my eyes roll back into my head as I passed out.

Aileene

I caught Alister before he could hit the floor and repositioned his body, so he was once again lying in bed. He was so vulnerable in this state and my anger burned like an inferno in my chest. I wished I could get my claws and teeth on those who caused such damage to my love. The door opened behind me and I crouched protectively over Alister's body and hissed at my intruder as I felt my hands turn into claws.

"Woah, Aileene, it's just me," the woman in front of me held up her hands showing me she didn't have a weapon.

"Sorry," I growled and ran my tongue over the dragon teeth that had sprouted in my mouth. "I'm a bit upset," I declared and shifted back.

Bernie laughed nervously, "I understand. Thanks for not shooting fire first and asking questions later. How's Alister?"

"Better?" I said with uncertainty. "He was conscious for about ten minutes but passed out after opening a small gate to Middle Earth for me."

Bernie joined me by the bed and we looked down at Alister's mangled body. I didn't want to tell him about the angry, red scars crisscrossing his body and face. The scar that bisected his face from his right temple to the left side of his chin thankfully missed his eye, but it was especially troubling.

Bernie put her arm around my shoulders and sniffed as she tried to hide her tears from me. She moved the rest of the covers away to expose Alister's body. Except for a pair of cotton shorts, he was naked, and we surveyed the damage together. Seeing him again like this, I was once again amazed that he'd survived. As bad as his front looked, I knew the back of his body looked even worse.

"Do you really think we can completely heal him now?" I asked timidly as my heart ached at the pain Alister had endured in the water.

"I think so, now that you have the magical energy from Middle Earth at your disposal. But I want you to reconsider my request to have my parents join us as we work on Alister; they have more experience with healing than I do."

"No," I growled reflexively and once again moved my body between Bernie and Alister.

Bernie didn't flinch away from me even though I could tell I had partially shifted again and could rip her apart with little effort.

She spoke softly to me, "Aileene, you know I love Alister like a brother and wouldn't ever do anything to hurt him, right?"

I nodded so she continued, "My parents love Alister like a son and won't hurt him either. You can trust us."

"I know," I said when I was able to control my emotions. "My instinct to protect Alister kicks in because he's vulnerable. I do trust you and your parents, they can enter."

She must have called them silently because the door opened, and Fritz and Frieda walked in. I was surprised when Frieda opened her arms wide and smothered me in an embrace. Fritz threw his arms around the both of us and I wept at their expression of love and support.

"Now, now, dear. It will be fine. We'll work together to bring Alister to full health," Frieda soothed as she rubbed circles on my back.

"I'm sorry," I sniffed after a few moments in their embrace.

"You have nothing to be sorry about," Bernie assured me. "I just about lost it when Shelley was blown up on Earth and you helped me focus enough to heal him. This is what we do for each other."

I nodded and asked, "How do we do this?"

"I think the best thing we can do is for Frieda, Bernadette and me to link our thoughts with yours to direct the deep healing. You use the energy from Middle Earth to power the spell. Where do you want to start?" Fritz asked.

I looked at the ugly scars across Alister's body and made my decision, "Let's start with the scar on his face so our enemy won't know how badly he was injured if we can't heal the rest."

I felt it when the link of three unicorn healers joined their minds with mine and I accessed the magical energy from Middle Earth. The rush of magic was so great, I staggered. Once my magical reservoir was filled, I touched the angry scar where it began at Alister's temple and whispered *Sanos* to trigger the healing spell. I traced the scar and was amazed to see it disappear under my finger as I moved my hand. The four of us worked in sync as I ran my finger along the scar until it disappeared.

When I finished, I disengaged the *Sanos* spell and looked at the Einhorns. "It worked," I grinned excitedly.

Bernie smiled at me and answered, "One down, a thousand to go."

I didn't care how long it would take, we would make Alister whole again and confront our enemies together. They would face the wrath of the High King of Theria.

Alister

I stood before the mirror and looked at the four thin silver lines crisscrossing my chest as I traced them with my fingers. The rest of my skin was smooth and didn't show any signs of the recent injuries I had suffered, and I was grateful for that.

"Hey, Stretch, are you flexing in front of the mirror again?" Shelley teased as he stood behind my right shoulder and looked where my hand rested on my chest. "Why did Aileene and Bernie leave those scars?"

"Aileene told me she wanted them to remind me that I'm not invincible and need to be more careful. She also wants them there to remind her that someone almost killed me which will fuel her retribution." I smirked at my friend in the mirror, "and she thinks they make me look tough."

Shelley punched me in the arm, "Seeing you ripped apart was probably the grossest thing I've ever seen, and I walked through the 'Hall of Horror' in Dimitri's fortress. Try not to do that again."

"I'll do my best," I said as I shrugged into my shirt. "How did you get the net off me?"

"I cut it off you while Bernie and Aileene kept you afloat. Every time I touched the net it ripped up my hands, I'm still surprised you survived," Shelley said as we made our way to the door.

We were heading to the foredeck where Hillaes was working with Aileene to see if they could create a magical defense against Royal Dragon bone weapons. It had been four days since the attack and we only had five days to produce a decent plan before we arrived in Cetacea. I hoped Lady Zhaleh hadn't been behind the attack but if she was, her rule in Cetacea would quickly come to an end.

The sun was shining overhead and I took a moment to breathe in the briny scent of the ocean. I sent up a silent word of thanks to An'Ceann for helping me survive and for the beauty surrounding me. I felt a comforting embrace in response as I made my way over to Aileene, Hillaes, Wu, Mkali and Bernie. My heart warmed when Aileene's eyes lit up when she saw me and the smile she gave me caused my steps to falter.

"Hello love," I said, and I kissed the top of her head after she threw herself into my arms. *Thank you for healing me, I feel much better.*

I don't plan on going through my long life without you, quit trying to get yourself killed, Aileene growled through our connection but the grin on her face told me she wasn't angry.

We walked up to the others and I saw the relief on their faces when we joined them. Even though Aileene and the Einhorns were the only ones allowed into my room when I was injured, I knew everyone had been worried about me.

"Alister, how are you feeling?" Hillaes broke the awkward silence.

"Much better, thank you. What are you working on?" I asked as I picked up one of the barbed hooks from the small pile at one end of the table. It was about five inches long with barbs along the curved end which ended in a jagged point. I shuddered in revulsion as I looked closely at the deadly weapon. This was one of the hooks that had ripped me apart and they'd all been made from the bones of a Royal Dragon.

"Aileene, Wu and I are trying to figure out a way to protect your skin and scales from these," Hillaes said pointing to the pile of hooks after I had finished studying the one in my hands.

Shelley wandered away to take up the third point of the protective triangle that my Knights created around our group. I smiled at my friend and was amazed at how serious he took his duty as one of my Knights.

"As I was saying before Alister joined us," Wu spoke up, "I've searched through the records available to me as The Historian and I haven't found anything that could protect a person from a weapon made of Royal Dragon bone."

"And I'll say it again, there may not be anything physical we can use but Therians tend to be a bit short-sighted when it comes to magical means of protection. You've admitted that Alister has an affinity for magic unlike any other High King or Queen in your history. He's also shown an amazing ability to construct spells in ways we haven't thought of before."

"How long has this been going on?" I whispered to Aileene.

"About an hour, as you can see, they have a difference of opinion." She grinned at me.

"Hold on you two, I think you're both right, but we have to figure something out that will work. What have you tried so far?" I asked.

Both Hillaes and Wu looked sheepish as Aileene answered for them, "They haven't tried anything yet. They've been arguing theories and haven't gotten to the practical yet."

"Okay," I said as I clapped my hands and rubbed them together. "Let's see what we can figure out, starting with a regular shield spell and go from there. Aileene, please cast the *Spheara* spell on me and then we can see if one of the hooks will pierce the skin on my finger."

Aileene scowled at me while she folded her arms over her chest. "I have a better idea, why don't you cast the spell on me, and we'll use my finger as a test subject?"

"I don't want to see you get hurt," I replied.

"And I want to see you get hurt again, especially after I've spent the better part of three days healing your mangled body?" Aileene answered coldly.

"But—" I began.

"And if you're thinking of saying something about me being a woman and you being a man then you can stop right there. I am a Royal Dragon and future High Queen of Theria, not some helpless female. Besides, according to your dream, I'm the one who gets killed by a weapon made from Royal Dragon bone," Aileene finished hotly.

"I don't know much about women, Stretch, but what I do know is it's better not to argue with them when they're right and have that look in their eye," Shelley said over his shoulder from where he was standing.

I looked at Aileene and softened when I realized she wanted to protect me as much as I wanted to protect her.

I pulled her into my arms and hugged her tightly. "I'm sorry. You're right, I just don't want to see you get hurt."

"I know, and it actually makes me feel good that you're so protective, but we have to figure this out. Better a little pain now than death later," she said as she squeezed me back.

We stepped back from each other and I cast *Spheara* on Aileene and she held up her hand. The shield covered her whole body and moved with her. Hillaes grabbed one of the hooks and moved to Aileene's right side where she held her arm away from her body.

"Alister, if I cut Aileene's hand, I would like you to heal her immediately and then we can adjust the shield until we find the right combination. Wu, please keep records of each experiment," Hillaes said as she took charge.

Wu had his tablet out to record the events and nodded at Hillaes.

"Are you ready, Aileene?" Hillaes asked and after Aileene nodded, she continued. "Experiment one, Spheara shield, regular strength, Aileene's right thumb. Here we go." Hillaes quickly drew the sharpened hook across Aileene's thumb and her indrawn breath of pain let me know the first experiment was a failure. I cast the *Sanos* spell and her thumb healed before the drop of blood fell to the deck.

"This is going to be a long day," I muttered and Aileene stuck her tongue out at me which made me laugh.

CHAPTER THREE

yndi
Earth

I laughed to myself as I once again imagined the faces of the sailors in the submarine I had come across shortly after I left Hawaii. Sailors are a superstitious lot and submarine crews are probably the worst. I shouldn't have tapped out the words to "Under the Sea" from the *The Little Mermaid* in Morse Code on the side of the submarine with a rock, but I couldn't help myself. I wish I could read the Captain's report he submitted to his superiors.

I'd eaten a late dinner in Hawaii and had taken two days to make my way towards Atlantis. For some reason, I felt compelled to check on the equipment I noticed the last time I was there but wanted to enjoy the journey as well. I loved the freedom I experienced while swimming, but I missed Jason. The last time we had dinner together I thought he was going to propose but he chickened out. If he had asked, I would have said yes, but there were still things we had to talk about. I have to let him know why I'm reluctant to return to Theria; that might be a good place to start.

My train of thought was derailed by a flash of light and a shockwave heading towards me, which was unusual because I was swimming around three-hundred feet underwater. I came to a full stop and waited to meet the displaced water rushing towards me. Using my sonar-like senses, I estimated the wave front would reach me in three-two-one.

If I had been on land, my breath would have been knocked out of my lungs, but I just curled in on myself and rode the wave until it played itself out. I looked to where the wave originated and saw a glow in the distance. I cautiously made my way forward and in five minutes could make out the ruins of Atlantis and see a swirling portal, glowing with a sickly-yellow light.

A sense of unease washed over me as I neared the portal and I felt like I was being watched. I looked around and couldn't see anyone, but I activated the pocket dimension on my necklace and retrieved my trident I'd stored there. Inching my way closer to the shining portal I saw myself reflected on the surface. My eyes were all black and teeth had elongated in response to danger. Even if I couldn't see a threat, my body's automatic response had kicked in and I knew better than to ignore the warning signs.

I'm not sure what was going on, but I needed to head to the surface and send a message to King Alister on the special tablet he'd given me, letting him know a dimensional gate had somehow opened on Earth. The planet could be in danger. As I was about to turn away from the portal, I saw movement reflected behind me and I spun around with my trident in my right hand and the claws of my left hand elongated. I was ready for a fight, but I wasn't ready for the sight that greeted me.

Two rows of mere-people in armor faced me, each one held a trident in his or her hand and were dressed in the livery of the Kingdom of Cetacea. When I turned around, everyone but the Captain of the Guard bowed deeply at the waist in my direction. The Captain of the Guard transferred his trident to his left hand, placed his right hand over his heart and inclined his head at me.

Lady Cynthia, he sent, *it is a pleasure to see you again.*

I refrained from rolling my eyes at his formality, but it wasn't his fault. *Hello, Captain Muir, you're looking well. I'm almost afraid to ask, but what are you doing here?*

He seemed surprised that I would ask such an obvious question. *We're here for you. Your mother sent us to escort you home.*

My shoulders slumped in defeat.

Alister

"What if you're looking at this the wrong way?" Shelley asked from where he lounged on the deckchair. He looked relaxed as he soaked up the sun's rays, but I could tell he was alert by the way he kept his body ready for action.

"What do you mean?" I blew out a frustrated breath and looked up from where I had once again healed Aileene's hand. We had been working on the shield spell for two days and we would arrive in Cetacea in three more.

"Take five and I'll let you know," Shelley answered.

I looked at Hillaes and Aileene to see if they wanted to take a break and when they nodded, I agreed. We moved into the shade and sat at the table set up there. Stewards brought us fruit juice and finger foods so we could eat and talk. It's always a good idea to have food ready when shifters meet; we eat a lot.

"Thank you, Jenesis," Aileene smiled at the young woman who served her.

"My pleasure, Lady Aileene," Jenesis replied with a curtsy.

"Sire, will there be anything else?" the man bowing to me asked.

"No, thank you Jansen, everything looks delicious," I said. I had tried to get the sailors to call me Alister until Fritz informed me I was causing more confusion than helping my people feel more at ease, I was still getting used to this.

"Okay, Shelley. Did you actually produce an idea, or did you just want a snack?" Bernie asked with a smirk.

"For your information, I have ideas—and I did want a snack," Shelley grinned. After emptying his juice glass, he continued. "How many attempts to create a shield against dragon bone have you made so far?"

Hillaes looked at her tablet and responded, "One-hundred-ninety-two."

"And how many have been successful?" he continued.

"Zero," Aileene answered, "What are you thinking?"

"Alister, remember the comic books we loved about the team of genetically enhanced superheroes and how each one had specific powers?" I nodded so he continued. "One of my favorite's was Diamond Girl. Even though she couldn't fly and didn't have some of the other cool powers, she could make her skin as hard as diamonds. What if instead of trying to create a shield, you try to harden your skin?"

The shocked silence around the table was only broken when Shelley asked for someone to pass the fruit tray.

"That might just work," Hillaes muttered to herself and began tapping on her tablet. After a few moments of silence, she grabbed an emmon from the center of the table and held it in her hand. Emmons are a round, dark-purple fruit which you peel like an orange. Also like an orange the deep red fruit inside is segmented and it can be juiced. It tastes like a cross between a pineapple and red grapes.

Hillaes looked at the fruit on her plate and took one of the hooks out of the pocket of her leather apron. The hook easily pierced the skin of the fruit. She rotated it ninety degrees, muttered *Adamantem* and tried again. This time she met resistance, but the hook still sliced into the fruit. She slumped in her chair. "I thought we were onto something," she said dejectedly.

"I believe we are," I said and held out my right hand for the hook. "My guess is this spell will work best on our dragon scales since we're already impervious to any other weapon we know of." Turning my left hand palm up, I looked at it and manifested dragon scales on my hand and arm. Concentrating on my hand, I muttered *Adamantem* and cast the spell Hillaes had explained to me. My hand didn't feel any differently, but I triggered the *Visus Magicae* spell I had created to see magical energy and noticed my skin was shimmering with a magical glow.

"Here goes," I said and dragged the hook across my palm—nothing happened.

"It worked," Aileene breathed excitedly and beamed at me. "Try it on me next," she said, and I handed her the hook. I cast the spell on her and gasped when she stabbed her palm with the hook rather than gently dragging it against her scales. The result was the same, the hook didn't pierce her scales.

Everyone at the table cheered and we enjoyed our success while I asked Jansen and Jenesis to bring us something more substantial to eat. Over the impromptu lunch we discussed what we should do next.

"We have proof of concept that the spell will work to keep you safe from dragon bone but we need to make sure it will work when you're in your dragon form," Bernie suggested as she took a bite from the double cheese burger on her plate. I listened as Hillaes, Aileene, Mkali and Bernie mapped out the next steps of our experiment. Shelley appeared to be having an eating contest, and since he was the only contestant, he was winning.

"Wu, something's been bothering me, and I hope you have some answers," I said when I finished eating.

"I hope so, too," Wu nodded as he picked at the salad he'd chosen.

"Shelley, please give Wu one of your burgers, I need him working at full capacity and that salad just isn't cutting it." I laughed.

"Thank you," he said as he accepted the offering from Shelley and hummed with pleasure as he took the first bite.

"Should I leave you two alone?" I teased.

"No, we're good," Wu grinned. "What do you want to know?"

"Where did this dragon bone come from?" I held up my hand to forestall the comment I knew Shelley was about to make. "Obviously, it came from a Royal Dragon but—," I paused trying to figure out how to ask my question. "Is there a Royal Dragon graveyard where the bones of my ancestors are buried? My parents haven't said anything about this before and I don't know what happens to our bodies when we die."

"I'm sorry, but I don't know that either. It seems that this is a secret only known to the High King or Queen and An'Ceann. This is probably another one of those things that you will learn about at the proper time; I don't have any answers for you," Wu apologized.

"I'll contact my parents later to see if they can give me some information because your response fills me with more questions. If the location of Royal Dragon bodies is such a closely guarded secret, how could our enemy get hold of one to make these weapons?" I held up the hook Aileene had returned to me and looked at it closely. "We retrieved ninety-seven hooks from the net and almost all of them were different sizes. Each one shows evidence that they were chipped to create the edge but I'm guessing the only thing that would have worked to make the hook would have been another piece of bone. How many of these bones does our enemy have? Do they have access to the lance I saw in my dream? I could go on for quite a while."

My friends shook their heads in concern, so I waved them off. "I have lots of questions, but no answers. I'll share what I can when I speak with my parents, but there may be things I cannot reveal to you," I said regretfully.

Once we finished our meal, we gathered on the foredeck and created enough space for Aileene to transform. She again insisted that she be the one to test the spell and I saw the wisdom of her request.

I'm going to trigger the Adamantem *spell then shift. I want to see if it will transform with me,* Aileene sent.

I triggered *Visus Magicae* and saw the magical glow on her skin as she cast the *Adamantem* spell. Then she shifted and that same glow spread across her scales like a fire spreads across paper when lit.

"How do you feel?" I asked as I walked up to Aileene and rubbed her jaw as she scent-marked me.

No different than I normally do, but you're pretty small, Aileene chuffed in laughter.

"Okay, I'm going to use a hook to see if the spell will protect your scales," I started.

Alister, I want you to do something for me and I don't want you to argue, Aileene sent. *I want you to manifest claws on your hand and use those instead of the hook. If the spell deflects your strike, we'll know it will work on the bone.* She sensed my hesitation; *I need to know this will work against a live dragon as well as against dragon bone. I trust you, if you cut me, you can heal me.*

I'd like to go on record that I hate this idea, I sent and pressed my forehead to her jaw.

Noted—Don't hold back, I believe the spell will work and I want you to drag your claws down my side.

"Fine," I huffed and moved next to her side and partially shifted. I grew about five feet in height and two feet in width. My arms were completely scaled, and my fingers ended in talons. *Here goes,* I sent then raked my claws against her side as hard as I could. My talons couldn't get through the protective spell and slid off without making a mark.

"It worked," Aileene shifted and jumped into my arms in excitement before I had the chance to transform.

Once I was human, I laughed and whirled her around. I looked into her shining blue eyes and was about to give her a kiss when I heard Shelley mutter, "Hey guys, I don't think Mkali should see things like that—oof."

"Don't mind him," Bernie said as she rubbed the hand she'd used to smack him in the stomach, "his mouth runs ahead of his brain."

"Tell us something we don't know," I laughed and gave Aileene one last squeeze.

Brarth opened the outer door to my suite and poked his head inside. "Sire, Jeffrey is here to see you. Is now a good time?"

I looked up from my tablet and the report I was reading about Cetacea Fritz had prepared for me. Standing and stretching my back I replied, "It's time I took a break anyway. Please send him in. Oh, and Brarth, can you also get us some coffee?"

"Absolutely," Brarth grinned and closed the door again. I moved into the sitting area and chose the red leather chair. Like all the furniture, it had been custom made to accommodate my size and I was embraced by buttery smooth leather as I sat. The door opened and

Brarth led Jeffrey to me while Gekur wheeled in the drinks cart which was loaded with everything necessary for afternoon tea. Even though I'd eaten lunch an hour before, I'd used a lot of energy this morning perfecting the *Adamantem* spell and was hungry again.

I stood to greet Jeffrey and he bowed low to me and spoke to the carpet, "You wanted to see me, Sire?"

Brarth arched one eyebrow at me and Gekur smothered a smile. They both knew how uncomfortable it made me when people bowed and groveled before me. I gave them both a withering glance which must not have been effective since they grinned back.

"Please rise and help yourself to something to eat and drink. You two as well," I said sarcastically to Brarth and Gekur who were already helping themselves.

"I informed Sirs Arktos and Einhorn that you were entertaining a visitor," Gekur mentioned as he loaded up his plate. "One of them will be along shortly."

"Do you need my help holding the door for you?" I asked when I looked at the heaping plates and cups of coffee the ogre brothers had in their hands. They had the grace to look sheepish at one another and nod. I laughed and held the door for them as they exited the room. "I hope you left some for me," I muttered as I closed the door.

There was plenty for me and I filled my plate and settled into my chair. Before I could start the conversation, Bernie and Mkali walked in to join us.

Alister, I know you like to keep things informal but Brarth and Gekur should not have both their hands occupied when they're guarding your door.

C'mon Bernie, who's going to—I stopped when she scowled at me. *Okay,* I conceded.

Her expression softened, *Shelley, Mkali and I talked this over. You need to trust us to do our jobs. I won't be too hard on Brarth and Gekur,* she sent, and I nodded.

"Would you like me to come back later?" Jeffrey asked nervously.

"No need," Bernie said brightly, "we just had to clear something up."

"Would you like a refill on your coffee?" Mkali asked. When Jeffrey shook his head, she took her post by the door while Bernie sat to my right.

"Thank you for coming," I told Jeffrey.

"I am yours to command, Sire. You have been kinder to me than I deserve. If I may be so bold—no, it's not my place to question. What would you have of me?"

Wu, please come to my suite, I sent before I answered the man sitting in front of me. "Jeffrey, I've asked Wu to join us because I think he has a perspective that can help you understand why I've shown you kindness. Before he gets here, I have something I need your help with."

"I will do anything," he said earnestly.

Bernie laughed, "I wouldn't be so quick to agree before you hear what he needs."

Jeffrey shook his head, "You don't understand. If the King asked me to jump off the ship and swim the rest of the way to Cetacea, that's what I would do. He gave me my life back; he gave me my family back. He has given me the chance to redeem myself and restore those relationships I destroyed when I worked for Dimitri. If it hadn't been for King Alister, I would have less than nothing."

Wu entered the room and saved me from further embarrassment.

"Wu, can you please tell Jeffrey the story of how we met on Middle Earth?" I asked and Bernie giggled at the expression on his face.

"Very well," Wu said as he sat and told Jeffrey the story of how he attacked Bernie and tried to kill her because Dimitri had threatened his family. He didn't stop there, he told him about our journey across Middle Earth and finished with the battle with Dimitri. Jeffrey sat in stunned silence as he heard the tale and even Mkali kept sneaking glances in my direction as Wu talked.

Jeffrey shook his head in confusion and addressed me, "I don't understand. Wu attacked you and tried to kill Sir Einhorn. How could you forgive him? How could you make him a member of your Inner Circle?"

"Jeffrey, both you and Wu were victims of Dimitri's evil and were forced to do things for the sake of your families. You both suffered and for that reason I chose to extend grace."

"But I oppressed those in Dimitri's fortress," Jeffrey hung his head in shame.

"True, but I also know you have worked to make things right with those you harmed since we freed everyone from the fortress. I also know that you defied Dimitri in secret and protected as many as you could from his wrath. How many did you hide when Dimitri ordered you to execute them?"

Jeffrey looked at me in surprise, "You know about that?"

"You'd be surprised at how many of those we rescued begged for clemency for you as they told us about what you did to save them. They also told me you protected and fed the children as often as you could, and you often took beatings on their behalf."

"There were some guards who liked to inflict pain and didn't care who they hurt as long as they got to damage someone," Jeffrey admitted.

Tears filled my eyes when I thought of the pain this man had endured at the hands of the sadistic guards. "Jeffrey, all I've done is given you the opportunity to make things right with those you wronged. If they've offered you forgiveness, you need to learn to forgive yourself as well. What you did was wrong, but great wrongs were also done to you. I'm sorry Dimitri was allowed to spread such hatred and evil. The only consolation I can offer you is I ended his reign of terror when I cut his head from his body."

I stood and knelt in front of Jeffrey. "On behalf of the Crown of Theria, I ask you to forgive us for failing in our duty to *Protect the Weak* when someone who should have protected you oppressed you instead."

Jeffrey looked at me in shock then took the hand I held out to him and shook it solemnly. I watched his resolve as we clasped hands. "Thank you, Sire. I do forgive you and will do everything in my power to help right the wrongs perpetrated on our people in the Kingdom of Theria and across the entire planet."

I smiled and pulled Jeffrey with me as I stood. I embraced him and kissed his forehead. "That's all I can ask of you," I said and retook my seat.

We talked for hours but we were no closer to figuring out which ruler or rulers had been working with Dimitri in plotting the rebellion against my father when he was High King. The protective shield that had covered the Kingdom of Theria may have delayed the plans of those who were bent on destruction, but the evil seed sown by the conspirators had been allowed to grow unchecked for fourteen years.

The rest of my Inner Circle joined me in my suite for dinner and everyone asked Jeffrey questions in different ways but always produced the same answers. Dimitri had worked with others; he had received the poison from another kingdom or kingdoms before he used it on my parents, but we didn't know who they were. We would arrive in Cetacea in a couple of days and as I got ready for bed, I considered the warning in my dream. We had produced a solution to the dragon bone but were still clueless on how to deal with the poison I was set to drink.

"I bring you a gift," An'Ceann said from behind me.

I whirled around and saw An'Ceann standing in my room. As usual, he was much larger than me and his presence filled my room, which seemed to expand to hold his essence. I looked at the corner of my bed and noticed pajamas that hadn't been there before An'Ceann arrived. I held them up and saw they were footie pajamas with a dragon's head for a hood. Even though An'Ceann appeared in his lion form, I could see he was smirking at me.

"Thanks a lot," I said as I held up the pajamas, "but I think I might be a bit old to wear these."

"That's not the gift," An'Ceann snickered, "but it would have been funny to see you put them on."

"Ha, ha, very funny," I muttered and gave him a hug. "It's good to see you."

"I'm glad to see you recovered from your injuries," An'Ceann said seriously as he bent his head to look me in the eye. "I think Aileene made a wise choice to leave those scars on your chest as a reminder of what you almost lost. You were close to death, closer than you've been before."

"Why didn't you help me?" I asked then winced at the accusation in my tone.

"But I did help you," An'Ceann said solemnly. "I gave you and Aileene to one another so you could be strong for each other. I also whispered to Shelley, Bernie and Mkali that they should confront you about trying to do everything on your own. If Shelley hadn't gone with you to attack the ship, you would have died in the water."

"But they could have ignored you. What would have happened if they hadn't listened, or if I hadn't listened to my friends. What would have happened if Aileene couldn't have healed me?"

An'Ceann stopped me with a reproachful growl, "We don't have to worry about those things because they didn't happen. Alister, there are far too many real things to concern yourself with than to make up 'what if?' scenarios. Suffice it to say, I helped you in the best way possible and leave it at that, okay?"

I bowed my head in apology, "You're right. Thank you."

He chuckled warmly, "You're welcome. Good job on figuring out the diamond skin spell, you were wise to listen to your friends."

"But we still have to figure out how to deal with the poison," I answered.

"That you do," An'Ceann agreed, "but, you don't have to have that question answered before you arrive in Cetacea."

I held my hand to my chest in surprise, "Did you just give me a spoiler?"

"Just a small one," An'Ceann laughed. "The reason I'm here is to give you the gift of knowing the answer to your question about the Royal Dragon graveyard."

"Thank you, I asked my father earlier and he told me that was something we would have to talk about in person and he couldn't give me any more details than that."

An'Ceann nodded, "Yes, and that's why I'm here. In the dark years before your ancestors chose to follow me, Royal Dragons fought and killed each other to establish their territories. The loss of life was staggering since not only would the dragons fight, their shifter armies would go to war as well. The bodies of Royal Dragons littered the battlefields and their bones were left to dry in the sun. Eventually those bones were used to make weapons and warring kingdoms would use those weapons to kill Royal Dragon hatchlings they considered to be their enemies.

"Once your ancestors, Dóchas and Síocháin, chose to follow my path I instructed them to collect all the dragon bone on the planet so I could destroy it. And before you ask, yes, I could have gathered it myself, but I wanted them to learn something from the exercise, and they did."

"What did they learn?" I asked hopefully.

"What I wanted them to," An'Ceann's laughter rumbled in his chest.

"Of course," I muttered.

"Since that time until now, when it comes time for a Royal Dragon to pass from this life, I take them to my kingdom first, so their bones aren't left on Theria."

I thought about what An'Ceann told me and about my own mortality. I knew I would probably live for hundreds if not a thousand years, but one day Aileene and I would make that journey to An'Ceann's Kingdom and our bones would be left there.

"That's—that's a lot to take in," I said quietly.

"I know," An'Ceann answered and put his paw on my shoulder.

"How do I get rid of the hooks made out of bone?" I asked.

"What do you think?" He answered my question with a question.

"I suppose dragon-fire would work?" I asked.

"I suggest you use inferno," he chuckled as he used the name Shelley and I had produced for my flame intensity.

After a moment I asked about the next thing that had been bugging me. "But, if all the dragon bones were destroyed in the past and no Royal Dragons have died on Theria since then, where did these bones come from?"

"From a place they shouldn't have," An'Ceann answered mysteriously.

"And it's up to me to figure that out?" I asked.

"Not alone—it's up to all of you to figure this out together," he responded. "If it's any consolation, I believe in you."

I looked at the glint of amusement in his eyes and couldn't help laughing. "Well, that's good. Will I see you again on this journey?"

"Possibly, but remember, even if you don't see me, I will be with you, always," he answered.

"Wait," I stopped him, "did you just quote Star Wars to me?"

He laughed, "Of course not. However, I think Star Wars might have quoted me."

"You said that about Spider-man too," I reminded him.

"I've said a lot of great things," he laughed and kissed me on the forehead. "I'm proud of you, Alister," he said and disappeared.

"Thank you," I whispered and finished getting ready for bed. I did not wear the footie pajamas.

I knelt amidst the carnage on the field of battle, weeping over the bodies of my two best friends. Bernie and Shelley had died back to back and even in death, they still held hands. They were surrounded by the bodies of enemy shifters—their attackers paid with their lives. However, it didn't matter in the end; everyone was dead.

Hearing a noise behind me, I turned to see a shadowy figure in a hooded cloak holding a golden goblet. I couldn't see the face of the figure but I knew it wanted me to take the cup and drink. The menacing specter compelled me to move toward it.

My outstretched hand, covered with the blood of my friends, trembled with the effort to fight the compulsion. Helplessly overcome, I took the cup and drained the bittersweet contents. My mouth and throat burned and I could feel the liquid travel into my stomach. The fiery pain was replaced by freezing cold and my limbs became numb. I heard a roar and saw Aileene streaking toward me as I fell to my knees, my vision darkening at the edges.

My eyes were fixed on my mate as a shaft streaked from the ground and struck her in the chest. Instead of sinking into her flesh, the missile exploded when it hit her hardened skin. I watched Aileene fly towards me and I smiled with the knowledge she would survive. My limbs turned to rubber and I fell face-first onto the bloody earth. I was roughly flipped onto my back and once again confronted by my faceless enemy, my body void of feeling or strength. My heartbeat faltered and stilled in my chest while my sight faded.

The last thing I heard before slipping into oblivion was one word. "Soon."

CHAPTER FOUR

*B*ernie, Shelley, Aileene and I enjoyed breakfast on the balcony outside my suite which overlooked the aft deck. We were contemplating the changes to my dream as well as the discussion I'd had with An'Ceann.

"So, Bernie and I are still dead?" Shelley asked solemnly.

I nodded and replied, "I am, too, but at least it looks like we've changed Aileene's future."

"I'm happy about that," Bernie added, "but I'd prefer to keep all of us alive if possible."

Aileene looked at the three of us with fire in her eyes. "We will survive, and our enemies will quake in fear when we find them. If I have to burn each kingdom to the ground to keep you safe, I will." She declared fiercely.

As usual, Shelley broke the silence. "You're cute when you get all protective and homicidal and stuff."

Aileene threw a biscuit at him and we all laughed. "I am serious though," Aileene continued. "We will make it through this alive. Alister's dream has already changed since we solved the issue with the dragon bone, I'm certain we'll be able to change the rest as well."

I leaned over and kissed Aileene on the cheek, "Thank you, love. I also believe we'll be able to change the future. We just have to figure out how to do each of these things," I ticked off each of the next points on my fingers one by one. "We need to reunite the kingdoms under the banner of the High King, we have to root out the leaders of the rebellion and deal with them and we have to figure out how to neutralize the poison that I am fated to drink at some point in the future."

"If by 'deal with them' you mean utterly destroy them, I agree with you," Bernie added.

Aileene and Shelley nodded in agreement. "Let me clarify my position on this," I added firmly. "Based on what I already know, these conspirators were in league with Dimitri and they are also guilty of the death and destruction committed by Dimitri. When they are unmasked, the only mercy I will show them is a quick death. They have committed treason and will pay for that with their lives. I will spare the innocent and those who have been forced to follow these unjust rulers, but the leaders have sealed their fate."

Both Shelley and Bernie looked at me with newfound respect and placed their right fist over their heart and bowed their heads and said in unison, "Yes, my King." I felt a frisson of energy leave my body and pulse outward at my declaration and their agreement. The air around me felt charged with electricity and it was clear that something momentous had happened.

Sire, is everything okay? Wu sent and by the reactions of my friends I knew he was broadcasting to all of us.

Yes, we're just talking over breakfast in my suite. Why? I asked.

You did more than that, you just pulled power from every shifter on the planet and made a royal decree. Do you remember when you were about to fight Minos and you claimed the kingship?

I remember that, but how do you know about it? You weren't there.

As the Historian, I have all of Gustav's memories that pertain to your rule. Anyway, in the same way you declared yourself King and used power to make that happen, you just used your power as High King to pass judgement on those who are guilty of treason. Every person on this planet heard what you said and now the traitors know their fate is sealed.

I had no idea, I stammered mentally and looked to my friends who nodded to let me know they had heard me in their heads, too.

Did you mean what you said? Wu asked.

Absolutely, those who are part of this conspiracy will pay for their treachery with their lives.

Good, that's as it should be. As King you can show grace and mercy, but you must also be just. Even though you have already made your royal decree, I will also note it in the records. Your word will be written as law, Sire. Wu added then he closed the mental connection.

"I didn't know you could do that," Aileene said with awe in her voice.

"Me neither. I guess I'd better be careful when I order something different for breakfast," I joked.

"Even though I agreed the guilty must be punished, now I'm even more convinced we need to do something. If your decree had that effect on me, what do you think it did to the guilty?" Bernie asked.

"Probably nothing," Aileene responded. "Those with evil intent believe in the rightness of their actions regardless of how they hurt others. They will know that the King has declared their fate, but they will be arrogant enough to think they will be able to prevail."

I turned to Aileene in surprise. "You seem pretty certain of that. How do you know?"

"You're not the only one An'Ceann talks to you know," she responded smugly.

"And he's shared some things with you that you can't tell me?" I guessed.

She smiled brightly, "I can't give you spoilers, as he likes to call them. But, it's not anything you won't figure out eventually, and if you don't, I can always nudge you in the right direction."

"You can nudge Alister?" Bernie asked, "I have to hit Shelley with a two-by-four to get his attention sometimes."

We laughed at Shelley's expense but since he laughed, I didn't feel bad. "I updated my parents on our progress and the changes to the dream, too," I said as I helped myself to more bacon.

"Which ones?" Aileene asked as she stole bacon from my plate.

"All of them—they were together for an early breakfast. They will try to figure out which of the rulers Dimitri had been working with," I said as I tried to protect the food on my plate. Aileene stuck her tongue out at me and lightning quick, snagged another piece.

"You know, there's a full platter in front of you," I pointed out.

"But stolen bacon tastes better. Everyone knows that," Aileene pouted.

"It's true," Bernie chimed in as she swiped food from Shelley's plate. "I think it's amazing that our parents have been friends with each other for hundreds of years. It gives me something to look forward to."

"That's assuming we all survive," Shelley added gloomily.

Aileene glared at Shelley. "You must not have been listening earlier when I told you we will all survive. As your future Queen, I command you to stay alive. I don't really care what happens to you, but I know Alister would be heartbroken if you died."

"Love you too, Sis," Shelley said and winked at Aileene.

After a few minutes of some serious eating I mentioned another topic. "According to An'Ceann we have a little time to work on the problem of the poison, but I'm stumped on what we can do."

"Can't you just neutralize the poison when you come into contact with it?" Shelley asked.

"Possibly, if I knew it was there. But I asked my mother and father what they remembered about the poison and they said they didn't know anything was wrong until after they'd ingested it. They didn't smell anything unusual and even the bitter-sweet taste was similar enough to the wine in their cups they didn't have any warning they were in danger."

Bernie looked thoughtful as she asked, "What do you remember about the poison from when you healed your parents?"

I closed my eyes and concentrated on that day. I remembered the despair I felt when I realized I didn't have enough magical power to heal their withered bodies. They had been without food and water for so long they were on the edge of dying. The poison filled their bodies with a stygian darkness that absorbed the healing energy the way black holes keep light from escaping their gravitational fields. I remember touching that darkness with my mind and feeling a sense of oily residue that coated my parents' bodies. It was only after I was able to overwhelm the darkness with the magical light I created that the poison was slowly driven out and destroyed.

"Do you remember when we were on that beach in California and stepped in tar?" I asked my friends. At their nods I continued, "It was hard to wipe off because it kept transferring to anything we touched? It's a lot like that. The poison felt oily, coating everything it touched and seemed to spread whenever I touched it with the spell."

"Would you recognize the feel of it if you encounter it again?" Shelley asked.

"I'm not sure, let me think about it," I finished lamely.

"Alister, I would like you to remember the events of that day, but this time broadcast your memories to the three of us. Maybe we'll see something you missed," Bernie suggested.

I reached out my hands to Aileene and Shelley and they connected their hands with Bernie's. I didn't know if we needed to touch but if I was going to relive those memories, I wanted the physical connection. I'm not sure how long we spent reviewing memories like game-day instant replays, but it felt like days had passed rather than hours. Not only did my friends experience the events, they also shared my emotions. By the time we had everything we needed, we were all exhausted and fell back in our chairs.

"That was intense," Shelley breathed and stood. He hadn't let go of my hand, so he pulled me out of my chair and gave me a hug. I soaked up the warmth of my friend and appreciated the support he gave me without having to say anything. I did laugh when he said, "I figured you could use a bear hug."

We slapped each other on the back and sat. Bernie leaned into Shelley and he put his arm around her. She had tears in her eyes when she looked at me. "Is that what you went through when you healed me?"

I nodded and felt Aileene lay her head on my shoulder and wrap her hands around my arm. "It wasn't as intense with you but in some ways was worse because I was just learning how to heal."

Aileene smiled at me and said, "One of the things I love about you is your willingness to give your all to help others. I am thankful that you were able to heal Mother and Father, but it wasn't wise for you to drain yourself to the point of death."

I nodded and kissed the top of her head, "I know, but I didn't have many options." I chuckled, "You'd do the same thing and you know it."

"You're right, but I also would have at least called out to my mate for help and an infusion of strength," Aileene said as she looked me in the eye. I was taken aback by the intensity of her gaze. "You are learning to let others help you, but it is imperative you don't continue to make the same mistakes and keep trying to protect the rest of us when we have abilities you don't." She leaned in and rested her forehead against mine, "The future of Theria depends on our survival. We have enough enemies trying to kill us, we don't need to assist them by being foolish."

Tears welled in my eyes because I could feel her love and support through our mate connection, but I could feel Bernie's and Shelley's as well. "Thank you all, you're the best."

"Glad you finally figured it out, I've been telling you that for years," Shelley grinned and punched me in the arm.

Síocháin 18, 10,257

Two days later we sailed into the main harbor of Cetacea. Thousands of people were cheering on the shore and the water was filled with every type of water shifter imaginable. Mermen, mermaids and cecaelia were lined up on either side of the ship and served to hold back the cheering crowds in the water and to guide us into the berth reserved for us. Aileene and I stood on the prow of the ship waving to the crowds. We were flanked by our Knights and the rest of our Inner

Circle stood behind us. Fritz and Frieda kept up a steady stream of mental instructions on protocol. I never knew there were so many ways to wave.

Sire, you and Lady Aileene should transform and escort the ship the rest of the way to shore, Fritz sent.

I also recommend you have Sir Arktos and Sir Einhorn accompany you. We will bring Squire Mkali with us when we disembark, Frieda added.

I grinned at Aileene and we made our way to the center of the foredeck to transform. Aileene and Bernie went first, but I shot myself into the air seconds after Aileene did. If the crowds were loud before, the cheering doubled in volume when we appeared in our dragon forms. Aileene and I flanked the ship, she flew to port and I flew to starboard.

Why don't you give the people a taste of T-Rex, Shelley laughed and Aileene let loose with an ear-splitting roar. The crowd was momentarily stunned but then their roar of approval rivaled Aileene's.

You enjoyed that, didn't you? I sent.

Of course, was Aileene's smug reply, *why don't you dazzle them with a display of fire?*

Hang on, Shelley, I sent and then beat my wings to ascend at a ninety degree angle. When I reached the apex of my climb, I arched my back and flipped over, so I was diving towards the ocean. I roared and shot flame towards the water below. I made sure to turn off the flame before it got close to any shifters in the water and I could hear Shelley whooping in delight at this display.

By this time, the ship was slipping into the berth and the sailors were making things secure. Aileene and I hovered over the foredeck and partially transformed so just our wings were manifest. Bernie and Shelley clung to our backs as we lowered ourselves to the deck, hand-in-hand.

The four of us walked to the gangway and took our places in the procession. The palace guards led the way followed by Miriam and Stavros Arktos, Wu and Hillaes, Fritz and Frieda Einhorn then Shelley, Aileene and I walked side-by-side and Bernie and Mkali followed behind. The guards peeled off and stood next to the Cetacean guards who were holding back the crowds. Before Aileene and I stepped off the ship, Fritz announced, "His Royal Highness, Alister Rex, confirmed High King of all Theria by An'Ceann, Opener of Gates, Righter of Wrongs, Avenger of Blood, Defender of Theria, Champion of Middle Earth, Servant of An'Ceann and Lady Aileene, future High Queen of Theria, Champion of Eutheria, Defender of Earth, Revealer of Plots, Protector of the Realm and Servant of An'Ceann."

Aileene had her hand in the crook of my left arm as we made our way down the gangplank and walked towards the woman standing in front of a golden throne created in the shape of an octopus. Her skin was the color of polished driftwood, had piercing green eyes and was dressed in a long lace-covered gown the blue-green color of open water. The lace looked like ocean spray. She looked proud and regal, but had a welcoming smile on her face. Her long purple hair was the color of a sea urchin and the golden crown on her head was decorated with pieces of coral and sea glass.

"Welcome to the Kingdom of Cetacea, we are honored that you have joined us," the woman proclaimed.

Just as we rehearsed it, Fritz's voice sounded in my head.

"Lady Zhaleh, the honor is mine. Thank you for graciously meeting with us today. If I can serve you in any way, I offer my services as High King of Theria." I looked at the woman standing to her right and could see the family resemblance. Even though I was surprised to see her, I didn't let that show on my face as I continued.

"If your daughter is any indication of how you rule your people, I am glad to make your acquaintance."

Or, you could just wing it—Fritz replied with humor. *Don't stop now, you've clearly impressed the woman.*

I looked over to Cyndi standing there and winked at her, she stuck her tongue out at me and I laughed.

Thank you for welcoming me and mine to your Kingdom, I promise to serve you well, I broadcast to every shifter across Cetacea.

"Your Majesty," Lady Zhaleh breathed and got down on one knee in reverence. The rest of her subjects quickly followed her example.

"High King, I pledge to you my loyalty and promise to serve you, the people of Cetacea and all Theria."

Aileene and I moved to where Lady Zhaleh was kneeling and each of us took one of her hands and helped her stand.

Bernie spoke into my mind, *there is no deceit in her words.*

"And I accept your pledge and gladly affirm your rule in Cetacea," I said as we led her to the throne and helped her get settled. Turning to Zhaleh's loyal subjects I shouted, "Long live Lady Zhaleh, ruler of Cetacea." To a person, those gathered bowed in respect to their beloved leader and I felt a sense of connection between Lady Zhaleh and her people. This was a healthy kingdom.

"Thank you, Sire," Zhaleh whispered. "Over lunch would it be possible to discuss a small problem I'm having that you might be able to help me with?"

Before I could answer Cyndi responded, "I don't know about anyone else, but I could eat. Hopefully, I'll have time to change out of this dress though."

We met in the formal dining room, which was reserved for visiting dignitaries; Cyndi was still in her dress. Lady Zhaleh had offered me the place at the head of the table but I had declined in favor of the seat on her right. Cyndi sat at her left and Aileene sat next to me.

"Lady Zhaleh," Fritz asked from his place at the middle of the table, "when we last spoke you said you were undecided about whether you would support King Phillip's abdication. What changed your mind?"

Lady Zhaleh looked fondly at her daughter as she answered. "Cyndi had a lot to do with my decision. She has spent the last few days telling me about King Alister and why he's a worthy High King."

"I told her about our time together on Earth and how you went out of your way to find me and then let me stay behind when you returned to Theria," Cyndi added.

"I'm curious about that," Aileene said, narrowing her eyes in annoyance. "You don't think you could have told us you were Lady Zhaleh's daughter while we were on Earth?"

Cyndi looked embarrassed, "I'm sorry, I know I should have but when I left home, I wasn't sure I would be welcomed back because I said some horrible things to my mother before moving to the palace in Theria."

"To be frank, I also said some things I regret and have spent every day of the last fourteen years hoping for a chance to make it right. When I heard Cyndi was on Earth, I opened a portal and sent Muir and some of my other guards to find her and bring her home."

"Wait," Stavros interjected, "what do you mean you opened a portal?"

Lady Zhaleh deflated in her chair, "We've had access to portal technology since the days Atlantis was a thriving community on Earth. My ancestors kept this secret from the High Kings and Queens and until recently I assumed it wasn't possible to open the portal without my knowledge or consent."

"If this were a movie, this is when the music would get more intense," Shelley whispered and Bernie and I nodded, Aileene rolled her eyes.

"Ignore them Mom," Cyndi laughed at her mom's expression. "It's a compliment if they tease you like this, it means they like and accept you."

"My apologies for interrupting your tale," I said. "I can't apologize for Sir Arktos, because there really is no excuse for him."

Shelley grinned unrepentantly and Lady Zhaleh laughed. "I can see you are very great friends, my husband and I had such friends before he was killed. I'm afraid I let those friendships fade away because the memories were too painful."

Cyndi held her mom's hand and silently encouraged her to continue.

"As I was saying, I've only recently learned that the portal has been randomly opening and closing for centuries but even more disturbing, someone in Cetacea has been using the portal as his private passage to

Earth, which he treats as his personal playground," Lady Zhaleh confessed.

"When did you discover this?" I asked.

"Just over a week ago. Once I discovered what had been going on, I asked Captain Muir to take a pod of twenty-four of my personal guards through the portal to find my daughter. I was surprised at how quickly they returned but it seems the portal was calling Cyndi home before we went looking for her."

"Remember I told you when I first arrived on Earth, I spent years exploring the oceans and found Therian equipment in the ruins of Atlantis?" At our nods she continued. "I've been thinking about that lately and grew concerned at what it could mean. I left my home seven days ago with the intention of looking into this mystery. I was quite surprised to find Captain Muir and the guards waiting for me."

"It sounds like An'Ceann had his hand in the timing of all this," Bernie concluded.

"You're probably right," I agreed.

"Okay, I understand you recently found out about the portal, but why didn't you inform my father?" I asked.

Lady Zhaleh looked puzzled, "I figured it wouldn't do any harm to wait until you arrived."

"I can understand that," I conceded. "Okay, my next question, is the portal still active?"

"No, as soon as we brought Cyndi home, I made sure it was shut down. There isn't any way to open it from Earth and now I'm truly the only one with access to the controls on this side."

"Wu, how is a portal different from a gate?" I asked.

Wu closed his eyes for a moment, which I'd come to learn meant he was accessing memories, but then answered. "A dimensional portal is created through technology and was first used to explore other dimensions around ten-thousand years ago. Therian scientists in Cetacea created this technology and connected this island of Cetacea to the island known as Atlantis on Earth. Those on Earth who believe Atlantis was an actual place look for ruins in the Mediterranean Sea near Greece. However, the actual location is near New Zealand."

"Thank you, Wu, but how is a portal different from a gate?" I grinned as I asked again.

Wu laughed, "I'm still getting used to all this knowledge at my fingertips, I get carried away."

"But on the upside, you'd do great on Jeopardy," Shelley muttered.

"The short answer is, a portal is created through technology, but a gate is created through the magic inherent to the High King. It was believed that all the portals had either been destroyed or were under the control of the Kingdom of Theria. This discovery could signal more problems for you, Sire," Wu finished.

"Let's worry about one thing at a time without inventing troubles we may not have," Miriam commented.

"I'll consult with my father later to see if he has anyone he can send to look into the malfunctioning portal. My second question is, do you know who has been accessing the portal to Earth?"

Lady Zhaleh looked embarrassed, "I do."

Please read Lady Zhaleh for me, she's not telling us the whole story, I sent to Bernie, Fritz and Frieda.

When she didn't continue, I decided to give her the full picture. "Lady Zhaleh," I said just above a whisper, "what I have to tell is extremely sensitive and only those with the highest level of clearance can hear what I'm about to say."

She looked at me with wide eyes but must have sent a silent command because most of her retainers and all the wait staff left the room. Cyndi was surprised to see Captain Muir still seated at the table but smiled slightly and chose not to mention anything.

When the room was clear I asked Hillaes to cast *Indicens* which created a shield of silence around the table so sound couldn't get in or out of the room. She nodded to say the spell was in place and we were free to talk.

"Fourteen years ago, my Father and Mother went to visit Dimitri who was a member of their Inner Circle. While there, Dimitri poisoned my parents and they only survived because they shifted into their dragon forms although they fell into deep comas. Once we received word at the palace of Dimitri's treachery, we fled Theria and headed to

Earth where we lived for thirteen years. Bernie, Shelley and I were unaware of our heritage and lived as humans. At the same time of our escape a magical shield covered the palace and the Kingdom of Theria so no one could leave or enter the kingdom.

"It wasn't until I defeated Dimitri and returned to the palace that I was able to lower the shield and bring stability to the Kingdom of Theria. We've recently discovered that Dimitri wasn't working alone and got the poison he used on my parents from another kingdom. I would like to believe that your pledge of loyalty is genuine, and you have nothing to do with the rebellion, but I don't know you and am not a fan of secrets right now. Please don't mistake my desire for peace as weakness. I will do everything within my power to reunite the kingdoms under my banner."

"And I will do anything I need to do to protect my mate and our people, even if that means I have to burn one of the kingdoms of Theria down to the dirt," Aileene growled.

I put my hand on her leg under the table.

Too much? she sent.

Just a tad, I replied, *but I appreciate the sentiment.*

"Sire, I'm not a traitor and before you told me, I didn't know anything about a rebellion," Lady Zhaleh answered nervously.

Truth, Bernie sent.

"Then what do you know about the one who's been accessing the portal?" I demanded.

Lady Zhaleh flinched at my tone but I could tell she was still reluctant to answer.

"Mom, please tell King Alister what he wants to know. Who is it?" Cyndi asked and her mom looked at her imploringly, while silently shaking her head.

"Zhaleh," Muir said softly, "if you don't answer the King, I will."

She whipped her head in his direction and I snapped, "Enough. Less than an hour ago you pledged your loyalty to me as High King. As your King, I am no longer asking, I am demanding you answer my question. Who accessed the portal?"

Tears streaked down Lady Zhaleh's face as she whispered, "My son."

Cyndi's face paled and she brought up her hand to hide her gasp of surprise.

"I don't understand," Cyndi said once she gained her composure, "how could it be Nestor? He died with Dad in the accident."

Lady Zhaleh shook her head, her shoulders shaking with her sobbing. Frieda got up from the table and put her arm around Cyndi's shoulder.

Muir stood beside Lady Zhaleh and placed his hand on her shoulder, she reached up and squeezed his hand then began to explain. "When your dad and brother got caught in the explosion, we thought both died. We recovered your dad's body but thought Nestor was buried under the rubble. After the funeral I had the debris removed so we could lay your brother to rest as well. It took six months to clear everything away, but your brother's body wasn't anywhere to be found.

"We discovered an underground passage filled with seawater and we assumed his body was washed out to sea. Over the years I thought I saw him out of the corner of my eye occasionally but whenever I turned to look there wasn't anyone there. I believed it was a mother's wish that her child was still alive. One night, about twenty-five years after the accident Nestor came walking into my study as if nothing had happened. He sat down and we talked for hours. I was unwilling to call anyone to join us because he said he didn't want anyone to know he was there.

"I must have fallen asleep at some point because when I opened my eyes, he was gone again. I wasn't sure if I had dreamed of the visit or if he had really been there. Cyndi, I'm so sorry I never told you this, I was so heartbroken when your dad and brother died, I didn't want to share this with anyone, even if it was just a dream."

"How long ago was the accident?" I asked.

Cyndi answered because her mom had withdrawn into her memories. "It was over a hundred years ago."

"Nestor would show up every decade or so and would only stay for a few hours. Whenever I pressed him to tell me where he went, he'd just laugh and tell me he was having the best time and was pulling the greatest prank ever," Lady Zhaleh smiled sadly.

"How can you be so sure Nestor is the one using the portal?" I asked.

"When he was a boy, he loved learning about the glory days of Therian technology especially how they created portals," Lady Zhaleh answered.

"Besides, the last time Nestor appeared, I saw him slip out of the study and I followed him," Muir added. "I was shocked to see Nestor alive but wanted to see what he was doing. I followed him into the tunnels and watched him open the portal using the old equipment. He slipped through before I could catch up with him."

Lady Zhaleh straightened in her chair and looked at her daughter. "I'm sorry I didn't share this with you, I know how much you loved your younger brother and it was wrong and selfish of me to keep this to myself. Please forgive me."

Cyndi stood and quivered with rage, "Forgive you? How dare you. You dragged me back to Cetacea for what? If King Alister hadn't demanded you tell him who used the portal you still would have kept Nestor a secret, wouldn't you?" Seeing the look on her mom's face was enough for Cyndi. She turned to me, "Alister, when you leave Cetacea will you please allow me to go with you? There is nothing for me here and Jason is waiting for me on Earth."

I inclined my head in agreement and Cyndi stormed out the door.

The only sound in the room was Lady Zhaleh softly crying into Muir's chest.

Cyndi

I didn't know where I was going but I knew I couldn't stay near my mom. I wiped angry tears from my eyes as I navigated the wide hallways in the palace. I wasn't paying attention as I walked into a wall of muscle and bounced off. I felt myself falling backward and imagined how ridiculous I would look falling in this stupid dress.

"There she is," I heard as I felt large hands grip my upper arms to keep me from falling.

"Brian," I shouted and jumped into the arms of the person standing before me.

"I see you're as enthusiastic as ever, I'm glad," he rumbled as he hugged me.

I stepped back and looked at the friend I hadn't seen since I'd left Cetacea for Theria about seventy-five years before. Brian was about six-foot-five and very muscular. His black hair was styled in a pompadour and had bushy sideburns that went half-way down his cheeks. He was smiling down at me and I knew I was grinning from ear-to-ear.

"Where are you going in such a hurry, little darlin'?" He asked with a drawl I didn't remember him having before.

"You've been to Earth recently, haven't you?" I asked suspiciously.

He paled and looked around nervously. "What makes you say that?" he asked.

"Because your hair, sideburns and even your accent remind me of an entertainer from Earth named Elvis," I laughed.

He lifted one side of his top lip and said, "Thank you, thank you very much. Now you want to tell me why you were barreling down the hallway without watching where you're going?"

I linked my arm with his and started along the hallway. "I'm going swimming and you're coming and you'll tell me how you managed to get to Earth, does this have something to do with the portal my mom has kept hidden?"

Brian was startled and blurted out, "She has a portal to Earth?"

"That's just one of the many secrets she's been keeping," I responded bitterly. "Now, tell me when you were on Earth and how you got there."

"I can't tell you everything, but I can admit I was on Earth until the mid-nineteen seventies. Since you know about Elvis, I'm assuming you've been there, too?"

As we walked along the hall, I told Brian about how I got from Theria to Earth and the life I'd built there. I found myself also telling him about the conversation with my mom and King Alister and the big reveal that my brother Nestor was alive and currently on Earth. I also told him that I'd be traveling with King Alister when he went to Earth and how angry I was with my mom. By the time I'd finished my story we'd exited the palace and were standing on a cliff overlooking the ocean. Brian took off his shirt so he could shift, and I noticed his back was filled with tattoos of vintage movie monsters.

"Is that the creature from the black lagoon?" I asked.

"Yep, he's my favorite. I'm a huge fan of monsters," Brian grinned at me over his shoulder.

"I really want to hear stories of your time on Earth," I said then dove off the cliff. Before I hit the water, I transformed into my mermaid form. I love the way I feel when I shift and how much quicker I am in the water. I moved out of the way so Brian wouldn't land on me.

Ready or not, here I come, he sent just before he dove into the water and transformed into an enormous kraken. I almost double in size when I transform, but Brian's transformation is utterly amazing.

Hey Brian, when you were on Earth, did anyone ever see you swimming around?

Only once. I surfaced too close to a passenger ship in the Atlantic that happened to be carrying some of the most famous movie stars at the time and some people saw me and took some blurry pictures.

Why did you get so close?

I could sense his embarrassment when he answered me, *I heard Marilyn Monroe was a passenger and I wanted a look.*

As we swam, I thought about Brian's story and I grinned at what I'd figured out. *How'd you like to come with us when we head back to Earth?*

I'd love it, but do you think your mom would let me go?

I'll put in a good word for you to King Alister.

Thanks, Brian sent, *but why would he let me come with you?*

Because you're the one who helped me figure out where my brother is, and you're going to help us bring him home.

CHAPTER FIVE

*A*lister
Earth
Scotland

Brian and I stood side-by-side at the top of Grant Tower on Urquhart Castle looking out at the calm waters of Loch Ness. We had to do some gate hopping to get to Loch Ness without anyone knowing about our journey. I opened a gate from the throne room on Cetacea to the one on Eutheria. After a quick reunion with Lord Moss, Aileene and I flew the others to the loch where I opened a gate to Earth.

The moon was hidden by clouds, but I could easily see details in the dark, as the world was a vibrant green and silver to my night vision. I'd asked my Knights and Mkali to stand guard at the base of the tower so I could talk with Brian in private. I could see Cyndi and Aileene walking along the shore below.

"Cyndi told me that you've been to Earth before and would like to stay with her," I began.

"You are correct, sir," Brian affirmed.

Sometimes the most important paths are the hidden ones, I tested Brian.

But hidden paths can also be dangerous, he replied, completing the Tionchar code phrase.

I suspected you might have been a member of Tionchar, I sent to Brian, *why do you want to stay on Earth?*

There are many reasons, Sire, but right now the most important one is to watch over Lady Cyndi. Even though she has rejected the Throne of Cetacea for now, she is destined to rule when Lady Zhaleh steps down. I also miss corn dogs and some of the things I can only get on Earth.

I laughed and turned to look him in the eyes. *Brian, I will let you stay on Earth on three conditions. The first is you contact Josef Shoals, the CEO of Rex Industries and take up your role in Tionchar again. An'Ceann and I have restructured things for past members of Tionchar who wish to extend their service and he will restore all your memories from when you were here before. The second condition is you will keep an eye on the oceans of Earth and investigate any anomalies you hear about. Even though Nestor is the only unexpected shifter currently on Earth, it's possible other creatures from Theria migrated here and they could cause problems.*

Brian nodded his acceptance at my first two conditions.

The third condition is you will help Cyndi and Jason and will watch over her. Josef will work with Cyndi to get her up to speed on the mission of Tionchar and make her a probationary member. She won't like having a bodyguard, but since she has known you her entire life, I believe she will accept you.

It will be my pleasure, Sire. Brian answered and saluted me by placing his right fist over his heart.

"That's settled then," I said as I hugged the big man. "Thank you for your loyalty to the Crown and for the love you've shown to Cyndi. She's going to need your strength and support to get over this betrayal by her mother."

We turned towards shore after hearing a startled scream followed by a splash and saw Aileene helping Cyndi out of the water where she had fallen. We could hear their laughter from our position.

"I'd better get down there and help her find her brother. I swear,

I've never met anyone as clumsy as she is," Brian said affectionately and walked down the stairs.

I looked down at Aileene and smiled as she waved at me, *are you coming down?* she sent to me.

In a few minutes, I'd like to let Cyndi and Brian connect with her brother first. He's almost to the loch, I sent.

Sounds good, Aileene replied and broke the mental connection as I heard Shelley walk up the stairs.

"So, we're here at Loch Ness to meet Cyndi's brother, who she thought was dead?" Shelley asked when he took his place next to me.

"Yep," I replied.

"And, he's been coming to Scotland for about a hundred years?"

"That's right." I agreed

"And his name is Nestor, but his sister called him Nessie when they were growing up?"

"Right again," I smiled at his growing impatience and waited for the inevitable.

"Dude, you're telling me that Cyndi's brother is the freaking Loch Ness Monster? The monster is real, and he's been pranking people for a century, this is awesome."

"I know, right?" I grinned and pointed, "and there he is now."

In the middle of the lake a head broke the surface of the water and kept rising on a twenty foot long neck. When the entire neck of the creature was out of the water, his humpback broke the surface, too, and I could also see his four flippers just under the surface. Wherever he swam he created whirlpools in his wake.

Cyndi and Brian, Nestor is in the middle of the lake at one o'clock from your current position, I sent to my team. *I'm going to ask him to wait where he is.*

Nestor, I sent to the plesiosaur shifter, *this is High King Alister of Theria please stay where you are, there are some people who want to talk with you.*

Yes, Sire, Nestor sent back, and he stopped moving forward. I watched Cyndi and Brian slip into the water and start making their way to where Nestor was waiting.

"C'mon Shelley, let's meet the others and wait on the shore until the family reunion is over."

Planet Theria

Unknown Location

He walked into the darkened chamber and knelt at the base of the throne, waiting to be acknowledged.

"Report," the voice hissed from beneath the cowl. He kept his gaze on the floor before him. He knew better than to try to look into the face of the one seated before him; to do so led to a horrible death.

"We attacked the HMS Beatrice as instructed but were unable to disable the vessel or inflict casualties on the King's entourage."

"That was to be expected. Was the netting deployed against the prince?"

"Yes, the mechanism worked flawlessly, and he crashed into the sea."

After a long pause the person sitting on the throne spoke again, "Since you hesitate, I assume you have distressing news. Do not make me drag the information out of you."

"Forgive me, Your Excellency, he was entangled in the netting and crashed into the sea. From the reports I received, he was mortally wounded while in the ocean but appeared on deck of the HMS Beatrice healed and healthy days later. My informant didn't know how that was achieved and the fools on our ship blew it up before the sensor link was complete. We don't have the data we were after."

"I see, and what about the others who I sent with you?"

"All dead, I made sure to activate the kill switches of those who hadn't done it themselves."

"I don't care about them but am disappointed we don't have the data," sighed the figure as it rose from the throne and stood next to the man kneeling on the floor.

"We can try it again," the man said, "I will personally make sure the data link is secure so you can gather the information you need."

The figure walked towards a staircase, "Follow me, I want to show you something."

He rose quickly and followed as his master ascended to the top level of the chamber. At the push of a button two steel doors slid open revealing a balcony overlooking a pit as black as midnight. The figure beckoned the man and he took his place against the railing, standing next to the figure.

"There isn't enough dragon bone to make another net. I only have one piece left and that has a special purpose. The netting was one weapon in my arsenal, but my greatest weapon is below."

He leaned over the balcony to see what was below and he could just make out the outline of a huge beast. He panicked when he felt a clawed hand grasp the back of his tunic and bend him even farther against the railing.

He could feel the warm breath of the person he'd sworn allegiance to whispering words that brought dread to his heart. "My pet is always hungry and I need to keep him fed so he will fight for me when it's time. Thank you for your loyalty and your final gift in the war against the High King." He heard a high-pitched whistle as his legs were swept out from under him and he felt himself falling into the darkness. His eyes were wide with terror as he sensed movement below and saw the gaping maw of the gigantic beast coming toward him as he fell to his death.

The person in the cowl smiled at the sound of crunching bones and the contented growls coming from below. The steel doors slid shut as the person left the balcony.

Alister

Loch Ness, Scotland

"How did you know I'd be here?" Nestor asked while we sat around the fire I'd made on the shore of Loch Ness.

"That was King Alister's doing," Cyndi explained as she bumped her brother's shoulder with her own. "He can connect with any shifter on a planet and he could sense you were coming here. Besides, Brian helped me put the clues together that you've been playing the Loch Ness Monster for a century."

Nestor laughed. "It started innocently enough but once I started, I couldn't help myself; it's so funny to see the humans react whenever they catch sight of me."

"How did it start?" Shelley asked with a grin.

Nestor's face fell and Cyndi put her arm around him in a hug. "Dad and I were working on one of his experiments when there was an explosion and the building collapsed on top of us."

Cyndi explained, "Our dad was always tinkering with various ancient machines found in Cetacea trying to get them to work."

"Dad's the one who showed me how to work the portal controls, he hoped I would follow in his footsteps and embrace science as my life's work. Anyway, whatever he did that day didn't go as planned and I thought we were dead. Fortunately, I wasn't crushed under the rubble but fell through the floor into a secret chamber. My memories are patchy, but I do remember waking up ravenously hungry and stumbling along to the portal control. The next thing I remember is being in my shifter form and swimming in the Loch.

"Years passed while I healed and finally figured out who I really was. By that time many people had seen me from shore and the legend of the Loch Ness Monster was firmly established."

"Wait a minute," Bernie interjected, "people have described seeing a creature in this loch long before you showed up here."

"I don't know about that, but I did find a passage from the loch under Inverness and out to the North Sea. Whatever creature had been seen before might have travelled that passage or even died before I got there. All I know is I've been having fun teasing the population for a long time. Anyway, once I regained my memory I headed to Atlantis and discovered the portal was still active. I slipped into the palace with the hope that Dad had survived just as I had. I was devastated when Mom confirmed he was dead.

"I'm sorry I left again but, by that point, Cyndi had gone to the Kingdom of Theria and I realized Mom had moved on as well. I'd show up every ten years or so just to check in but always slipped away before anyone but Mom knew I was there; at least that's what I thought until I met Cyndi and Brian tonight."

"What are you going to do now?" Aileene asked.

"I guess I'll go home," Nestor said as he rubbed his chin. "I've had fun playing the monster but it's time I grew up and headed back to Cetacea. Sis, I know you're not coming, but I hope you'll visit from time to time."

Cyndi made a non-committal grunt. "Alister, what do you want me to do?"

I thought about her question before answering. "I want you to stay on Earth and do the things we talked about. It's even more important now that we know there's been a portal open from Theria for so many years. Since your brother is heading back to Cetacea, I'll trust him and your mom to watch over the portal on the Therian side."

Cyndi tackled me in an enthusiastic hug, and I had to laugh at her exuberance.

"Thank you, I won't let you down," Cyndi said.

"I won't either," Brian agreed.

"I'm glad you're alive, I've missed you," Cyndi said as she hugged her brother. "The King has a way we can stay connected while I'm on Earth. I'll visit whenever I can."

Once Cyndi and Nestor finished their goodbyes, I opened a gate to Cyndi's private beach and Cyndi and Brian stepped through. They turned and waved then I closed the gate behind them. Shelley and Bernie put out the fire and when they were finished, I opened a gate back to the throne room in Cetacea and we stepped through.

As usual, I closed the gate behind me as Aileene and I were the last ones to enter the throne room. Since I had turned to talk with Aileene I didn't notice there was a problem until I slipped in a puddle of blood on the floor.

"What happened here?" Nestor asked as he looked about the throne room in concern. There were piles of rubble and body parts scattered across the floor. The walls were scorched, and it looked like bombs had exploded in the room. Nestor rushed to a crumpled body lying near the overturned throne and by his wail, I assumed it was his mom. He fell to his knees and pressed his ear to her chest.

"She's still alive," he shouted. His eyes were wide in panic as he turned to me. Aileene and Bernie rushed to his side and knelt next to Lady Zhaleh to try and heal her.

It felt like we'd been standing, frozen in place for hours, but we had been in the throne room for less than a minute.

"Guard the entrance," I commanded Shelley and he shifted and ran to the door. *Stavros, report,* I broadcast mentally.

Stavros is a bit busy at the moment, Alister, Frieda answered, *but I'm glad you've returned.* I could hear Stavros' roar farther in the palace followed by the screams of those I assumed he was fighting.

What happened? I asked.

Shortly after you left, an envoy arrived from Marsupia claiming to have an urgent message for you from Lord Elandorr. Lady Zhaleh kept him waiting for hours but he finally demanded to see you. Lady Zhaleh granted him a private audience and shortly after he entered the throne room there were multiple explosions followed by attacks on land and against the HMS Beatrice. I'm not sure what happened to Lady Zhaleh. Fritz and I are tending to the wounded while Captain Muir and Stavros are fighting the invaders.

I'm on my way, I sent and prepared to gate to Stavros' position.

We need a gate to Middle Earth for the magical energy, Aileene sent to me along with a mental hug.

I opened a pinhole gate and gave my next command, "Nestor, Aileene and Bernie will tend to your mother. You need to defend your people in the water. Their defenses are about to be overrun, and we don't need more enemies in the palace."

Nestor rose, took one last look at his mother and opened the hidden passage that led to the ocean.

"Shelley, you're with me," I said and opened a gate to Stavros. While this wasn't the first battle I'd been in, this was by far the bloodiest. We were in the courtyard and the ground was littered with body parts and the air was filled with shrieks, explosions and the screams and moans of those wounded in battle. The combatants swarming through the breach in the wall didn't have weapons other than those they had in their natural forms.

I watched in horror as an alicorn dove from the sky. The multicolored feathers of its wings fluttered in the forceful wind and sunlight glinted off its golden horn as it rushed towards the ship. The majestic creature crashed into a line of our soldiers, exploding on impact. The defenders were flung about like bloody rag dolls and lay unmoving on the ground. Rage consumed me at the loss of life, and I transformed into my half-form of a fifteen-foot tall humanoid dragon on two legs. I roared my anger to the sky and issued the command to fall back. Those who were able to move ran towards me and I cast *Spheara* to protect my people.

Tend to the wounded, I commanded and used the shield to push the enemy away from our fallen soldiers. I waded through the carnage towards the quickly re-forming enemy line.

Submit, I mentally shouted and burst into flame and advanced towards those who had attacked us. With a mighty roar, the enemy shifters raced towards me to overwhelm me. Those that didn't at once burst into flame when they met my burning body detonated the explosives strapped to their backs. I tried to douse the flames covering my scales, but my rage fueled the inferno.

If you surrender, you will be spared, I mentally implored the shifters who continued futilely to attack me, but it was no use. I had no choice but to protect the wounded in the courtyard and the innocent people in the palace who would die if I didn't stop the advancing enemies. I tried to force the shifters to transform into their human forms, but something drove them onward in a frenzy. They dashed upon my scales like ocean waves on rocks; the loss of life was terrible, and I did my best to spare as many as I could. However, whenever I managed to render someone unconscious, they exploded anyway.

Please, stand down, I mentally shouted, *your life will be spared if you surrender.*

I was hit with a wave of despair coming from the few remaining soldiers running towards me.

Sire, I would if I could, sent one of the young tiger shifters running towards me, *but if I did, my family*—his voice was forever silenced when the explosives he carried on his back detonated.

I dismissed the *Spheara* spell and told Shelley to climb on after I fully transformed to my dragon.

Shelley and I are heading out to the ship to see if they need our help, I sent to the defenders inside.

The palace is secure, Muir informed me.

Lady Zhaleh is healing and will recover, Aileene informed me, *however I think Bernie and I will be more effective with the wounded in the palace. Find whoever did this and make them pay.*

I will, I called and catapulted us into the air. *Captain Jormis, report.*

Sire, we've managed to repel all boarders, but we took heavy casualties before your sorceress started attacking the enemy from a distance.

On our way, I sent before closing the connection. I followed the plume of smoke rising from the HMS Beatrice and quickly flew to the harbor.

Nestor, how goes the battle underwater?

We're holding the line, but enemy reinforcements are still swimming in.

Any explosions?

No, Sire but every time we incapacitate one of the enemies, they die.

Alister, drop me off at the ship then go help Nestor. Shelley sent.

Rapidly approaching the ship, Shelley and I used the Gimli maneuver we'd perfected to drop him safely aboard. The ship was listing to starboard from damage sustained in the attack. The decks were covered with dead and wounded members of our crew. I saw this in the seconds it took me to fly over the ship, wheel back into the air then fold my wings and arrow into the water.

Using my tail like a crocodile, I swam to where Nestor was in his huge plesiosaur form dispatching mere-people who were trying to hack their way through our people with their weapons. I shot through our line and used my wings to bowl over the enemy the same way I did when I flew. The line of defenders fell in behind me as we took the battle to the enemy.

Take prisoners if you can, I sent to my people, but it didn't do any good. Even though none of these shifters carried explosives on their bodies, they died anyway. I heard a high-pitched sound and all the enemy soldiers stopped swimming and began to slowly sink to the ocean floor.

Our side cheered when they realized the danger had passed but I was crushed by the death and destruction.

Nestor, please gather our wounded and bring them to the palace. Gather the dead and bring them as well. I don't want a single shifter left in the water.

Yes, Sire, Nestor answered soberly. *How's my mom?*

After consulting with Aileene I answered, *She's healed and asked the same thing about you. I asked Aileene to let her know you are well. I have to get back to the ship.*

With that, I swam rapidly to the surface and shot out of the water and into the air.

HMS Beatrice

Seven days later we gathered on the aft deck to honor the fallen. As I stood to address the mourners, I thought back to the devastation wrought by the unprovoked attack. The ship had sustained considerable damage but that was nothing compared to the loss of life. I looked to my right and saw the forty-seven shrouded bodies laid out on the deck, forever silent.

A tear trailed down my cheek as I looked where Brarth and his brother Gekur lay mute; I'd never be able to serve Brarth his coffee again in this life. They had continued to fight even though they were seriously wounded because they wanted to protect others from evil. They died side-by-side, the same way they'd served in life.

Nearby lay Ensign Gibbs. I never got the chance to thank her properly for saving my life. Each of the forty-seven died bravely, while protecting the weak. We would honor them with a burial at sea, which was the custom in Cetacea. On deck were the friends, family members and those who fought alongside these brave men and women. Their sacrifice would be forever remembered.

Even though we were honoring our fallen, we had performed a similar ceremony for the five hundred and twenty-six enemy combatants yesterday. Although they had viciously attacked us we deduced that they may have been forced to do so. Each of the shifters that attacked us on land had been fitted with an explosive backpack which could either be detonated remotely, by the wearer or when the wearer died. We also discovered that each of the shifters who attacked us by water had been killed remotely by an injection of poison when they were captured or rendered unconscious.

We also found two HMS Beatrice crew members who were poisoned in the same way. Both were in possession of equipment that proved they were traitors and had murdered their fellow shifters. They must have been unaware they were sealing their own fate when they destroyed the others.

"Today we gather to honor our fallen brothers and sisters. They gave their lives so that others may live. This loss of life is grievous to all of us gathered here. Here lie sons, daughters, brothers, sisters, husbands, wives, fathers and mothers. Their deaths will not be in vain. For those of us who survive, we owe it to them to live our lives in honor and a recommitment to *Protect the Weak*.

"I make a solemn promise to you that we will find those responsible for these heinous deeds and bring them to justice. If our cowardly enemies follow the same pattern, some of those we face will be forced to fight against us while others willingly follow those who are evil for their personal gain. Our enemies do not value life, not even the lives of those who they claim as allies. Even though we value life, we will not stand idly by and allow evil people to destroy what others build. We will prevail, we will not stop until the evil is rooted out and our people can live in peace without the fear of being forced to harm others." I opened myself to the shifters sitting on deck and then continued to connect with every shifter on the planet as I made my declaration. *We are coming for you, workers of evil and we will stop you. Those who choose to stand with evil will pay the same price as those who orchestrated this travesty. You have been warned. I, Alister Rex, High King of all Theria declare this to be true.*

I felt the pulse of power leave my body and travel down the individual connections. I watched those seated before me lean back in their chairs as though they had been hit with a gust of wind and those standing on deck took a step back. I turned towards the shrouded figures and knelt on one knee before them.

An'Ceann, I sent, *please give these brave men and women my message, thank you for your sacrifice, it will not be in vain.*

A sudden wind blew over the deck and I heard everyone sigh in relief as the scent of flowers wafted over us. I recognized the fragrance from my dream of An'Ceann's kingdom. Even though I felt comforted by An'Ceann's presence I wept openly for our loss. Aileene knelt next to me and took my hand as we cried together.

We sat in the conference room aboard the ship on our way to Marsupia. We could easily make the trip in slightly over two days, but Captain Jormis plotted a three day journey so we could be on the lookout for other attacks. The shipwrights of Cetacea had repaired the Beatrice so well, it was virtually impossible to tell there had been a battle on board merely a month before. We'd spent another three weeks in Cetacea touring other duchies in the kingdom.

We didn't encounter any enemies the rest of our time there, but we did have to recount details of the battle everywhere we visited. I had to smile and laugh along with the others who shared their stories but inside I was seething. Even though I made the effort to be kind to everyone I met on Cetacea it was difficult. I was relieved when we finally set sail for Marsupia on the fifteenth of Damlar, and left Cetacea behind us.

I was sad, consumed with rage and ready to explode. When I was younger, I remember seeing a documentary on volcanoes and when they erupt, lava can form tunnels with a brittle crust. They look whole but just under the surface molten rock continues to flow onward. If someone stepped on the crust, they would fall through to their deaths; that was probably the best way to describe how I was feeling and how brittle my emotions really were.

"Um, Alister—," Shelley said. When I looked at him, he pointed to his face and made a circular motion.

"What? I'm not in the mood for stupid games," I snapped and gripped the arms of my chair so hard I could hear the wood creak under the pressure.

Shelley straightened his back and looked me in the eyes, "Well, for starters you have smoke coming out of your nostrils and your eyes are rather dragonish. We've also been waiting for you to answer Captain Jormis' question but you're just sitting there grinding your teeth. Would you like to share with the rest of class what's bothering you?"

I stood so suddenly my chair was thrown backwards where it crashed to the floor. I placed both of my fists on the table and leaned towards Shelley and hissed my answer. "What's bothering me is that almost six hundred people were killed in Cetacea for no reason and that's not including the hundreds who died attacking us on the way there. We don't know who's behind these attacks and no one has any ideas how we figure it out. On top of that, I'm still having that stupid dream about all my friends dying every night and I'm sick of it." My chest was heaving with the emotion of my angry outburst.

At some point during my rant, Shelley stood too, and we were almost nose-to-nose. "Are you feeling better now?" he asked cheekily and waggled his eyebrows at me as he stared into my eyes.

The absurdity of Shelley's response hit me like a physical blow and laughter erupted from my mouth. It felt like a dam had burst and my emotions rushed out in a torrent. I felt Aileene's arms encircle my waist and she laid her head on my back. I felt her tears soaking through my shirt as she held me tightly.

"I'm sorry," I mumbled after a few minutes. The circumstances hadn't changed but I felt both exhausted and lightened by my outburst.

I sat back down in the chair that someone had thoughtfully replaced and looked around the room.

"Before you apologize again, you need to know we were expecting something like this," Miriam began, "you've been bottling up your emotions and we figured you would eventually have an outburst."

"Actually, we took bets on when it would be," Shelley smirked.

"And who won?" I laughed.

Mkali smiled sheepishly and raised her hand.

"Son, being High King is difficult enough without carrying the actions of everyone on the planet on your shoulders," said my father. I looked around in surprise to see if he was in the room but noticed my parents were looking at me from a screen mounted on the wall.

"We made some upgrades to the communication system when we refitted the ship," Captain Jormis added.

"We're all angry about the treachery and the deaths caused by those intent on destruction; you don't have to bear this burden alone," Mom said from where she was standing by Dad.

"Between those with you on the ship and the four of us back at the palace, you have plenty of people to help you carry this," Mother added.

I believe we've already talked about this, my mate. Even if you choose to shut everyone else out, you may not do that to me. We are in this together love, and our enemies will tremble when they see us coming to right these wrongs.

I looked around the room and was once again overwhelmed with the love and support of everyone here and on-screen. I was ashamed that I had let my rage overwhelm me again and had to be reminded of a lesson I had already been taught.

Oh, little dragon, An'Ceann's voice sounded in my head, *if you think you must only learn a lesson once until you've mastered it, you are sorely mistaken. Rely on those who have already walked before you to guide you in the path of wisdom. You'll make the same errors again, but the true test of growth is how long it takes you to realize you're wrong, admit your mistakes and make things right. I'm confident you'll find a way.*

"Thank you," I said to An'Ceann and everyone else within reach of my voice. "I allowed my rage to overwhelm me. Please forgive me."

As I looked around the room at my friends and family who nodded agreement and smiled encouragingly at me, I felt better.

"What do you say we order some food and really get down to some serious planning? We've got plans to thwart and nefarious villains to defeat," Shelley smiled broadly.

"You've been looking for a way to use the word thwart, haven't you?" Bernie asked as she turned to her boyfriend.

"Of course," Shelley laughed. "I don't want all that knowledge I've gained from reading comic books to go to waste, now do I?"

"That would be tragic," Bernie muttered as she rolled her eyes.

The sound of laughter filled the room and gave me hope for the future.

CHAPTER SIX

Theria
Kingdom of Marsupia
Damlar 18, 10,257

Shelley and I stood by the railing watching the harbor grow as we sailed closer. Bernie and Mkali were with Aileene as she finished getting ready. Fritz recommended we arrive in style and wear some of our courtly clothing. I was dressed in a green tunic with a dragon embroidered on my chest with red and gold thread. I also had a sword fastened about my waist with a gold belt. My black trousers were tucked into supple leather boots that came up past my knees. I wore a mantle the same shade of green as my tunic embroidered with the names of each High King and Queen from Dóchas and Síocháin until Aileene and me.

Shelley was fidgeting and pulling at his collar and I grinned when I looked at my friend wearing clothing befitting a Knight of the High King.

"I'll trade you the collar for the crown I have to wear," I said softly to Shelley.

He looked at my diamond and gold crown and shook his head.

"No, I think I'll let you wear that monstrosity. Are those dragon claws pointing to the sky?"

"I think so—this thing must weigh ten pounds," I muttered, and my friend laughed.

"You boys can turn around now," Bernie called out behind us and I gaped at Aileene when I saw her.

She was resplendent in a green gown that was studded with rubies, emeralds and diamonds in the shape of a dragon on her bodice. Her auburn hair was curled and hung loosely over her back and shoulders. She was wearing a belted sword that matched mine and wore a crown proper for the future High Queen of Theria. Her sapphire-blue eyes crinkled in amusement when she looked at me and I realized my mouth was agape.

"You, are, gorgeous," I said slowly as I looked at my future mate.

Aileene blushed and looked away shyly. "Thank you, you look pretty good yourself."

Shelley stepped in front of me and asked, "What about me? How do I look?"

"You look like a doofus," Aileene laughed but I heard Bernie mutter, "Looking good, Shelley."

"Should we leave you two alone?" I asked Bernie and Shelley.

"Yes," our friends exclaimed in unison.

"Nine-year old here, remember?" Mkali teased and we laughed.

Captain Jormis blew three short and one long blast of the ship's horn to signal we were coming close to shore.

"Shall we go M'lady?" I asked and held out my left arm to Aileene.

She curtsied and placed her right hand on my forearm, "Lead the way M'lord."

We made our way into the salon and stood before the closed doors that led to the starboard gangplank, lined up the same way we did when we went ashore in Cetacea.

"Something's been bugging me," Shelley said behind us.

Fritz had planned more pomp and circumstance for us this time before we went ashore so I knew we had time for a conversation.

"What's that?" I asked.

"How can Nestor shift into a plesiosaur if his parents were mere-people?"

I hadn't really thought about it, so I didn't have an answer; thankfully Wu spoke up.

"Most times shifters run true through family lines but occasionally, a child is born who can transform into a separate form in the same species. For example, in my family I have a cousin who can transform into a saber-toothed tiger although his parents are normal tigers and so are the rest of his family members. Another example is the Rock family." Wu finished.

"They're part of the wolf guards at the palace, right?" Aileene answered.

"Correct, their eldest son, Sawyer, is able to transform into a dire wolf which is larger and more powerful than a regular wolf and his partial shift form looks like a werewolf you've seen in Hollywood movies. We're not exactly sure why this happens but something within the genetic make-up of these individuals causes this anomaly and they have a form different than anyone else in their family."

"That's so cool," Shelley said with awe in his voice, "I look forward to talking with your cousin and Sawyer when we get back."

"So, Nestor is one of these special shifters who transforms into a unique form and is a plesiosaur, that's pretty awesome," Bernie added. "But what happens when one of these special shifters finds their true-mate?"

"Again, nine-year old standing here," Mkali giggled and we all laughed.

"Erm—" Wu started but was interrupted by the royal fanfare played by the trumpeters signaling it was time for us to make our way to shore.

I would love to continue this discussion later because there's something I would like to ask you, Wu sent to me and I nodded to show I heard him.

Aileene reached out to grab my hand and we intertwined our fingers. I looked at her curiously at the break in protocol and she looked at me with a mischievous smile. *Trust me, my mate.*

Always, I agreed and brought her hand to my lips so I could kiss the back of it. Her laughter filled me with pleasure, and I was so lost in her eyes that I almost missed our cue. Commander Chelsea and Lieutenant Davis, who were dressed in my livery, stood by the doors ready to open them once Fritz finished announcing our titles. They had volunteered to join my guard in place of Brarth and Gekur and I was grateful for their service. Cetacean palace guards replaced the lost crew members and members of my guard who had been killed.

The women smiled widely and threw open the doors when Fritz finished announcing us; he'd added to our titles since the last battle. Aileene and I moved forward. The crowd along the shore had been cheering but silenced when we walked into the sunlight and the light reflected off the jewels sewn into our garments and crowns. After a few moments of silence, the crowd began cheering again.

As we walked down the gangplank to the stone pier, I looked at the crowd and was struck by the clear line dividing the groups. To the left of the pier elves stood in rows without expressions on their faces. They were richly dressed in blue and silver garments which looked to be made of expensive fabrics. To the right of the pier stood fae folk of all species, shapes and sizes. I recognized some of the forms like gnomes, brownies, dryads and goblins but there were so many more that I didn't recognize. These creatures were dressed in various outfits and were quite the contrast to the uniform elves. They were also cheering wildly while the elves stood silent.

King Alister, Lady Aileene welcome, chorused tiny voices I assumed were coming from the small fairies flying towards us.

I laughed and told my guards to let them come. They danced around Aileene and me and we were peppered with tiny kisses on our foreheads. Aileene held out her hand and one of the fairies landed on her palm while the rest settled on our heads and shoulders. The fairy looked up from Aileene's hand and smiled. Aileene laughed in delight and it was wonderful to see my future mate interact with this diminutive fairy.

Sire, Galan, Lord Elandorr's Majordomo is asking if those pests are bothering you and Lady Aileene.

He is, is he? Please inform him that Lady Aileene is holding a conversation with one of our subjects and we will join him on shore when we finish.

Very good, Sire, Fritz sent, and I could tell he was annoyed with Lord Elandorr and his people already.

I smiled as I watched Aileene have a conversation with this fairy. She was four inches tall and was clothed with light. Her colorful wings resembled those of a Monarch butterfly, and she had a rapier in a scabbard which was attached to a golden thread tied around her waist. Her strawberry-blonde hair was piled on her head in a bun and was also fastened with another blade of grass. After a moment, Aileene held her hand in front of us so both of us could look at the diminutive fairy.

King Alister, may I present to you, Brooklyn, Queen of the Pixies.

I inclined my head in respect, *Your Majesty, it is a pleasure to make your acquaintance.*

It is my pleasure to make your acquaintance as well, she replied and inclined her head in response. *It would please us if you and your people would join us for a feast in your honor.*

That would please us, too. Lady Aileene and I accept. However, our schedule has been arranged by Fritz and Frieda and I would ask your people to arrange things with them.

Brooklyn's laughter sounded like the tinkle of silver bells, *Well spoken, Sire, it shall be done.*

She leaped off Aileene's hand and was joined by her guards and the others in her court and flew over the water to shore. One pixie flew over to Frieda and landed on her shoulder, I assumed they were revising our plans. We continued walking towards the elf standing at the end of the pier. Behind him was a wide path of the same stone as the pier, leading into the forest. The trees had smooth white trunks and the leaves were viridian green that reflected the sunlight. The trees on either side of the path created an archway that glowed with the sunlight shining through the canopy.

The elf standing before us had long black hair that hung in braids down his back. His piercing gray eyes reflected centuries of experiences, but his pale skin was smooth and wrinkle-free. He wore the same silver garment as the rest of the elves, but he had a red sash crossing his chest from his right shoulder to his left hip. His voice, when he spoke, was precise but held an undertone of derision.

"Prince Alister and Lady Aileene, I am Galan, Majordomo to Lord Elandorr. He bid me welcome you to his kingdom of Marsupia. My Lord was detained with pressing matters so was unable to greet you upon your arrival. If you will follow me, I will have one of the servants escort you to the quarters reserved for you. My Lord will inform you when he can grant you an audience."

Aileene squeezed my hand and I could feel her rage through the connection we shared. I stared intently at the elf standing before me who was so puffed up with his own self-importance, he didn't realize the danger he was in.

Fritz, I don't want to undo all your hard work. Is there anything I shouldn't say to Galan?

He's all yours, Alister. I can't believe the level of disrespect Lord Elandorr is showing you through this man. Fire away.

I smiled at Galan and he must have seen something in my face that caused him to step back. "Congratulations. You were trying to be insulting, condescending and offensive and you managed it well. You may report back to Lord Elandorr that we have accepted the invitation of Queen Brooklyn to join her people and will be staying with them. When Lord Elandorr's schedule is clear, he may find us there. At that point, I will decide if he is worthy to retain his seat on the throne of Marsupia."

"You dare—" Galan spluttered but stopped when I stepped into his personal space and loomed over the now nervous elf.

"We were attacked in Cetacea by an envoy claiming to have come from Lord Elandorr. I am not here to gain his approval to accept my authority as High King. An'Ceann crowned me himself and that's enough for me. You may be suffering from delusion as to why I am here. My tour of each kingdom is to decide which rulers should stay in power, which should be replaced and which should be tried for treason and pay the penalty if found guilty. We will also be looking for any who abetted traitors and deal with them as well.

"A contingent of my guards will escort you and Fritz Einhorn back to Lord Elandorr to ensure there isn't any confusion about my message. Lady Aileene, my Knights and I will stay with Queen Brooklyn. I hope our next meeting is better than this one. You are dismissed," I said as Aileene and I brushed by the shocked elf.

"M-my apologies, Sire," he stammered, "I only communicated what Lord Elandorr ordered me to."

"That's no excuse. You knew what he asked you to do was discourteous and unnecessary and I could sense you enjoyed the opportunity to put me in my place. But what is even more disturbing to me is the division I see before me and the insulting language you used to describe people under my protection. You can be sure I will be looking into the way those in charge of this kingdom have been protecting the weak."

If the wave of fear coming from Galan was anything to go by, there were a lot of things that needed to be changed within the Kingdom of Marsupia.

"How did it get so bad?" Mother asked. We were sitting in their suite at the Royal Palace. Aileene and I had slipped away to have this face-to-face conversation. We'd been in Marsupia for two weeks and uncovered disturbing information. While there weren't any collaborators in the rebellion, we'd uncovered evidence of systematic speciesism and oppression of the fae folk by the ruling elvish government.

"According to Queen Brooklyn and the other leaders of the fae folk, this policy of separation has been going on for hundreds of years, but it was only after the Kingdom of Theria was cut off from the rest of the planet that the true oppression began," I said.

"We also found out that your foster mother opposed the subjugation of the fae folk but once she was gone there was nothing left to stop those in power from creating laws to remove rights from the fae folk," Aileene said with anger in her voice.

"Son, we had no idea this was going on," Father said. "Since the rulers always insisted on face-to-face meetings rather than meeting remotely, we only received the reports given to us from the ambassador sent from Celand Elandorr."

"And because I was so hurt by my foster parents' behavior towards me, we were reluctant to travel to Marsupia to meet them and see this injustice for ourselves," Mother said guiltily.

"We believe that's what they were hoping for," I answered, grieving that my mother had been hurt by her foster parents again.

"What have you decided to do?" Father asked and I looked to Aileene for confirmation that we agreed on the plan.

"We want you and Mother to come back with us to Marsupia. Even though we know Alister is High King, there are many within the elvish community who don't recognize that and will only accept your word," Aileene said.

Father and Mother looked at each other and it was clear they were having a private, mental conversation. Once they stood, I opened a gate to the fae folk encampment where we'd been staying in Marsupia. "Meet you there, I have something to do first," I said and waved as they stepped through. I could hear the cheers of the fae folk before I closed the gate behind them. I had a lot to do, but I mentally called out to my mom and dad. I could use some hugs from them to help me deal with the evil we'd uncovered in Marsupia.

Suttain 1, 10,257

We walked into the throne room on Marsupia to confront Lord Elandorr. Predictably, he tried to bluster when he saw Aileene and me walk in side-by-side but sank back in his chair when he saw those who followed me into the room. Directly behind Aileene and me walked Lady Malonne Farhana-Elandorr, then my father and mother. After my father and mother stepped through the gate to Marsupia, I went to

Florida and retrieved Malonne so she could be here for this. Behind them my personal guards led a group of twenty elves, who made up the nobility, into the chamber and shut the doors on another group of my guards who stood outside the chamber.

Aileene and I stopped at the bottom of the dais that led to the thrones and faced Lord Elandorr. Shelley and Bernie walked past us and physically removed Elandorr from the throne and brought him down to the floor to stand next to his wife. Aileene and I walked up the stairs and I sat on the throne while Aileene stood by my side.

"Celand and Malonne Farhana-Elandorr, rulers of Marsupia we are here to determine the course of action we must take against you for your dereliction of duty to protect the people of Marsupia," I began.

"I have done no such thing," Celand answered angrily but Malonne hung her head in shame. The other nobles in the room murmured amongst themselves until my father roared, "Enough," and strode to stand before the ruling couple.

"Your duty was clear; you were to protect the weak among you and you failed to do that," Father ground out while smoke poured from his nostrils.

"Sire, I don't know what lies your son has been spreading but you can ask anyone in this room to see if I've neglected my people and they will tell you this just isn't true," Celand answered hotly.

"I'm not the one you need to convince; you are on trial before the High King and the judgment is his," Father said as he took his place next to mother.

"But, how can he be High King if the rulers of the other kingdoms haven't accepted him as such?" Celand asked.

"I already gave you the answer about this two weeks ago, you just didn't care for what I said," Fritz reminded Celand.

"That doesn't matter," I said and Celand turned back to face me. "You suggest I ask anyone in the room to see if you've neglected your people so that's what I'll do. Please invite our guests to join us," I said and Commander Chelsea and Lieutenant Davis opened the door. Queen Brooklyn flew in first followed by representatives from the gnomes, brownies, hobs, pucas, dryads and goblins. They lined up on the other side of the aisle from Celand and Malonne and faced the throne.

"What are you doing? They don't belong here," shouted one of the noble elves.

I turned my gaze towards that group, and I could tell my eyes were blazing. "Of course they belong here; these are people of Marsupia and fall under the protection of the Lord and Lady of this land. Apparently, you have forgotten why you serve and you seem to think you are here to be served. Unless you would like me to make an immediate judgment on your sentence, I suggest you remain quiet until it's time for you to give your testimony," I bit out as I looked at the one who interrupted the proceedings.

Turning back to the fae folk I spoke softly, "Queen Brooklyn, please take your time to answer the following question. Have you or your people been neglected by any in this room? Please be specific."

Queen Brooklyn shimmered and in the place of the normally tiny pixie there now stood a statuesque woman with butterfly wings on her back. She was still clothed in light and she looked at me with her large eyes the color of amethyst.

"Before I begin, I would like to give a brief history of our people. The distinguished gentleman said we don't belong here, but we've lived on Marsupia for thirty thousand years. We were here when the first elf landed on these shores and many of us are older than the people standing in this room. It is true that we didn't originate on Theria but rather escaped here from the planet you call Grebalar, but we call Faerie. We left there to escape persecution and an endless war between the Light and Dark Fae. However, we aren't the only ones from Grebalar. Even though it has been lost to the sands of time, the elves originated on Grebalar as well."

There were gasps in the room at this revelation and I growled for silence.

"Even though we look nothing alike, we have more in common with the elves in the room than we do with the shifters on this planet," Queen Brooklyn announced.

"How do you know this?" Malonne asked.

"Because some of the fae folk in this room are those who went back to Grebalar to help the elves escape." The room was deathly silent as people thought about this revelation.

Did you know any of this history? I asked Wu.

No, but I am updating the records as we speak," he answered.

"Thank you for that information, and I look forward to learning more, but could you please answer my question?"

"Of course, Sire," Queen Brooklyn answered with her tinkling laughter. For the next three hours, each of the leaders of the fae folk gave detailed descriptions of systematic abuse, injustice and cruelty they had faced at the hands of the elves. They talked about being driven from their homes when an elf wanted what they had and how they started a new community in the woods. They shared how the laws had been changed fourteen years earlier removing all rights from the fae folk and they had been treated little better than slaves.

They told how their people were often beaten or jailed for the slightest infraction without trial, often without any evidence or way to defend themselves. There were separate laws for elves and fae folk and there wasn't any way for the fae folk to get justice if they were wronged by elves. The evidence was complete, overwhelming and damning. I was exhausted, sad and angry after listening to the testimonies of the people in the room. "They speak the truth," Bernie affirmed, and I could tell she was trying not to cry. To be honest, so was I.

"Do you have anything you would like to say in your defense?" I asked Celand, my voice rough with emotion. He was seated next to Malonne on one of the benches Frieda arranged to be brought in thirty minutes into the trial. Celand stood, body rigid, with his hands fisted by his sides.

"King Alister, my wife had nothing to do with these atrocities as she has been absent from the kingdom for the past fourteen years. I ask that she not be included in your judgment," he said but instead of the haughty expression I'd seen on his face before the trial, his eyes looked haunted.

Malonne stood and grasped his hand in hers, "Sire, I am complicit in this as I saw the injustices before I left Marsupia but did nothing about them. I may not have known how badly the fae folk were being treated while I was away, but I did nothing to stop the division while I was in power."

Celand looked at his wife and I could tell they were having a mental conversation which was perfect since I was having a conversation with my parents, the Einhorns and Aileene at the same time. After about five minutes of silent deliberation Celand and Malonne turned back towards me and Celand cleared his throat.

"Sire, Malonne and I have no defense for our actions and are guilty of dereliction of the duty to lead all our people and to protect the weak among us. Furthermore, we are also guilty of not rooting out injustice when it reared its ugly head. Our indifference to the suffering of others has led our people astray and instead of setting the example of how to serve others, we allowed oppression in this kingdom. We accept your judgment and the consequences for both our action and inaction."

"Do you agree?" I asked looking at Malonne.

"I do, Sire," Malonne said as she looked me in the eyes. Both Celand and Malonne were pale and shaking as they stood before me.

Closing my eyes, I sought all the elves and fae folk living in Marsupia and connected with them using my power as High King. I could feel Aileene's presence in my mind and she soothed my roiling emotions as I made my proclamation.

Be it known that Lord and Lady Elandorr, by their own admission, have been found guilty of the crime of dereliction of duty in their failure to protect the weak among the citizens of Marsupia, namely the fae folk. Their titles and lands will be stripped from them and their estate will be used to make restitution to those who have been wronged. They are hereby banished from the Kingdom of Marsupia and will make further restitution to the peoples of this land at a designation of my choosing. Let it also be known that further investigation of injustices against my people will be carried out and the guilty parties will also face justice. I, Alister Rex, High King of all Theria, by the authority of An'Ceann and with his blessing, do hereby decree this to be.

Furthermore, I urge us to use this time to reconcile all peoples of Marsupia to bring about healing to this land so we can stand in unity to the principles handed down to us from An'Ceann. I sent a pulse of energy through the connection to each shifter and sent a sense of profound sorrow for the things we'd discovered.

"Please clear the room and place the rest of these elves under house arrest," I said to the guards and waited until the elves and fae folk were out of the room. I cast the *Spheara* and *Indicens* spells together to create a soundproof shield around the room.

"Where are you sending us, Sire?" Celand asked after he stood. He placed his hand on Malonne's shoulder and she grasped his hand with her own.

"Earth," I responded and Celand looked at me with shock but Malonne had a hopeful expression. "For the past fourteen years, Malonne has worked with autistic children and adults on Earth. Many of these children have been marginalized, discriminated against and treated poorly by others. You will work together to help these children. Not only that, you will also work with some of my people I have on Earth influencing humans to improve their societies.

"While we work to improve the lives of elves and fae folk on Marsupia and eliminate the injustice, prejudice and racism that you have allowed to grow in this kingdom; the two of you will be working to eliminate the same things on Earth. You will have opportunities to use your power and gifts to bring healing to divided communities in the United States. There is a lot of hatred and division so you will endeavor to bring peace, love and healing for the next century."

"Thank you for your mercy, Sire," Celand said as he bowed low.

"Queen Brooklyn was actually the one to suggest this course of action. She genuinely believes you can do better on Earth than you can do on Marsupia and I hope you use this opportunity to better yourselves and the people you serve. Shelley, please give them the tablets."

Shelley walked over and handed two of the tablets used by Tionchar. "These are secure and can be used to send messages to Wayne and Josef, who will be your contacts on Earth. You will also be able to send and receive messages to Theria when gates are opened. Wayne will contact you with more instructions." I rose from the throne and walked down to stand in front of them. "Let me make this clear. If I receive any reports that you have used your power or position for any purpose other than healing, you forfeit your lives. Do you understand?"

Both Celand and Malonne nodded and I opened the gate to Josef's office at Rex Industries in Phoenix, Arizona. Wayne and Josef were waiting for the former rulers.

"It's good to see you," I said to my friends, "I just wish this was a happier occasion. They're all yours."

We'll make sure they know what needs to be done, Josef sent to me.

Thank you both, I sent back.

That's what we're here for, Wayne quipped, *we live to serve.*

Celand and Malonne walked through the gate and I shut it behind them. There was a collective sigh of relief from everyone still in the throne room.

"Do you think they'll learn their lesson," my father asked.

"I hope so. Mother seemed to think Malonne had changed during her time on Earth. Hopefully, Celand will, too." I sighed, "I suppose we'd better see what we can do with the rest of the so-called nobility."

"Can we at least get some lunch first?" Shelley asked. "I'm going to need more energy if we have to listen to more stories like we've already heard."

"That's actually a great idea, I'm surprised you came up with it." Aileene smiled at Shelley.

"I told you Bernie's been training him," I joked.

Everyone laughed but I could tell it was forced as we all felt the pain from the testimonies we'd heard that morning.

Aileene

I wanted to find Alister but rather than call out, I followed the mate bond and found him near the fountain in the center of the castle garden. We were staying in the northwestern part of Marsupia in the duchy of

Tarwa. This was the final stop on our month-long tour to root out oppression against any of the fae folk. Fortunately, the worst of the oppression was contained in the southern part of the kingdom near the capital city of Farhana.

Alister was in deep discussion with Duchess Falenas Omalen, of Tarwa. Falenas was a tall, stately elf with smooth brown skin and depthless brown eyes the color of dark umber. She easily smiled and her laugh was infectious.

"Ah, Lady Aileene," Falenas bowed when she saw me walk up behind Alister, "I take my leave to check on the preparations for the farewell feast."

"How are you?" I asked as I smoothed Alister's hair away from his face when he turned to face me. His green eyes sparkled with humor as he looked at me and for a moment I was lost in his gaze. He took my hand in his and kissed the back of it and we sat together on the lip of the fountain.

"I'm doing better now that I know not all elves are jerks," Alister said with an edge, "but I still can't believe the Farhanas allowed the injustice to continue for so long."

"I know, and that breaks my heart too," I said but then added with a smile, "it was evident they were self-centered when they named the capital city after themselves."

Alister laughed and I leaned my head against his chest, and he put his arm around me. I loved to hear him laugh and was pleased I could ease some of the pressure he'd been under.

After a minute of silence, Alister began to talk. "Even though I didn't realize it at the time, my parents, and the other members of the Inner Circle, were teaching me how to be a just king when we lived on Earth. Whenever there were examples of injustice in the news, we would discuss why it was wrong to treat people differently based on skin color, religion, gender or even who they loved. I was taught that it was important to love people and treat them the way I would want to be treated.

"There was a large mirror in the hallway in our house and it was the first thing I'd see when I came in and the last thing I'd see when leaving the house. Next to the mirror was a framed quote by a man named Edmund Burke. The quote is, 'The only thing necessary for the triumph of evil is for good men to do nothing.' Every time I looked at the mirror, I saw the quote and wanted to be the type of person who would do something to stop evil."

I sat back and looked into Alister's troubled eyes. "You are that man, Alister. You may be High King because An'Ceann crowned you, but you are worthy of the crown. Since we met, you've been relentless in stomping out evil wherever you find it; even to the detriment of your health. I know you're disappointed that some of the elves actively oppressed the fae folk and others stood by and did nothing. But I also want to remind you that many others, like Falenas, actively worked against the laws passed by Celand Elandorr.

"She protected her people and allowed fae folk from other duchies to settle in her territory. She banded with other dukes and duchesses so there were actually fewer duchies following the unjust laws than those that did."

Alister sighed deeply, "I know but I was hoping that the shifters of Theria were above such behaviors."

I couldn't help laughing as I thought of all the things we've already been through, "Oh love, I'm not laughing at you but I think you're forgetting how many shifters have tried to kill you or oppress others since you found out the truth about your heritage."

Alister hugged me and chuckled and I imagine he'd also thought back to everything he'd seen so far. "You're right, but—you know—elves. I was hoping for something different from elves. In all the stories the elves are always the good guys."

"Well, there are a lot of good elves," I stood on my tiptoes and kissed him on the chin "and they jumped at the chance to be part of the coalition government you established with Lady Falenas and Queen Brooklyn as co-leaders. They are excited to reform the laws on Marsupia."

"And since Queen Brooklyn contacted other rulers of the fae folk to be part of the government, too, I do feel we've left Marsupia better than we found it," Alister admitted.

"Now all we have to do is root out the traitors who want to kill us and take over Theria, no big deal," I said with a wink. "Are we heading to Metatheria next?"

"I've changed our plans a bit, but I think you'll like the surprise," Alister said with a grin.

"You know how much I love surprises," I giggled.

"Yep," Alister agreed and kissed me.

CHAPTER SEVEN

Dóchas 1, 10,257

We stepped through the gate I'd created at Falenas Omalen's home on Marsupia and entered the throne room on Eutheria. Lord and Lady Moss stood to greet us and Aileene rushed over to hug her foster father. She also hugged a clearly pregnant Bronwyn Moss who we hadn't seen on our quick trip to Loch Ness.

"How far along are you?" Aileene squealed in delight.

"Six months. We waited so long to get married, we didn't want to wait too much longer to start a family," Bronwyn said proudly.

"I'm going to be a big sister?" Aileene said excitedly. "Alister, we're both getting new siblings to spoil. This is going to be amazing."

Everyone laughed with Aileene and congratulated the expectant parents. I loved seeing this side of Aileene. She was a fierce dragon but could also get excited about simple pleasures. I was glad I decided to make Eutheria the next stop on our journey where we would spend the entire month of Dóchas with people we cared about.

After everyone had gathered in the throne room, I closed the gate and we followed James and Bronwyn Moss to the dining room. I excused myself after everyone was seated because I had to get my second surprise. Conversation stopped a few minutes later when I brought my mom and dad into the room. This caused another round of hugs and a few tears from Bronwyn when she realized Mom was there to help her through the first step of her pregnancy.

"Alister, I thought we were heading to Metatheria next," Shelley said after we all finally sat down to eat.

"I figured we could visit Eutheria first then Metatheria next month," I answered before taking a bite of the roasted sprìosh. "Besides, it's been a while since we've hunted, and I happen to know where we can get more of this delicious meat."

"Captain Jormis will wait another three weeks in the port at Tarwa then set sail for Metatheria. The journey will take twelve days or so. He'll drop anchor about fifty miles off-shore and the King will open a gate back to the ship. This will allow us time to travel across Eutheria to allow the dukes and duchesses the chance to meet the King and Lady Aileene and hopefully confuse our enemies," Stavros explained.

"If your captain sails your ship to Metatheria, how will you get there? Will you fly?" Bronwyn asked.

"Alister can create a gate to the ship," Aileene answered proudly and took a big bite of the rare meat on her plate.

"That's impressive, Son," Dad beamed at me. "Not even your father had the kind of control over gates that you do."

I ducked my head in embarrassment but was pleased by the compliment from my dad. Before I could answer, Wu piped up.

"Actually, there hasn't been another High King or Queen that has the control over gates like Alister does."

"And Wu and I have been talking about Alister's magical abilities and we've discovered that no one else in Therian history has had the ability to wield magic or create new spells the way Alister does," Hillaes added.

Shelley stood and bowed to both Wu and Hillaes before sitting. "Thank you both for confirming what I've always known; Alister is a super freak." He smirked at me before I hit him in the forehead with a roll.

"I may be a super freak, but at least I'm not super weak," I shot back and stood.

"Oh, brother," Bernie muttered. "Can we at least finish dinner before the two of you throw down?"

Shelley and I were glaring at each other when I heard Bronwyn mutter, "oh, dear."

Turning to our host I apologized, "I'm sorry for my uncouth friend. His behavior was completely unacceptable. I will make sure to teach him a lesson after we finish this delicious meal." I sat and continued eating.

"B-b-but you were the one to throw the roll," Shelley spluttered.

"Yes, but you're the one who tried to catch it with your forehead. As your king, I'm quite embarrassed. I expect more from one of my Knights." I grinned smugly.

"Well, Your Majesty, I will be more than happy to accept instruction from you after dinner on acceptable behavior." Shelley smiled and began shoveling his meal into his mouth.

Bronwyn looked distressed but Mom patted her hand. "Don't worry, dear, they've been like this since they were children. After everything they've been through, they need to blow off some steam."

"True that," Shelley said and held out his fist for a bump.

Even though I knew we were being silly, I felt lighter than I had for a long time and felt comfortable acting like this with the people surrounding the table. I considered everyone there family and was glad we'd be spending the month together in Eutheria.

Aileene and Bernie laughed at me when I groaned as I sat at the breakfast table. The only thing that made me feel somewhat better was Shelley looked worse than I felt. After dinner the night before, we trooped outside so Shelley and I could get our battle on and found it was snowing. There was enough on the ground for us to make snowballs, so we started with a snowball fight. Even though it had been the beginning of summer in Marsupia, winter was setting in on the northern hemisphere of Theria. It had taken me some time to connect the months on Theria and Earth, but Dóchas was the same as December.

Shelley and I wrestled, boxed, sparred and generally had a great time beating each other up. We began our bout with a crowd but by the time we were finished there were only a few people left outside, the other observers had moved inside where it was warm.

"Even with your enhanced healing it's obvious you're both in pain. Why don't you let us heal you?" Bernie asked.

"Because, now they're competing to see who gives in first and who can tough out the pain," Aileene said in an exasperated tone.

"Idiots," Bernie muttered and Shelley and I grinned at each other.

"That's fine for you, but since we're always connected through our mate bond, I get to feel what you do," Aileene said to me. I looked at her and noticed the tightening around her eyes which showed she was also in pain.

"I'm so sorry, I didn't think about that," I apologized, "please go ahead." I said and held out my hand to her.

I sighed in relief as the aches and pains disappeared.

"I win, Stretch," Shelley crowed then winced when he tried to give me a fist bump.

"Yeah, you win," Bernie said painfully.

Shelley turned to her in alarm. "Wait, are you feeling my pain, too?"

Bernie bit her bottom lip and nodded shyly.

"So, that means we have a mate bond, too?" Shelley asked in wonder.

"Well, duh," Aileene said and reached over to punch Shelley's arm. He didn't even react but kept looking at Bernie with a goofy grin on his face. "Men," Aileene muttered and cast *Sanos* to heal Shelley's aches and pains.

Shelley kept looking at Bernie and finally asked, "How long have you known we're true mates?"

"Pretty much since Alister and Aileene met. Once I felt the truth of their bond, I could recognize ours. Were you really as clueless as you like us to believe?" Bernie asked.

"No," Shelley grinned widely, "I suspected it when Gustav told us about true mates, but I knew for sure around the same time. I didn't want to say anything until you were ready."

Shelley reached across the table to take Bernie's hand and they looked lovingly at one another and I could tell they were conversing in thought-speak. Grinning at Aileene, I started to eat my breakfast.

So, I thought to her, *you were feeling my pain?*

Yes, usually I can block it out but combine your physical pain with the residue from the dream you had last night, and I wasn't doing a good job with my mental shields.

I'm sorry, I thought as I stopped eating and looked at her.

She looked at me and giggled. *I'm sorry for laughing but you have some egg on your face. You're almost as messy an eater when in human form as when you're a dragon.*

I laughed while I wiped my face, *Yeah, but you find me irresistible.*

Aileene grinned cheekily and sent me a wave of emotions through our connection and embraced me with her mind. *You're right, I do.*

I smiled to myself and continued eating. It was nice for the four of us to spend time together. After a few more minutes of silence I interrupted Bernie and Shelley's mental conversation. "I had the dream again last night but there were some significant changes."

This caught the attention of my dining companions and Aileene looked at me with concern. "That's why my mental shields aren't as strong as normal," she remarked. "What happened?"

"Well, it started as usual with the armies arrayed against each other but instead of seven armies attacking everyone else, they were arrayed into two sides. Theria, Eutheria, Cetacea and Marsupia were lined up on one side of the field of battle and Sirenea, Metatheria and Carnivoria were lined up on the other. The armies clashed and many people died, but not everyone this time."

"What about us, did we die?" Bernie asked.

"Some did, and some didn't. In fact, one person from each mated pair of the Inner Circle survived."

"That's progress," Shelley commented.

"But that's not all, is it?" Aileene asked.

"No, the death toll was still terrible, and the dragon bone missile still bounced off Aileene's skin but this time when I died from the poison all life on the planet was wiped out as well," I said sadly.

"Well, that sucks," Shelley responded after we'd been silent with our thoughts for a few minutes. "It seems like we've still got to continue reuniting the seven kingdoms and make sure you don't die. Piece of cake," Shelley added before stuffing more eggs and spriosh bacon in his mouth.

"I will not accept death and defeat for any of us," Aileene declared, "I don't care if I have to rip the last three kingdoms apart, I will find and punish those responsible for the rebellion."

"I won't accept defeat either, but we need to make sure we only punish the guilty parties," I said gently.

"When I find those who have caused you pain like this, they will not survive," Aileene said with finality.

"Very well, then we'll find them before they can destroy Theria," I agreed. That apparently satisfied Aileene because she smiled brightly and continued eating.

"Hey, what were you and Wu talking about for so long after the fight last night?" Shelley asked, changing the conversation.

"He wanted my permission to propose to Hillaes," I smiled.

Both Aileene and Bernie "awed" and started talking about wedding details.

"You knew Wu and Hillaes were interested in each other?" I asked confused.

"It was obvious," Aileene said, rolling her eyes.

"They've been looking at each other differently since we came back from Earth," Bernie added.

"Wait, I'm confused," Shelley interrupted. "First of all, why does he need your permission to propose and second, isn't Hillaes human? How does that work?"

"I'll answer the second question first. When we're in our human form, for all intents and purposes we are completely human. They could get married and Wu would stay human as long as Hillaes was alive. However, because Hillaes is human, she would die within seventy or eighty years, and neither of them want that. Wu asked my permission because he wants me to petition An'Ceann to transform Hillaes into a tiger shifter."

My friends were stunned by that announcement but of course, Shelley spoke first. "An'Ceann can do that? Of course, he can do that, he can do anything, but this is something he would actually do?"

"According to Wu, this has happened in the past when there were more interactions between the different dimensions. Wu can always ask An'Ceann himself, but he wants to follow tradition and has asked me, as High King, to make the request on his behalf. Of course, I've agreed and plan on asking An'Ceann the moment I see him next."

"Wow," Bernie breathed, "this is so cool. Who would have thought this would be our life when we were growing up on Earth?"

"I'm very happy for Wu and Hillaes, everyone should be as happy finding their true mate as we are," Aileene smiled at me.

I felt the same way she did, so all I could do was grin back at her.

"Where are we?" I heard Aileene ask so I opened my eyes and saw the bright, blue sky of An'Ceann's Kingdom. Somehow the sky always felt bigger here, so I knew at once where we were. What surprised me was that Aileene was here with me. Normally, I would be here alone with An'Ceann. I sat up and looked at my future mate and couldn't help laughing when I looked at her tousled hair.

"I know you aren't laughing at me because you know that would be very unwise," Aileene said to me with narrowed eyes as she tried to comb her hair with her hands. "Think about your answer carefully, Alister. Once we're married, you'll be waking up next to me for centuries and I'm sure you would rather not sleep on the royal couch." She grinned evilly.

I gulped but was saved by An'Ceann speaking to us before I could answer. "A bit of advice, never laugh at how a woman looks when she wakes." An'Ceann smiled and Aileene tackled him. I loved watching how free she was in expressing her love and appreciation for

An'Ceann. I was overwhelmed with feeling blessed to have such a wonderful person in my life.

"Not that I'm not grateful, but why are we here?" I heard Aileene ask.

"Walk with me," he answered, and I moved up next to Aileene and grabbed her hand in mine.

"I do think you look beautiful, even with bedhead," I snickered.

"You're such a charmer," she giggled and An'Ceann laughed.

"You couldn't have done anything differently to save the shifters who were killed by their masters during the battles," An'Ceann began after we'd walked in pleasant silence through a field of glowing purple flowers.

I felt a weight lift off my shoulders that I didn't know I was carrying and Aileene squeezed my arm when she felt my emotions lighten.

"Furthermore, almost all of those killed volunteered for the attacks even though they didn't know they had devices to take their lives when detonated," he continued.

"Thank you for sharing that with us, Alister has been carrying this with him for a long time," Aileene said.

An'Ceann smiled and answered, "I know."

"That explains a few things," I remarked. "Muir reported that their investigation on Cetacea had stalled but they had confirmed none of the attackers were citizens of that kingdom. They were all water shifters but must have come from somewhere else in Theria. And, of course you're not going to share with us which kingdom they came from."

An'Ceann shook his golden head, releasing beams of light from his mane. "I won't tell you that, but I can confirm they didn't come from Cetacea, Marsupia, Eutheria or Theria," he smiled mischievously.

"That's a lotta help, we'd guessed that ourselves already," I muttered sarcastically.

"I'm glad I could confirm your hypothesis," he laughed and Aileene and I laughed along with him. We stopped near the edge of a forest filled with trees unlike any I'd ever seen before. Their trunks were pale green and glowed softly. The lavender colored leaves of each tree stirred as though a breeze blew through the forest, but the air was still. They emitted a faint fragrance that reminded me of freshly-baked chocolate-chip cookies and a sense of profound peace emanated from the forest. I had a desire to explore the depths of the woods but An'Ceann's voice stopped me before I could step closer.

"I'm proud of the way you handled the problem on Marsupia."

"Why didn't you stop the injustice yourself?" Aileene asked with a hint of accusation.

His eyes softened as he asked, "What would you have me do, Daughter?"

"Punish those who were unjust to the fae folk and make sure they could never harm others the same way again. Free the oppressed from the yoke of evil and enact restrictions so it couldn't happen again," Aileene answered fiercely.

"And how would that be any different from what you did?" He asked gently.

"It—" Aileene began then trailed off in thought. "I guess it wouldn't be any different, but you could have done it much sooner than we did."

"But you're assuming I wasn't doing anything at all. I was working with those who choose to follow my ways. They are the ones who protected the fae folk and put their own happiness on the line to help them. There will come a day when I will once again take charge of Theria but until then, I work through those who claim me as their High King." An'Ceann gave Aileene a lion's kiss on her forehead. "My dear, you have great passion and are fiercely protective of those you love, and you have a huge heart. Thank you for caring so much. One of the ways I help others is to work through you."

"An'Ceann, that's something I wanted to talk to you about as well," I said.

"You don't say," he smiled at me.

"My father was surprised you interact with me so directly. He said he's only had a few face-to-face conversations with you over the centuries."

An'Ceann lay down on the grass and rolled to his side. Aileene and I sat and leaned against him, basking in his warmth.

"He's right and he's wrong," An'Ceann began. "I've had many conversations with Phillip that he doesn't remember because as he's grown older, he's less open to my influence, but I do. Besides, during his reign he hasn't had to face the challenges you have since learning who you are. Phillip hasn't done anything wrong; you just understand you need to rely on my strength more than you do your own."

We were quiet after that as I contemplated what he said. It was so peaceful laying here I wasn't sure I wanted to get up.

"Was there anything else you wanted to tell us?" Aileene asked, breaking the lengthy silence between us.

"Hmmm," he purred, "please inform Wu and Hillaes that I wish them the best and know they'll be happy together."

With that, he disappeared and Aileene and I fell backwards since our support went away.

"He always does that," I muttered. "I wish I would have asked him who our enemies are."

"Do you think he would have told you directly?" Aileene asked.

"No, I suppose not," I answered and closed my eyes to enjoy the warmth of the sunshine a little longer.

Dóchas 21, 10,257
  Eutheria

Lord Moss and I were in the new communication room in his castle. One of the changes I was making as High King was requiring each ruler use available technology to stay in contact with the Kingdom of Theria and each other. I appreciate tradition but I believe some of the problems we'd met could have been eliminated if their ways to receive information had been more efficient.

We stood in front of the ten foot wide monitor, which was only an inch thick, and right now looked exactly like the blank wall it was mounted on. It used extraordinarily little electricity and produced almost no heat while running. When Rex Industries releases this technology on Earth, we'll make another fortune.

"Uncle James, please initiate contact with my father, Captain Jormis, Lady Zhaleh, Lady Omalen and Queen Brooklyn."

The scene on the monitor changed and instead of the image of the wall, it was now divided into six sections that showed the people I wanted to talk with, plus my own image so I could see how I appeared to them. The picture was so clear, it was as if they were in the room with us.

"Thank you for joining us this morning. I have some updates for you and want to check in to see if you have any for me," I began.

After the greetings were over, I shared with them the changes to my dream. For some it was the first time hearing me describe what I'd been dreaming but for others this was old news. We talked about what it could mean but we all agreed that we were moving in the right direction even though if I died, all Theria would die with me.

When I finished, my father gave his report. "We've finished analyzing the materials and bodies you sent us and made some interesting discoveries. Those who died of poison had evidence of microscopic capsules in their bloodstream which contained poison derived from the Orquidea Brilhante flower which is native to Metatheria."

"So that means one of the conspirators is from Metatheria?" Shelley asked from where he and Bernie were standing guard at the door. Mkali was outside the door with Chelsea and some other guards.

"Not necessarily," Father replied. "Even though the flower grows in the wild in Metatheria it can flourish in greenhouses. In fact, we have flowers from every kingdom in the Royal Gardens at the palace."

"Was this the same type of poison used on you and Mother?" I asked.

"No, so far we haven't been able to find the poison used on us and any of the known poisons don't affect us."

"And how do you know that?" I asked suspiciously.

My father looked uncomfortable as he admitted, "I've been serving as a test subject. I may not be High King any longer, but I refuse to let you face these dangers alone. If I can help figure out which poison could affect you, I'm doing it. Besides, I figure if I'm poisoned you can gate here quickly enough to heal me." He grinned as he finished.

I was touched by my father's love and his willingness to put himself in danger to save me.

"What's the news in Marsupia?" I asked, my voice rough with emotion.

Brooklyn and Falenas sat side-by-side and after a quick, silent conversation, Brooklyn spoke. "Things are progressing well. We've set up the joint government in every duchy and so far, things are moving along peacefully. Those who committed the greatest atrocities have been imprisoned and are awaiting trial while investigations are underway. There were also some fae folk who attempted to take the law into their own hands, and they have been imprisoned as well."

"Those of us who remember the time when we coexisted peacefully as equals are letting people know how things should be. We're reviewing the history being taught in some of the duchies and making sure the information is correct. I'm ashamed to admit I didn't have any idea how bad it had gotten in some parts of the kingdom," Falenas admitted.

"Thank you for your work; it seems like we are making strides, but it will take years to undo the damage that was caused by the Elandorrs and those who followed their own prejudices," I added.

"We've finished our investigation on Cetacea," Lady Zhaleh added, "and it looks like everyone associated with the rebellion was killed in the attacks. None of the water shifters had relatives living here, and in some cases only shared a distant ancestry with my people. We're confident Cetacea is secured from any conspirators."

The rest of the rulers, including my father, nodded in agreement with her assessment.

"Captain Jormis, what is your status?" I asked.

"We set sail for Metatheria tomorrow. The weather may be rough in a few spots, but we should be in place before the beginning of Faollich."

"That's the same as January, right?" Bernie whispered to Shelley and he nodded.

"Thank you, Captain." I continued, "Uncle James, could you please report on what we've been doing on Eutheria?"

"With pleasure," he said as he addressed the others on the monitors. "King Alister, Lady Aileene and the others of his Inner Circle traveled to every duchy in Eutheria and met with the dukes and duchesses. The Einhorns utilized their talents to find the truth and we feel confident each one is supportive of the High King. Even though we moved quickly through the kingdom, we were able to visit everyone we needed to."

"You forgot to share the best news," I prompted.

He smiled widely and announced, "I'm going to be a father." After everyone congratulated him, he continued. "Fiona helped Bronwyn through the process to lay her first egg. They're currently curled up together to keep the egg warm." He beamed with pride and I put my arm around him in a hug.

"Alister, what's your next move?" Father asked.

Smiling widely, I answered, "We're going to celebrate Christmas."

Carnivoria

Lord Carmanor

There were five male shifters standing in a fighting circle. The tallest one was in the center of the circle. He was eight feet tall, stripped to the waist and looked human except for his amber eyes which were glowing slightly. He wore a pair of loose fitting pants; his feet were bare, and he didn't hold a weapon in his hands. He slowly pivoted in the circle and kept a wary eye on the four partially shifted werelions who prowled about him.

They charged him at the same time, and he was confronted with four fighters coming at him from different directions. At the last moment he leapt straight up and kicked the head of the man who rushed him from the front. There was a crack and the shifter dropped to the ground in a boneless heap. The shifter to his right tried to slash him with his claws but he twisted in mid-air and the shifter's attack missed its mark by inches.

He dropped back to the ground, landing on his feet and grabbed the one who had missed his chance and used his body to shield himself from the other two who pressed the attack. He slammed his forearm and elbow into the back of that shifter's head and he also dropped to the ground.

He faced the remaining two shifters and smiled wickedly. The sun reflected off his bald head and his ebony skin glistened with sweat. He turned slowly so he continued to face the two left standing, but rather than wait for them to make a move, he rushed the one on his left and inflicted punishing blows to his abdomen and ribs. Before the other fighter could attack, he lashed out with his right foot and caught him in the throat with a backward kick.

Turning his attention to the shifter who was trying to rally to attack him he blocked a punch by grabbing the shifter's wrist then calmly broke his elbow with a punch from his other arm. The shifter screamed but his pain was soon cut off by an uppercut that tossed him off his feet and he was unconscious before he hit the dirt.

The victor examined the shifter who couldn't breathe due to a crushed larynx but kept walking to a woman who was seated on a golden throne in the shade.

"My Lord, if you continue to damage your playthings in this fashion the healers won't be able to put them back together again," she said.

"Bah, Kudanganya, what is the point in sparring if I don't treat it like a real battle. If these warriors of mine aren't strong enough to survive a little friendly practice, they don't deserve to live. If they die, they die."

"Of course, dear," she said as she kissed her husband. She looked over at the shifter with the frown on his face who stood near her throne. "What do you think, Joshua, do you think Lord Carmanor is too hard on your soldiers?"

"Lord Carmanor knows my feelings on this subject. I believe it is unnecessary to inflict such physical damage on those who are loyal to his lordship and the Kingdom of Carnivoria," Joshua said in disapproval.

"Lighten up, Josh," Lord Carmanor laughed as he watched the shifters he defeated being treated for their injuries. "Don't make me question your training methods. As Captain of the Guard I expect better from you. Well, since I don't have anyone else to spar with, I guess it's your turn," Lord Carmanor smiled wickedly.

"As you wish," Joshua intoned as he shifted into his half form. As a were-rhinoceros he was almost as big as Lord Carmanor.

"Don't hurt him too badly dear, he is your most loyal subject," Lady Kudanganya trilled.

"I'm not making any promises, I have to get ready for Prince Alister's visit. He's going to have to defeat me in a physical battle before I'll submit to his authority."

"Run along Joshua, I've been looking forward to seeing my husband give you a beat-down for a long time."

"As you wish," Joshua bowed his head and made his way to the battle circle.

CHAPTER EIGHT

Dóchas 24, 10,257

Logs blazed in the fireplace at the far end of the hall, lighting up the entire room. The walls and ceiling were festooned with garlands of evergreen and red berries from the aveous trees. The berries smelled like baked apple and cinnamon and reflected the light from the candles in sconces. The dinner tables had been pushed against the walls to make room for dancing. We had feasted on roast pig, beef, turkey and goose imported from Earth along with sprìosh and gambon from Theria.

Even though Christmas wasn't celebrated in Theria I had always liked the holiday and the meaning behind why we celebrated. I'd always been fascinated by the idea of the all-powerful God leaving his place in eternity and choosing to be born as a helpless baby so he could save everyone. Since I had been raised with the principle of protecting the weak, I couldn't think of a better example of this played out through the Christmas story.

Aileene danced with her foster father, Lord Moss, and my heart warmed to see her wide smile. She was dancing the same way she approached everything else in life, with complete joy, enthusiasm and abandon. She wore a long velvet dress trimmed with red and silver ribbons. Her auburn hair shone in the candlelight and I was proud that she called me hers.

"Why don't you just ask her to dance?" Mom asked me as she slipped her arm through mine.

"I'm enjoying watching her dance with Uncle James. I'll get my turn later," I laughed. "Where's Dad?"

Mom snorted, "I wore him out, so he stepped outside to catch his breath. Thank you for planning this party. It won't be too long before your siblings are hatched, and your dad and I won't get any time to ourselves for a bit."

"I'm sure Aileene and I would be happy to babysit—drakesit—watch the kids, while you and Dad go out," I teased. "When we get back after this round-the-world tour."

"Are you worried about the danger forewarned in your dream?" Mom asked as she squeezed my arm.

"I'd be lying if I said no," I commented. "However, I think the dream has helped remind us that we have to be on our guard. I think we'll be ready for danger when it comes."

Mom was silent for so long I turned to look at her in confusion. She had tears in her eyes, and she shook her head at my silent question. "It's nothing," she said. "I was just thinking about how much you've all had to grow up in such a short period. You've only known about your heritage for a year and a half and you've already had to fight major battles on Theria and Earth and assumed the mantle of High King.

"We're all so proud of you, Son. Your dad and I, along with your father and mother. We've had a lot of time to talk about things since we stayed behind at the palace and we all agree that we couldn't have handled things any better than you. Even though you're new to this, you've done an amazing job. We just wish you could have enjoyed your childhood more."

I put my arm around her and kissed the top of her head. "You and Dad did so much to prepare me for this task, thank you. Shelley, Bernie and I have talked, and we've agreed that we wouldn't change a thing, even if we had to cut our childhood short. I mean, just look at Shelley. Half the time he still acts like a kid," I laughed.

"I heard that Stretch," Shelley yelled as he and Bernie danced by where Mom and I were standing.

"See what I mean?" I grinned, "we don't feel like we've missed out. We've gained far more than we've lost," I said as I looked again at Aileene. I could tell she heard me because her eyes blazed for a moment as she walked towards me.

"Mom, I'm going to steal Alister from you, he owes me a dance," Aileene said as she hugged Mom and dragged me onto the dance floor.

"See you later," I called over my shoulder, "and thank you for everything."

Aileene kissed my cheek and whispered, "And I feel like I've gained more than I've lost as well."

I grinned and twirled Aileene into the crowd so we could join the dance.

Faollich 03, 10,258

HMS Beatrice

We stood on deck as we approached Castelleon Harbor where Lady Lynx had agreed to meet us. If we were on Earth we would be sailing into Rio de Janeiro, Brazil and I was struck by the sheer beauty of the dense jungle that covered the shore. There were so many shades of green represented by the trees I was awestruck by the variety. There were also flowering bushes covered with vibrant flowers of yellow, purple, pink, red and an iridescent orange. The jungles pulsed with life and even though I couldn't see any animals through the vast foliage, I could hear a myriad of sounds that were coming from shore.

The water in the harbor was turquoise and so clear I could see the white, sandy floor of the ocean below. Our underwater guard easily kept pace with the ship as we approached the shore. We also had guards in the air led by Erich the Eagle. I hadn't seen him since the battle with Dimitri and he joined us when we left Eutheria. So far, we'd added to our guards each time we left one of the kingdoms and it was gratifying to see the various shifters work together.

Shelley, Stavros and Miriam were communicating with the guards above and below to coordinate our security. We'd decided to show a force of strength when we approached Metatheria, in case there were people wanting to do us harm. We'd also decided that we would drop anchor far out into the bay and Aileene and I would fly ashore. I would open a gate back to the ship so the rest of our people could disembark; Fritz and Frieda felt this display would strengthen my position as High King.

Castelleon Harbor was in the Duchy of Lobisomem and was the capital city where Lady Lynx ruled. Her husband Lord Saltu lived with her but wasn't co-ruler. The rule had passed along her family line and that suited her husband quite well. During his briefing, Fritz informed us that Lady Lynx was planning to retire and asked for my help to choose her heir from one of her twelve children. Frieda added that Lady Lynx wasn't prepared to accept me as High King before meeting me, but neither was she opposed to my rule. In many ways, she was ambivalent, and I would need to prove myself to be a capable leader. They didn't think she was part of the conspiracy of rebels but couldn't guarantee that.

We've reached our designated location, Sire. I'm about to drop anchor. Captain Jormis sent from the bridge.

Thank you, Captain, Aileene and I will get into position.

As Aileene and I walked to the fore deck, I connected to each shifter on the continent of Metatheria. I thought back to how long it took me the first time I tried this but now could connect with little effort. I sent a calming wave through each connection to let them know I had arrived and was almost overwhelmed by the wave of joy that was returned, and I diverted that energy to my power reservoir. Smiling at the welcome I'd received, I stopped and opened a micro gate to Middle Earth and linked it to the doorway between the deck and the interior of the ship. I wanted easy access to magic for our party while we were in Metatheria.

The rush of magic through the gate was instantaneous and those of us who could use magic would be able to draw from Middle Earth, even though we would be on land. Those who would go with us to shore were gathered in their natural forms and wouldn't transform into humans until we stood before Lady Lynx and her husband Lord Saltu. I smiled as I looked at Wu and his new wife Hillaes in their tiger forms. We'd celebrated their wedding the day after Christmas and I was happy they'd found each other.

I was distracted by Shelley standing on his hind legs scratching his back against the ledge running around the bulkhead.

What? Apparently, the salt air makes me itchy.

"You big oaf," I laughed, "we've only been back on the ship for a few hours. We stepped through the gate from Eutheria this morning."

That must be it then, he sent smugly, *it was snowing in Eutheria when we left and now, we're in tropical weather. I must be shedding my winter coat.*

"We don't have all day for you two to finally get around to challenging each other to the 'fight of the century'," Aileene interrupted before Shelley and I could get our rhythm going. She even used her fingers to make air quotes.

"You know us so well," I laughed, and Bernie snorted and stamped a hoof. "And you, my dear, just want to transform into your dragon to make potential enemies quake."

Aileene turned to me with a predatory smile, showing too many teeth, and answered, "And you know me so well." She laughed, ran towards the bow and leaped up and over the rail, diving towards the water below. She roared as she transformed, and her majestic green dragon skimmed the waves before soaring into the sky.

Grinning, I followed her example and manifested my wings as I flung myself from the prow of the ship. My wings filled with air and with powerful strokes I quickly climbed until I was a hundred feet over the water. I fully transformed and roared in exaltation. Everyone on shore was being treated to their first sight of Royal Dragons for at least two decades. Our dragons had continued to grow, and we had grown larger than my royal parents. I was almost eighty feet long and my wings stretched seventy-five feet tip to tip. Aileene was large for a female Royal Dragon and was over fifty feet long and had a forty foot wingspan. Although we were huge, we could maneuver extremely well in the air.

Even though I couldn't see Aileene I could feel her through our bond, and I knew she was above and behind me, her sense of glee blazed through our connection and I knew she wanted to play. She nipped my tail as she flew past, so I gave chase. We lost ourselves in the sheer joy of flying free and being in each other's presence in our dragon forms. At this point, nothing worried me, and I knew both of us were covered by the *Adamantem* spell. We put on a brief aerial show before flying side-by-side towards the shore.

That was fun, promise me we can do that again later, Aileene sent.

Absolutely, but we should bring our Knights with us when we do, I responded.

Aileene laughed, *you just want to see if you can make Shelley puke, don't you?*

Of course, I answered and flared my wings so we could land at the spot that had been cleared for us. The moment our feet touched ground, we transformed and walked together through the cheering crowd towards the pavilion which had been set up within the jungle clearing. Aileene and I stopped and I concentrated for a moment to open a gate back to the deck of the ship where the rest of our party waited.

The crowd quieted as our guards and inner circle walked through the gate in their natural forms. Some of our flying shifters landed and joined the others while a dozen of our aquatic shifters walked out of the surf and stood with us as well. The last few shifters through the gate carried extra robes for those shifters who didn't have thought medallions and would need some type of clothing when they shifted. The last person to assemble was Captain Jormis in his ice dragon form. I sent the mental command, and everyone shifted while I closed the gate.

To the right of the pavilion there was a wide path paved in cobblestones. This boulevard was lined with towering palm trees interspersed with flat-roofed buildings and led to a golden structure that looked like an Aztec pyramid, although it was easily twice the size of any I had seen in history books. As we walked towards the person sitting within the pavilion I smiled and waved at the crowd of cheering and dancing shifters who celebrated our arrival. Music was playing from somewhere and I couldn't help swaying to the beat of the drums.

When Aileene, our Inner Circle and I entered the pavilion, Lady Lynx stood from her golden throne and threw her arms open in greeting. She was in her half form and it was clear she was a jaguar shifter. Her piercing golden eyes had slitted pupils like a cat and her fur was jet-black. She stood over six and a half feet tall and smiled broadly with a mouth full of sharp teeth. Her cloak looked as if it were made of peacock feathers, her arms were covered with golden bracers and a plumed headdress adorned with colorful feathers rounded out her impressively regal outfit.

"Welcome to Metatheria. Peace, safety and friendship from me and mine to you and yours while you are our honored guests," she growled and spread her arms wide. Even though I was surprised to hear a human voice coming from the mouth of a cat, I didn't let it show on my face.

"We accept your hospitality and pledge to protect you and yours with all our power. Furthermore, I give you my personal assurance, that I serve all those loyal to the High King of Theria," I promised.

She laughed and shifted to her human form. "I see Fritz has coached you well. I am loyal to the High King but whether I accept you as such remains to be seen. You must first satisfy me that you are worthy of the role."

Aileene stepped forward and looked intently at Lady Lynx. I could tell that they were having a silent conversation but Aileene had shut me out. Aileene must have gotten her point across; Lady Lynx blanched and Aileene smiled sweetly at the ruler of Metatheria.

"Yes, well—you must be tired after your long journey. My people will show you to your rooms and I will see you at the feast held in your honor," she said while looking at me. Silently she added, *If I could have a few moments of your time before the festivities tonight, I would greatly appreciate it.*

Of course. Would you like to speak now?

No, thank you. I will come by your room in an hour, please ask Lady Aileene to join us. I like her; she's fierce.

Yes, she is. I sent with pride and severed the connection. Lady Lynx bowed deeply to us and swept out of the pavilion, followed by her attendants.

"Your Highness, my name is Paulo. If you will follow me, I will show you to the royal guest suite." Paulo was dressed in the livery of Metatheria, a snarling golden jaguar on a black background. As we followed him out the back of the tent, I mentally asked Aileene what she'd said to Lady Lynx.

Nothing much, I just reminded her we are here more to decide if she meets your approval rather than seeking her approval for you to be High King. I also quickly told her why Celand and Malonne were banished from Theria and would spend the next century working off their exile rather than be executed as they deserved, she answered seriously. *I didn't like her insulting tone. In case you don't know this by now, I don't do subtle very well,"* she smiled and bumped my hip with hers.

Laughing I sent back, *And that's one of the many things I love about you.*

Bernie

"Can I ask you something?" Mkali asked as we stood guard outside Alister's room. Even though we had plenty of guards who could take this duty, I felt it was important for Mkali's training for us to do this together. I was impressed with her dedication to duty, but I also liked hanging around with her. She was the kid sister I'd never had.

"You just did. I gotta admit, I thought you might ask something tougher," I teased.

She giggled, "No, silly. I wanted to know what you thought of Lady Lynx; do you think she's part of the rebellion?"

"Hmmm, I don't know. I hope not, but I didn't really get a chance to test her when we met. My parents don't think she has anything to do with it but I'm learning the older a shifter is, the easier it is for them to be deceitful."

She was silent as she thought about what I said but I could tell there was something else she wanted to talk about. "What else is bothering you?"

"I'm still worried by King Alister's dream. Do you think we're going to die?"

Moving next to Mkali, I put my arm around her and squeezed her shoulders. Even though she was only nine, she was also a warrior, so I didn't want to lie to her but also didn't want to cause her more anxiety than necessary.

"I don't think so," I said softly. "It's always possible that we won't be strong enough to overcome what our enemies have planned but I know Alister and he will do everything in his power to keep everyone safe."

"Even if he puts himself in danger," Mkali muttered darkly.

I laughed and told her how many times Alister had stood up to bullies even before he knew he was a dragon. She laughed when I told her about the encounter we had with David Barnes back on Earth and she was silent when I told her about our encounter with Minos on Middle Earth. Even though she had heard some of these stories before, they took on special meaning for her now.

"None of us know what tomorrow will bring, but I can promise you that Alister, Aileene, Shelley and I will do whatever we can to make sure you survive."

"And I will do everything I can do to make sure the King is safe. I know he is more powerful than the rest of us put together, with the exception of Lady Aileene, but he needs us to watch his back to protect him from treachery and that's one of the things I can do as a knight in training."

I looked at Mkali in awe. Sometimes I forgot that she had known who and what she was from birth, unlike Alister, Shelley and me who had forgotten our true nature for thirteen years. Mkali stood tall, proud and looked more mature than any nine-year-olds would have looked on Earth. She wore the livery of the High King and her quiver and bow were strapped to her back where she could easily reach them when she transformed into her centaur form. Even while we talked, she kept facing forward and her eyes were watching for potential threats.

"Mkali, I may not say this enough, but I'm proud of you and I know King Alister is relieved you're also watching his back. Some people may underestimate you, but we don't; I'm glad you're on the team. Whatever happens, we'll fight side-by-side to protect the people we love and protect those weaker than ourselves."

She stood taller at my words and her lips turned up in a small smile. I know I just affirmed that she was a warrior, but it took everything in me not to give her a hug and make promises that I may not be able to keep. If I knew Alister, he had a few more things planned to keep us safe while we defeated the enemy; I just hoped he wouldn't put himself in too much danger protecting us from harm.

Alister

Shelley and I were covered in mud and lying along the riverbank. What had started off as a morning swim had turned into an epic mud wrestling match. We were still panting with exertion and both of us were grinning widely and glad to be with each other. Bernie and Aileene would join us soon but neither of us had the energy to jump in the river to wash off.

Even though we'd stayed up too late enjoying ourselves at the feast held to honor our arrival, we'd gotten up early because of my stupid dream.

"What did Lady Lynx want to talk to you and Aileene about yesterday?" Shelley asked as he stretched then wiped some mud off his face and threw it at me.

"First of all, she apologized to Aileene for the haughty attitude she showed me when we met her earlier that morning."

Shelley laughed, "I love how Aileene is quick to take offence on your behalf but is also willing to quickly forgive if the person is sincere with their apology."

"Me, too. It was hard for me not to crack up when she told Lady Lynx although she accepted her apology, she wouldn't be happy with her if she did it again." Shelley and I laughed when I described how Aileene said this while smiling, showing all her teeth and Lady Lynx took a step back at her expression. "Once Aileene looped her arm through Lady Lynx's and dragged her over to the couch and poured her a cool drink, she began to relax and told her why she wanted to talk with us. She wants to retire and leave one of her children in charge of Metatheria, but she doesn't know which one to choose."

"We met all of them at the party last night, didn't we?" Shelley asked.

"Yes, we did. Each of her children is a duke or duchess of one of the twelve duchies in Metatheria. Anyway, she told us she wanted my help to decide which one would be best because she loves her children and doesn't want to have to choose one over the rest."

"Huh? That doesn't really make sense to me. She knows her kids better than you would, and she knows what her kingdom needs."

"That's what I think, too, but Fritz and Frieda explained that sometimes people get too close to a problem, so they have trouble seeing the solution, especially when it comes to family members," I answered then put my hands behind my head and watched the fluffy, white clouds drift lazily in the sky. "Soooo," I broke the silence after a few minutes, "do you want to talk about your mate bond with Bernie?"

"Not really," Shelley sighed, "but that's not going to stop you bugging me about it, is it?"

"Nope," I laughed.

"Fine," Shelley grumped.

"I thought you'd be happy to know you two have a mate bond."

"I am, but just like you and Aileene, I'm not ready to get married and I don't want to disappoint Bernie."

"Has she said she wants to get married now?" I asked

"No, but what if she does? I don't want to hurt her feelings. I mean, I love her and really look forward to spending the rest of my life with her, but I think we're too young to get married. We're only nineteen, actually, we'll be twenty in June, I mean Ceitain, but I think that's too young. I was going to talk to my dad about it, but he and Mom have been busy working on security arrangements for the rest of our time here in Metatheria and I didn't want to bother him. But then again, I suppose he would be the best one to talk to after all; he and Mom have been married for hundreds of years and know a lot—I'm rambling, aren't I?"

"Yep," I said and popped the 'p', "but I get that. I was a bit freaked out when I found out Aileene and I were made for each other, but I've gotten used to the idea and find it really comforting. There are a lot of benefits to a mate bond and I know it will only get stronger once we're married. I like the connection we share, and I know you will too, once you get used to it. There's no reason for you and Bernie to rush into marriage.

"Believe it or not, there is more pressure on Aileene and me to get married sooner rather than later because traditionally the High King is married before taking the throne. My parents were married in the morning then my dad was crowned king later the same afternoon."

"I didn't know that."

"I didn't either, until Lady Lynx brought it up yesterday and Fritz confirmed it to be true. She asked for the honor of holding our royal wedding while we were visiting her kingdom and I was so startled by her request I choked on the juice I was drinking. Aileene laughed at my discomfort and told Lady Lynx that we appreciated the offer but would hold the wedding at the palace in Theria."

Shelley was silent for a moment as he digested what I'd told him and then started laughing so hard he had trouble catching his breath.

"It's not that funny," I muttered, and he laughed harder. After a bit I joined in and we laughed until tears streamed down our faces. Every time I thought we had ourselves under control, one of us would start giggling again and that would start a new wave of laughing; and that's how the girls found us, holding our sides and rocking back and forth on the muddy bank of the river.

It took a good five minutes for us to explain what we were laughing at because each time one of us would try to tell the story, we would start laughing again. We finally wound down and were able to gasp out the story of my meeting with Lady Lynx from my perspective. When Aileene embellished her retelling we all started laughing again. It really wasn't that funny, but it was great to laugh with people I loved. Aileene gave me a sly grin and I knew she felt the same way and what she'd been doing by telling the story the way she had. When she stood and walked away from us, I knew she was up to something, but I was enjoying the warmth of the sun and hanging out with my friends too much to care.

I should have cared; I really should have. Especially when the sun was blocked, and I could sense mischief coming from Aileene through the connection we shared. I opened my eyes in time to see Aileene in dragon form curled in on herself and hurtling towards the water. She hit the water and a tidal wave crashed over the three of us on the bank before we could move. Aileene's laughter sounded in my mind and I knew she was broadcasting to Bernie and Shelley as well.

So that's how you want to play, I mentally shouted, *now you're going to get it.*

Bring it dragon-boy, Aileene taunted and the three of us ran for the water to continue our game.

Hillaes

Claw

Wu and I held hands as we walked away from Garket and Tandy's house. It was great spending a week with my brother's family, but I was ready to spend the last week of our honeymoon by ourselves. We were heading back to my home about a half day's walk from Garket's, but we were planning on shifting into our tigers once we were in the woods, away from prying eyes. We'd shared information about my transformation with Garket and Tandy but weren't going to share with anyone else. Wu was smiling as we walked in contented silence and I bumped him with my hip and asked him what he was thinking.

"I was thinking about the kids and how much they love their Aunt Hillaes."

"They love their Uncle Wu, too," I laughed. "Az and Isobel were your shadows the whole time and even baby Gustav would stop crying whenever you held him."

"I do have a way with kids," Wu answered smugly. "It's an honor your brother named his youngest child after Gustav. I know he would have been pleased."

I nodded and we kept walking. The warmth of the sun felt good on my face and I silently thanked An'Ceann for the gift of making me a tiger shifter so Wu and I could grow old together.

"How much longer do you need to create the things Alister asked you to?" Wu asked.

"It'll only take me another day to complete. We have another seven days before Alister opens the gate so we can rejoin everyone on Metatheria."

Wu chuckled, "Alister constantly amazes me with his thoughtfulness. Not only did he send us back to Theria for a week so we could spend time with my children, he opened another gate for us so we could spend three weeks on Claw to visit with your family."

"Even though he gave us an assignment, he didn't need to give us a month when we could have accomplished everything in about a week, and he certainly didn't need to drop everything he was doing to make this happen for us."

"That's just the kind of person he is. He works hard to serve others. I know I've told you the story of the first time I really met him; he changed my life instead of taking it as I deserved. I'd do anything for him," Wu declared.

"If we hadn't fallen in love, I would've been willing to permanently relocate to Theria just to follow Alister. Life is certainly more interesting around the King and I look forward to seeing what he'll accomplish. He's already made a positive impact on Claw when he killed Minos and he definitely changed Earth for the better by getting rid of our enemies there." We were far enough into the woods that we couldn't be seen, so I stopped, turned towards my husband, put my arms around his neck and tiptoed up for a kiss. Before our lips touched, I smiled and pushed him away. "If you want a kiss, you'll have to catch me," I laughed and shifted into my tiger.

I was new to shifting but I already loved my powerful body and the way my senses sharpened with the change. My tiger eyes couldn't see as much detail in the daylight but I knew I would be able to see much better in the dark. Besides, the details I missed with my eyesight were compensated by my sense of smell and amazing hearing. My powerful muscles bunched beneath me as I took off running through the woods towards my house. I knew I wouldn't be able to maintain this speed for long, but I hoped to get a jump on Wu to keep away from him.

Tricky, I like it, Wu laughed in my mind and I could sense him shift and start after me.

After running at full speed for a few minutes I knew we were getting close to my house in the woods. I skidded to a stop as I scented something unusual in the air.

Don't tell me you give up, Wu sent as he slowed and stalked towards me.

I smell something and don't know what it is, I sent as Wu joined me. He paused long enough to rub his head and jaw against mine but then narrowed his eyes in concentration.

I smell humans. They recently passed this way and seem to be heading for your house. We should approach cautiously.

We walked side by side, aware of our surroundings and looking for any sign of danger. Since Wu had identified the scent as human, I could distinguish at least five different scent patterns. I didn't know why so many people would come to my home, but I assumed they were up to no good. Wu and I stopped when we were still far enough into the forest to stay hidden but could see my home and the two men trying to break the front door. I was angry at this violation and I could feel my lip lifted in a silent snarl.

Wu leaned against me and I was calmed by his physical presence. *We should shift. I can hear three people trying to stay quiet on this side of the house and I think it's safe to assume the rest of the house is surrounded, too. Based on their attempt to break-in I think we can surmise they're not here for peaceful purposes.*

I stifled my snort and shifted, grateful Alister had provided me with a thought-medallion so I was clothed after I shifted. I grabbed Wu's hand, cast *Spheara* over us so we were protected, and calmly walked towards my home with my husband by my side. As we exited the woods, I could hear men moving at our back and following us into the clearing. The men who had been trying to break down the door stopped and walked towards us. The larger of the two let out a shrill whistle as he walked and grabbed a double headed axe he'd leaned against my porch.

He was muscular, stood about six feet tall, which was large for someone on Claw, and wore a leather tunic studded with silver squares. He had a sword in a well-worn scabbard on his left hip, dark breeches tucked into his boots and a silver medallion around his neck with an image that looked like flames. He wore the same wide-brimmed hat as the rest of the men surrounding us, but the red feather stuck in the hat band was larger than the rest, marking him as the leader. His narrow eyes glinted with malice and his yellowed teeth showed through his bushy black beard as his smile appeared in the form of a grimace.

He stopped about ten feet away from us and I recoiled from the stench of his unwashed body and what could only be the scent of hatred. I could hear the unmistakable sound of crossbows being cocked behind us and was glad we were protected by the *Spheara* spell. He was joined by the men he had called with his whistle, so we were surrounded by eight armed and dangerous men. The leader took another step forward and smiled cruelly and spoke, "Hello witch, today you die."

CHAPTER NINE

'm not sure what he expected us to do with his declaration, but I'm quite sure it wasn't us doubling over in laughter.

"This is serious, witch," he growled, "your execution has been ordained by the Order of the Crimson Flame and will be carried out this day after you confess to the charges levied against you."

He held out his axe and the man on his left stepped forward and took it from him while he pulled a scroll from his belt. Unrolling the scroll, he began to read.

"Hillaes Vonner—"

"Chen," I interrupted.

"What?" he asked.

"My last name is Chen, we just got married," I answered while Wu snickered.

"It doesn't matter," he replied, annoyed at my interruption, "Hillaes Chen, you are hereby charged with using witchcraft and consorting with demons. You have been found guilty by the Order of the Crimson Flame. The penalty for these crimes is execution which I, Captain Maddok Thornhart, will bear witness to as it is carried out after your confession." He rolled the scroll and stuck it back in his belt while glaring at me, probably because I was smirking at him.

"Dear, would you like to say anything before I answer?" I asked Wu and he shook his head and smiled at me.

I'll follow your lead, my love. My guess is we've added another duty to our plate while on Claw?

You have that right, I snorted. *I don't know where this Order of the Crimson Flame came from but it's our duty to stamp them out before we meet the others in Metatheria.*

Will the items you're working on be negatively affected if we leave them for another week? Wu asked and I shook my head.

They'll be fine but I'll check on them after we finish with these goons, before we dismantle this organization—

Thornhart interrupted me by clearing his throat to get my attention.

"What?" I glared.

"How do you plead?" he asked, confused by my lack of reaction to what he considered a serious situation.

"I plead you are woefully unprepared and uninformed. However, I have a few questions for you."

"You are in no position to ask questions," he screamed, spittle flying from his mouth.

"Humor me. You have us surrounded and I believe I deserve some answers before you murder us."

"Very well, ask your questions, we'll prolong your deaths by an hour for every minute you waste," he replied magnanimously as he spread his arms wide. The men surrounding us laughed wickedly which further fueled my anger.

"Magic isn't outlawed anywhere on Claw. Where does this Order of the Crimson Flame get their authority to execute anyone?" I demanded.

"It doesn't have to be illegal to be immoral. Those of us who see things clearly banded together to create the Order and it's on our authority that we carry out our decisions."

"And how many witches have you executed?" I seethed.

"Our hunter group has taken down forty-two so far. You and your husband will make forty-four," said the man standing to the right of Thornhart.

"Why would you execute me?" Wu asked curiously.

"Two reasons," Thornhart sneered. "The first is, you are guilty by association and deserve death as she does. And the second—because we can."

The men surrounding us chuckled darkly.

"So, you're basically a bunch of murderous outlaws who deserve the death you've given to so many others." I heard a crunch and realized one of the men behind me tried to strike me with the butt of his crossbow. It didn't do any damage to me but based on the sound, he now had a broken crossbow.

"I've heard enough," I said with steel in my voice into the stunned silence after the failed attack. "As to the charges, I am not a witch, but I am a sorceress and that is much worse for you." I manifested a fireball in my left hand and took a step closer to Thornhart. "Wu, I'm going to introduce the ones in front of us to my crimson flame. Would you please take care of the ones behind us?" I asked as I began to throw firebolts towards the men standing there.

"My pleasure," Wu growled as he transformed. The men screamed as he attacked.

I had to be careful to keep one of these murderers alive so we could find out the location of the rest of the members of this evil order. As his agents, we would make sure they felt the wrath of King Alister as we took vengeance for those innocents they had slaughtered. As crossbow bolts hit my shield and shattered on impact, I gave those murderers my full attention. They were going to regret interrupting our honeymoon.

Garwan 17, 10,258

Alister

Pé Grande, Metatheria

"Do you want another, or are you too stuffed?" Shelley asked me.

Hmmm—I'm pretty full but I think I have room for one more.

Shelley tossed the dead capybara and I snapped it out of the air and bit down with a satisfying crunch. I sighed contentedly and lay down again to bask in the sun. Aileene was stretched out next to me already dozing, having also eaten her fill.

"How lazy can you be?" Bernie muttered disgustedly then turned to Shelley with her hands on her hips. "And you're not helping, mister. If Alister's hungry he can feed himself."

They're having an eating contest, Aileene responded. *Alister told Shelley that he could eat thirty of these tasty, what did you call them?*

"Capybara," Shelley answered.

Right, capybara. Well, after we'd already hunted these delicious creatures, Shelley and Alister began arguing about how many Alister could eat in one sitting and they settled on thirty. That was the last one, so Shelley agreed to help Alister finish the last one.

"I didn't think he could really eat that many, even though he's an enormous dragon. I have to admit, I'm impressed," Shelley grinned.

It's been a while since I've been able to eat enough to fill my dragon belly, but I think I should have stopped at twenty-eight. I feel like I could burst.

Poor baby, Aileene crooned and settled into a more comfortable position for her nap.

"And how was your lunch?" Shelley asked Bernie.

"Delicious. I found some tasty grass in the clearing near the castle and enjoyed the peace and quiet while the three of you went hunting. Are these really like the capybara they have on Earth?"

Yes, although these are much larger, I answered. *Wu told us this is one of the animals that can be found on Earth, Theria and Middle Earth although they range in size among the dimensions.*

"How weird," Bernie said. "When I saw pictures of them on Earth, I always thought they looked like large hamsters, how are they?"

"They taste like chicken," Shelley grinned, and Bernie laughed.

I'm going to lay in the sun for a bit to aid my digestion, I said and stretched my body out to catch as many rays as possible.

"How long have we been in Metatheria again?" Shelley asked.

"Forty-six days," Bernie answered, "and we've visited eleven of the twelve duchies during that time. We have four days here and then we head back to Lobisomem so Alister can give his recommendation to Lady Lynx on who should be her replacement."

"Have you really gotten to know each of the dukes and duchesses well enough in the four days we've spent in each duchy to make your choice?" Shelley asked.

I hope so, but I really won't know until we've spent time with Duchess Opaline here in Pé Grande. We're meeting Obaline and her nobles in a few hours.

Aileene laughed even though she didn't open her eyes. *Do you think you'll be ready to eat again by the time we meet them for dinner?*

Ugggh, I groaned mentally, *don't talk about eating.*

My friends laughed at my discomfort but after a moment I joined in because I had done this to myself.

After about five minutes of contented silence, Bernie spoke up again. "Wu and Hillaes sure look happy together. It sounds like they had a great time on their honeymoon and especially liked wiping out the Order of the Crimson Flame from Middle Earth before they rejoined us."

Shelley laughed, "When they told the story about the soldiers attacking them and how their swords and crossbow bolts kept bouncing off their shields, I had a hard time keeping my laughter in check."

Did they meet us in Grifo when we met with Duchess Sylvie? I asked.

No, they joined us two weeks ago so that was when we were in Duendes with Duke Osiston, Aileene muttered sleepily.

"You never told us what you wanted them to do for you on Middle Earth," Shelley said.

You're right, I haven't, I sent with a smile. *Nice try, Shelley, I'll let you know when it's time.*

"It was worth a shot," Shelley said and even though my eyes were closed, I could tell he was frustrated by the mysterious mission. Apparently, I'd learned some things from An'Ceann.

I felt Bernie and Shelley lean against my side and figured it wouldn't be long before they were napping. "How's the dream?" Bernie asked, yawning.

I'm still having it but there have been some changes for the positive. Now I'm the only one from our team who dies and Aileene takes my place as the ruler of Theria.

Aileene growled angrily so I sent her soothing emotions through our connection.

We've discussed this, my love, you will not die because I won't allow it.

I don't plan on dying but since I'm still having the dream, there must be something we're missing. I'm confident we'll figure it out but at least the rest of you survive and Theria isn't destroyed.

"Well, that's something at least," Shelley muttered, "but I'm not happy about any of us dying. You have an entire division of unicorns from each kingdom loyal to you combing through Metatheria for traitors, any luck yet?"

According to Fritz and Frieda, they haven't found any traitors among the leaders in any duchy on Metatheria, Cetacea, Eutheria or Marsupia. However, they have found a lot of people unhappy with the monarchy and how things went downhill while my parents were comatose. We've still got a lot of work to rebuild trust but there doesn't seem to be any factions actively plotting against us in those kingdoms.

"Unless Duchess Opaline and her nobles are corrupt we'll probably find the traitors in Carnivoria or Sirenea," Bernie added.

We should just fly there, confront Lord Carmanor and Lady Baolong, then burn their kingdoms to the ground, Aileene growled. I opened my eyes and saw smoke trailing from her nostrils and her eyes were blazing. I lifted my head and rubbed my jaw along hers to help calm her down.

We will confront those we find who are part of the plot to destroy Theria. They already have blood on their hands and we'll make them pay. But we cannot take our anger out on innocents.

I know, Aileene sighed, *but I'd rather wipe them out before they get a chance to hurt anyone else.*

"We all would," Shelley growled. "We all take our responsibility to *Protect the Weak* seriously and are willing to lay down our lives to protect you and Alister."

Thanks, bro, love you too, I sent to Shelley and opened a connection to Bernie and Shelley so they could feel the emotions that both Aileene and I were feeling because of their loyalty. I also wanted them to know that I would do everything I could to protect them, too.

"This has been great and all, but what do you say to a nap and then Alister can try to go for the world record for capybara consumption," Shelley said.

But I already set the record at thirty, I mentally groaned.

"Then we'll set the new world record at thirty-one," Shelley finished.

"Whatever—just make sure you don't wake up Aileene and me with your shenanigans," Bernie yawned.

"I like that," Shelley laughed, "I have a new nickname, Sir Shenanigan."

Sounds good to me, Aileene muttered, *now go to sleep before I get up to a shenanigan of my own and roll over on you.*

"No need for that," Shelley laughed, "I'm shutting up now."

I'll believe that when I see it, I said and smiled to myself as I lay down to take a snooze.

Lady Baolong
  Sirenea

"My Empress, Elmas Forelock, a representative from the High King is here and requesting an audience," a servant bowed before me awaiting my answer.

"I don't recognize that boy as High King," I hissed and felt a hint of pleasure as I watched my servant shiver in fear.

"My apologies, Empress, you have made your wishes quite clear. Elmas Forelock claims to be here on behalf of High King Phillip."

He flinched as I stood from where I was reclining, and I felt my lips twitch in the barest hint of a smile. I walked to where he bowed with his face to the ground. I caressed the left side of his face and gripped his chin and gently tilted his head so he could look into my eyes. "What is your name," I asked gently.

"Han, son of Zhang, Empress," he stammered nervously.

"Han, son of Zhang, you don't need to fear me," I chided gently.

"Yes, Empress," Han smiled tentatively as I patted his cheek.

"Bring him to me," I commanded and sat to wait for my guest's arrival.

Within minutes the door was opened and in walked a tall man wearing the livery of the High King. His shoulder length black hair was gathered loosely behind his head with a tie of some sort and he looked cool, competent and more like a warrior than a diplomat. I could smell that he was a unicorn shifter and he smiled warmly at me when he stopped.

"Lady Baolong, I greet you on behalf of High King Phillip and Queen Beatrice and wish you well."

Inclining my head slightly at his greeting I stayed silent and waited for him to continue. Based on the tightening of his eyes he wasn't expecting me to keep quiet. I looked coolly at him until he continued talking.

"I have been asked by the High King to update you on Crown Prince Alister's delegation—"

"Don't you mean High King Alister?" I interrupted him coldly.

He was unruffled by my interruption and continued smoothly, "King Phillip realizes you don't yet recognize Crown Prince Alister as High King so for now he is willing to remain High King in your eyes until you affirm Crown Prince Alister."

I smiled, "Very well, I accept the concession, continue."

"The delegation will arrive in Sirenea mid-Ceitain—"

"That is over three months away, and completely unacceptable. Is the prince attempting to insult me by delaying his journey to my kingdom?" I fumed.

"Not at all, M'lady, the journey from Metatheria to Carnivoria will take almost a month so they will not arrive there until the end of Mart. If Crown Prince Alister spends the rest of Mart and the months of An'Ceann and Giplane touring Carnivoria, the earliest he can be here is Ceitain fifteenth. Your kingdom is geographically one of the largest on Theria and Crown Prince Alister wanted to visit you last so he didn't have to rush through your kingdom," Forelock answered and bowed at the waist. Enough to show me the proper respect but not so low he debased himself as he was standing for the High King.

"Rise," I commanded before he had a chance to straighten on his own. The twitch of his lips as he straightened let me know he knew what I was doing. "Please tell me, what are your plans now that you've delivered your message? Do you plan on returning to Theria at once?"

"If I could impose on your hospitality, I would appreciate the opportunity to refresh myself before returning to the High King."

I leaned forward and cupped my chin with my palm as I considered his request. "How many are in your party?"

"I have twenty others with me, Lady Baolong, along with my valet."

"You will be my guests while I work on a proper response to send King Phillip. It's a shame the prince won't be here sooner, but perhaps you should remain here until he arrives. I will think about it."

"As you wish, M'lady," Forelock answered.

Unicorns usually make the best diplomats since they excel at discerning truth from lies. Perhaps Forelock would be willing to aid me in rooting out some issues I'm having with the loyalty of some of my people. I'll have to think of the best way to convince him to help me. I don't have any unicorns at the present time. I sent a mental command to my servants waiting outside the door and they entered the chamber and flanked Forelock. "My people will show you to your rooms. Let them know where to find your luggage and they will bring it to you. You may go now; I will see you at dinner."

He bowed again and left the room. I smiled to myself after the doors closed behind him. This was an unexpected turn of events, but I would be able to use it to my advantage. Thankfully, I had time before the delegation arrived. Rising, I slipped through the hidden door at the back of my chamber and took the stairs that would take me to my workroom; I had preparations to make.

Alister

Garwan 24, 10,258

We were gathered in the feast hall for our last night in Metatheria to celebrate the coronation of the new ruler. The chefs had prepared traditional dishes from each duchy in Metatheria and my friends and I were voting on our favorites. Aileene and I tended to prefer the spicier dishes but there wasn't one thing we were served we didn't enjoy. Before we left, I'd planned on asking one of the chefs to join the Royal Kitchen in Theria. Not only did I feel it was important to be able to enjoy more culinary choices from the regions across the planet, I realized we needed to learn more about the different cultures within my Kingdom.

While the feast had been delicious there was underlying tension in the room from the nobles as they expected my decision on who would be the next ruler of Metatheria. Each of Lady Lynx and Lord Saltu's children were in attendance along with their spouses and children. I enjoyed watching them interact with each other with laughter, teasing and genuine love and respect. After the fiasco we'd seen in Marsupia, it was a pleasant change to see the rulers of one of the kingdoms caring for their people and one another.

Children ran around the room in their human and shifter forms. It was amusing to see so many varieties of jungle cats and kits in the same place. Every adult in the room laughed when Wu and Hillaes transformed into their tigers and they were pounced on by the children in their feline forms.

You're being stalked, Aileene's mental sending was laced with humor.

You don't say, I grinned and turned to look at the young jaguar crouched behind me. "Good try, Kimbur, you almost got me that time."

"Young lady, what did I tell you about stalking King Alister?" Duchess Opaline called from her seat from the other side of the table.

You said not to do it. But Mama, King Alister doesn't mind, Kimbur broadcast to the room.

I stood and crouched next to the young black panther and scratched under her chin then gathered her in my arms. "It doesn't matter if it doesn't bother me, you need to listen to your mama." Sitting back down, she settled in my lap and closed her emerald green eyes and rumbled contentedly.

"My apologies, Sire, it seems like my daughter has a mind of her own," Duchess Opaline apologized.

"She takes after her mother," her husband said with a twinkle in his eyes.

Opaline's parents and siblings laughed while she blushed.

"King Alister," Duke Groose of Bruxa asked, "do you have enough information to make your decision on which of us will rule Metatheria next?"

I'd planned on standing to answer the question but Kimbur flexed her claws to hold onto my breeches so instead I scratched behind her ears and got comfortable in my chair.

Nodding, I answered, "When your mother told me she needed my help to determine who would take her place as ruler of Metatheria I was skeptical. I figured if a mother didn't know who was the most fit to rule, how could I make the determination. After spending time with each of you while touring your duchies and meeting your people I concluded that each of you would be a fitting replacement for your mother." There was a murmur from each of the dukes and duchesses sitting around the table as they looked at each other. "However, I also came to realize that only one of you actually had the desire to rule the Kingdom of Metatheria and would make the best replacement."

I took a sip of my drink which was a blend of regional fruit juices and a hint of spice and looked around the table at the expectant faces.

Would you like to make the announcement, or would you prefer it if I did it? I silently asked Lady Lynx.

If you'd please, Sire, I'd appreciate it.

Very well, if you'd be so kind as to take your granddaughter from me? I'm fairly sure she's asleep.

Chuckling, Lady Lynx rose from her chair and picked her sleeping granddaughter from my lap and settled her feline form in her arms.

Rising, I stood behind the chair Lady Lynx had vacated. Lord Saltu looked at me meaningfully, smiled and rose from his chair as well. He knew that I would announce his wife's replacement and his chair would be taken by the spouse of the new ruler of Metatheria. He joined his wife near my chair to pet Kimbur's head. I was happy for the couple that they would be able to enjoy their remaining years together without the pressure of rule.

"The new ruler of Metatheria is Lady Morwenna, formerly Duchess of Provocador. Please rise and take your place among your brothers and sisters who are Dukes and Duchesses in your kingdom." There was a collective sigh amongst the others gathered in the room and her siblings began to lovingly tease her about her new position. They were happy for her and would support her in her new role. She stuck her tongue out at them and sat down. I stood behind her and placed my hands on her shoulders. Aileene joined me and did the same thing to her husband Botma.

"May your rule be long, may you be a blessing to your people and the land, may An'Ceann give you his grace and may you always *Protect the Weak* in the Kingdom of Metatheria. By the authority granted to me by An'Ceann as the High King of all Theria, I hereby crown you Lady Morwenna, ruler of Metatheria." I placed the Metatherian crown on her head and her parents, siblings, husband and children stood and joined me as I said, "Long live Lady Morwenna."

"Thank you, Sire," Morwenna said quietly, "I will not fail in my duty."

"I never doubted you," I whispered, "now what do you say we celebrate your new role?"

"Sounds good to me," she laughed. And the celebration began.

Lady Baolong

Sirenea

I was already seated at the head of the table when my guest was ushered into the room. He smiled pleasantly as he took his seat and I raised my hand to forestall any questions while I continued to eat my meal. Before long, a nameless servant entered the room bearing a tray covered with a silver lid and placed it in front of the emissary from Theria. With a flourish he removed the lid and presented the entrée prepared as instructed.

"What a beautiful bowl," Forelock breathed as he examined the dish on the platter, "I've never seen anything like it."

Smiling enigmatically, I nodded at him and gestured for him to eat. I could tell that he was puzzled by my continued silence, but I'd planned this moment carefully and didn't want to speak before he took his first bite of the fish-noodle course.

"Do you know why Theria is the seat of the High King," I asked gently.

Since his mouth was full, it took Forelock a moment before he could answer. "Because that's where An'Ceann established the throne when Dóchas and Síocháin pledged their loyalty to him and vowed to follow his ways."

Even though I wanted to shout at Forelock for spouting the nonsense we'd all been taught for the last ten thousand plus years, I decided to instruct him on his ignorant beliefs. I took a sip of my wine before I began.

"That's what we've been taught for millennia, but I discovered the truth after my husband's death almost twenty years ago." I stood and leaned towards Forelock and he leaned back in his chair. Perhaps I wasn't controlling my emotions as well as I thought I was, but no matter, it's good for him to fear me. "My husband, Lord Zhào, was a visionary and an example of what a true ruler should be. Before he died, he arranged for me to rule in his place and entrusted me with the last book written by Zhèng the Merciless, the last Royal Dragon who ruled Sirenea. He was only defeated by the combined might of Milleadh and Síocháin." I waved away his objection, "I know he changed his name to Dóchas after he abandoned the way of the dragons but before that he was Milleadh the Dragon of Destruction.

"I don't object to the fact that Milleadh and Síocháin defeated Zhèng, but it was intolerable that Sirenea was subjugated and enfolded into the new High Kingdom. My husband told me the only reason the High King rules is because he is a Royal Dragon and is only susceptible to harm from another of his kind. Did you know that there are clutches of Royal Dragon eggs hidden in each kingdom?"

When Forelock didn't respond I stalked towards him and continued, "Of course you didn't, this is one of the most closely guarded secrets in all Theria, and you don't have enough clearance to know such things." I ran my fingers through his hair, my nails scoring his scalp. Even though I could feel his quiver of fear, he didn't move. I grabbed his hair and yanked his head back so he could look at me again.

"In his book Zhèng wrote how to force a Royal Dragon egg to hatch but warned that any dragon forced to hatch wouldn't have a human side and would be little more than a mindless animal." I moved again and leaned against the table and looked into his eyes, which were wide with fright.

"What he didn't know is how difficult it would be to accomplish. Out of the thirty dragon eggs left in Sirenea, only one male and one female hatched. The bowl you were so enamored with was created from the female's shell. Unfortunately, she died after five years, but we were able to make some deadly weapons with her bones." I raised my right hand and showed him the claws I wore on my fingers like extensions of my own nails.

"Before you ask what happened to the other dragon, I'll tell you." I leaned forward so closely our noses almost touched and I caressed his face gently. "He's healthy, enormous and completely loyal to me. In fact, you'll be pleased to know that the others you brought with you will be meeting him shortly and you'll get a chance to see him in action, it's quite exhilarating. If your precious Crown Prince Alister makes it this far, he will be meeting my pet as well."

I sighed then straightened and strode back to my chair and sat. "Unfortunately, my spies aboard his ship met their demise so I'm not getting regular updates on his progress."

"Don't you have anything to say?" I mocked. "No, I don't suppose you do since you are completely paralyzed. You see, one of my hobbies is making poisons tailor made for various shifters. Fortunately for you, this specific poison is only a paralytic which locks down your body and thought-speech and has an antidote. The poison I've sent to Lord Carmanor doesn't have an antidote and is based on the poison I gave to Dimitri all those years ago." I smiled as I imagined the argument Forelock would be making if he were able.

"I will get away with this because if Carmanor poisons Alister and Aileene I'll only have to deal with the King's Inner Circle. If Carmanor fails, the only thing connecting me to him is his word and since he'll have the poison, who'll believe the one who originally gave the poison to Dimitri. Either way, I win. Oh, and that was so thoughtful of you to send the message to Phillip asking him and Beatrice to join us at the end of the month of Ceitain, but if Carmanor is successful we won't have them to worry about."

I leaned forward in amazement as I saw a single tear roll down Forelock's right cheek. "Hmmm—it looks like I have to work on the formula for this poison, if you can produce a tear, what else can you do? Never mind, I'll give you the antidote after we watch my pet eat and I have you settled in your cell. You can tell me what you're feeling, and we can work on the formula together, won't that be fun?" I laughed as I smelled the scent of terror wafting from his paralyzed body.

CHAPTER TEN

Alister

Mart 28, 10,258

Kingdom of Theria

"Again," my father said as he stood over my prone form. Groaning, I rolled to my side and began to rise. Before I could get to my feet, he lashed out with his foot to kick me in the ribs. I flattened myself on the ground and rolled toward his planted leg. He didn't have time to compensate for my sudden move as I surged to my feet and lifted him with my shoulder between his legs. He sucked in a breath at the sudden pain and I continued my movement and drove him into the ground. We hit so hard; my teeth rattled in my jaw.

Unwilling to let him gather his strength I straddled his body and pinned his arms with my knees. I placed my fist on his throat and growled, "Yield."

"Never," he returned and partially shifted which shocked me long enough for him to grab the front of my shirt and throw me into a nearby tree.

"Watch the garden," Mother warned and when Father turned to look at her, I hit him with the rather large branch I'd knocked down with my body. It shattered against his scales and I saw a wicked gleam in his eye as he slowly turned towards me. I partially shifted, too, and we rushed each other and began to grapple. Even though I was taller than my father, he was more muscular than I and had centuries of fighting experience. If I didn't think of a way to use my magic to my advantage, he was going to beat me—again.

Even though he was slowly overpowering me and pulling my arms apart, I grinned as I thought of the perfect spell. I wrenched my right arm out of his grip, his talons ripping furrows across my forearm, and placed my right palm in the center of his chest.

I shouted, *Stark,* and blasted my father away from me. I'd learned enough about magic to know the word I used only served as a focus for my intentions. I'd created a repulsor spell that worked a lot like the beam Iron Man shot from his hand, so I named the spell after Tony Stark. I thought about all this in the split second it took for my father to fly away from me and tumble across the ground.

Before he could recover from my magic spell I pounced on his back and bent his arms so he couldn't attack me again.

"I yield," he groaned, and I rolled off him. He turned on his back and we lay side-by-side panting from our exertion.

"Time?" I asked weakly and Shelley's shadow fell over me as he stepped into my field of vision.

"That was your longest battle yet, I'd say it was about—"

"Forty-two minutes," Bernie called.

"Forty-two minutes," Shelley echoed. He grinned and dropped water skins on our chests and walked away.

My father chuckled, "Good job, Son. If I didn't hurt so badly, I'd pat you on the back."

After taking a long drink of water, I answered, "And I'd let you if it wouldn't hurt my cracked ribs."

The sun was once again cut off and I squinted my eyes to see Aileene and my mother standing side-by-side, frowning down at us.

"Is all this completely necessary?" Mother scowled as she waved her hand at the destroyed garden.

"Yes dear, it is," Father declared. "You know that Lord Carmanor will demand a contest of physical prowess with Alister in human form and we want our son to put his best foot forward. I'm fairly confident now that Carmanor won't wipe the floor with him."

"Thanks," I groaned and propped myself up on my elbows, looked around and winced at the destruction surrounding us. It looked like a herd of buffalo had stampeded through here.

"And don't get me started on how bad the two of you look," Aileene scolded. "You're bruised, bloody and from the waves of pain coursing across our mental connection, Alister is in agony."

"But did you see I finally beat him?" I tried to motion towards my father with my head but instead sank back with a groan.

"I'm very impressed," Aileene muttered and began to heal me. *I am enormously proud of you. Since Father declared that your physical training had been limited because you'd never fought against a male Royal Dragon, you've been sparring for the last week. Even though this is the worst beating you've taken, you won.* I felt the rush of pride and love come through our connection. *And if his groans are anything to go by, he's hurt as badly as you are,* Aileene chuckled and went back to work.

"I'm assuming you're laughing at my misfortune," Father groaned, "but you've earned the right. That spell you used at the end was quite effective, it felt like you kicked me in your dragon form. I'd like to see it again, as long as you're not using it on me—"

"What have ye done to me garden?" a shrill voice interrupted my father. I opened my eyes and propped myself on my elbows again to see two very annoyed looking garden gnomes glaring at us.

"Uh oh," Mother laughed, "now you two are really in for it."

"I just planted those flowers last week," scolded Gwenivar.

"And I finally managed to get the lawn just the way Queen Beatrice likes it," Noelle said crossly.

"Oooh," Gwenivar stomped her foot on the ground, "ye smashed the Bofruit trees. They'll never be ready for the Summer Solstice. If ye weren't the king, I'd tan yer hide." Gwenivar shook her finger menacingly at my father.

I stifled a laugh when I saw the diminutive gnome poking him in the chest while she scolded him.

"I'm not king anymore, he is," Father jerked his thumb in my direction, and I schooled my face so I wouldn't face the wrath of the gardeners.

"Well, yer Majesty," Noelle said through gritted teeth, "I think we should ask Clovella and Seannafair what they think about all this wanton destruction to these trees. I'm guessing the dryads aren't going to be too pleased with either one of you."

Aileene and Mother laughed at our misfortune, gathered their things and began to walk away. Before they got too far, they turned around and Mother tapped her index finger against her chin and asked Aileene. "My dear, what do you think about adding a water feature to this part of the garden?"

"What a splendid idea," Aileene grinned mischievously as she rapidly clapped her hands. "I think a gazebo overlooking the water feature would also be amazing. What do you think, ladies?" she asked the garden gnomes.

"Lovely, just lovely," Noelle beamed.

"I'll get the boys started on that project right away," Gwenivar smiled at my mother and future mate but then scowled when she turned back to my father and me.

"Have fun, boys. We'll save some dinner for you," Mother waved over her shoulder as she and Aileene walked away arm-in-arm.

"Well, this didn't work out quite the way I planned it," my father whispered.

"Yeah, but it's totally worth it since I beat you," I grinned.

"You say that now, but you've never had to repair a garden under the watchful eyes of garden gnomes and dryads. I have nightmares about the last time I had to do it and that was almost five hundred years ago." He shivered at the memory.

The color slowly drained from my face when I looked at the frowning faces and crossed arms of the gnomes then saw Shelley and Bernie sitting on the torn-up lawn with wide grins on their faces. This was going to be an exceptionally long day.

Bernie passed Aileene and me bowls of popcorn when we sat on the couch for movie night. Since this was the last night we'd be in Theria, the four of us decided to watch the latest rendition of The Lion King. Shelley said it was important to watch because it was about betrayal and how jealousy could eat someone up from the inside so badly, they'd kill their own family member. Bernie picked it because it takes place in Africa and that's basically where we were going tomorrow when we departed for Carnivoria. Aileene said she wanted to see it because she liked watching movies where animals talked.

"So, how was babysitting Isthe and Geordan so your mom and dad could go on a date?" Bernie asked.

Aileene tried to answer but started laughing so hard she couldn't get the words out.

"That good, huh?" Shelley asked sympathetically.

"Let's just say, I don't think my parents are going to let me watch the twins anytime soon," I grimaced.

"That's because you taught them how to manifest their flame and they destroyed most of the furniture in your parents' suite," Aileene finally managed to wheeze out.

"How was I to know they were too young to control their fire?" I whined.

"Alister, they're barely five months old. How would you expect babies to have any type of self-control?" Bernie asked with a giggle.

"Well, I know that now, obviously, but I've never been around baby drakes before. They're pretty big in their drake forms, I kinda forgot they were babies. Besides, Mom didn't say anything about keeping them away from fire in her written instructions," I finished lamely.

My friends gaped at me, so I threw up my hands in surrender, "Fine, I'm a terrible big brother. I should have known better than to show Fire Drakes how to use their fire."

Shelley, Aileene and Bernie laughed at my expense but Aileene put her arm around me and squeezed reassuringly.

"Don't worry about it, hon. There really wasn't any harm done and Mom and Dad aren't mad at you. It's pretty normal for dragon-type shifters to destroy things with their fire when they're young."

"Or when they get upset when an imaginary dragon dies in a movie and they incinerate a television," Shelley muttered.

"Exactly," Aileene exclaimed with a gleam in her eye. "Mom and Dad were hoping to escape the wanton destruction for a year or two. You just sped up the process."

"At least one good thing came out of your debacle, Shelley and I know better than to let you watch our kids when they're little." Bernie laughed but then thought about what she'd said and tried to back away from her statement. "Um, I mean—one day, you know, when—I mean if we get married, we'll want to have kids—"

I was watching Shelley's face as Bernie was trying to unwrap herself from the conversational knot she'd tied herself in but rather than looking uncomfortable, Shelley just sat there with a goofy grin on his face.

"You," he paused, "you want to have kids with me someday?"

Bernie's face was beet red and she was staring at her hands in her lap. Everyone was silent as she gathered her thoughts. To be honest, I felt a little embarrassed to be present for such an intimate conversation between my two best friends.

Bernie snapped her head up and looked directly into Shelley's eyes. "Yes, I do. One day, after we get married, I want to have kids with you. I love you, you big ol' teddy bear and I want to spend the rest of my life with you. We already know we're true-mates, so of course I want to raise a family with you." She smiled shyly and even though I didn't think it was possible, Shelley's grin grew wider.

"I love you, too, Bernie, and want to spend the rest of my life with you."

They looked at each other with such love in their eyes, I had to do something to break the moment. "So, do you want to get married right now? As King, I have the authority to do it before we leave for Carnivoria tomorrow," I teased.

Since I was hit with throw pillows from three different directions, I guess the answer to my question was 'no.'

"Okay, okay it was just a suggestion," I laughed and raised my hands in surrender. My comments must not have bothered my friends too much because they cuddled together on the couch as we watched the movie. Once it was over, I turned on the lights and looked at Bernie who was still staring thoughtfully at the TV.

"I can understand Scar's motivation for killing Mufasa and Simba, he figured if he got them out of the way he could become king. What I can't understand is what the conspirators hope to gain by killing the two of you," Bernie looked at us curiously. "I get why they need to kill you, Aileene. If they killed Alister and you were still alive, you would rain down fire and death on everyone in your grief."

"You're right about that," Aileene agreed.

"And I would do the same thing if Aileene died and I was left alive," I growled.

"Now, that's true love," Shelley quipped trying to lighten the mood.

"Ha-ha, now hush," Bernie told Shelley and kissed the back of his hand. "But won't King Phillip and Queen Beatrice do the same thing if the two of you are killed?"

Casting the *Indicens* spell, I waited until I could tell the shield of silence had settled around the room before answering her. "Well, normally that would be true, but my father and mother shared some information with us last night that changes things. They didn't want us to share with anyone else, but we argued that since our enemies seem to know it, we should tell our allies as well. We're going to share with you, but you must keep it to yourselves. Are you willing to swear an oath of secrecy as our Knights?"

Bernie and Shelley nodded solemnly and swore the oath that Aileene gave to them. When she was finished, I explained.

"If I die and Aileene doesn't, then she would become High Queen and rule Theria. If Aileene dies and I don't, then I would rule Theria as High King."

"That's not much of a secret, I'd already figured that out," Shelley muttered.

"Yes, but what you don't know is since Alister has already been crowned High King by An'Ceann the lives of King Phillip and Queen Beatrice are linked with his," Aileene said. "If both Alister and I die, then they die, too. If the conspirators are successful in killing us, there won't be any Royal Dragons left alive on Theria."

Shelley raised his hand, "Wait, you mean to tell me your parents will die if you do?"

"Yes. You see, since Royal Dragons are essentially immortal, we get to choose when we leave this life and journey to An'Ceann's Kingdom."

"Wow, so you could live forever if you wanted to?" Bernie asked in awe.

"I suppose so, but most Royal Dragons choose to leave this life once the last member of their Inner Circle has already made the journey. What would be the good of living forever if the ones you love the most have been gone for centuries?"

"But something happened when Alister rescued his parents from the brink of death, he shared so much of his life force with them so if he dies then they'll die, too." Aileene explained.

"Now, we're guessing here, but it would seem our enemies suspect something along these lines and that's why they think they'll get away with it if they kill both of us," I said.

"Wait, you shared a lot of your life force with Bernie, does that mean she'll die if you do?" Shelley asked, alarmed.

"I really don't know," I answered. "Since you, Garket and Gustav were also healing her, she might be okay. But that gives me even more of a reason to make sure I don't die."

We fell silent with our thoughts for a few minutes while the implications of this sunk in. As usually, Shelley was the one to break the silence.

"But they haven't taken your magic into account," Shelley grinned triumphantly. "They don't know you've created a spell to protect you and Aileene from dragon bone weapons."

"And that will be their downfall," Aileene grinned so fiercely I almost felt sorry for our enemies—almost.

Shelley

Giplane 28, 10,258

Carnivoria

The lead hatari shot its tongue towards the side of the road and snatched the young ngiri that had frozen in place trying to avoid the dangerous predator. The ngiri squealed once in fright before it disappeared into the maw of the hungry lizard. I started to sing "The Circle of Life," as I usually did when I watched one of the large lizards grab an opportune meal. Hatari are used for transportation on Carnivoria and can either be ridden like a horse or hooked to wagons and carriages. They look a lot like twenty-foot-long monitor lizards, with lime green skin, razor sharp teeth, a tongue they can use to ensnare prey the same way a frog does and a terrible disposition.

Joshua joined me as I sang the song until Lord Carmanor roared for us to stop. Even though he was in the carriage behind ours, he could hear us clearly due to his enhanced shifter hearing. Joshua and I looked at each other and grinned widely. The Captain of the Guard and I had developed a friendship over the two months we'd been travelling across Carnivoria and found that we had the same sense of humor. Alister enjoyed our banter, Lord Carmanor did not.

Is there a particular reason you're trying to annoy Lord Carmanor? Alister mentally asked me.

Yep, I don't like him and don't think he can be trusted. I figure if I can keep him thinking I'm an idiot, he'll underestimate me.

Does your new friend also think you're an idiot?

No, but I don't think he likes Carmanor very much either. He's loyal to him because of his position and he's an honorable man but something's bothering him.

See if you can figure out what it is. I don't like Carmanor much either, but he hasn't done anything that would cause me to remove him as the ruler of Carnivoria.

Not even separating the men from the women?

We had been apart from the women in our group since arriving in Carnivoria. Lord Carmanor was surprised that Bernie was one of the king's Knights and Mkali was her squire. While he showed respect to

Aileene, he treated the rest of the women as lesser beings. The only exception was his wife, Lady Kudanganya, whom he held in high regard. I'd since found out it was because her fighting prowess was such that she bested almost everyone in combat, except Lord Carmanor himself.

Alister growled through our mental connection, *I may not like his attitude towards women, but it doesn't appear he's mistreating them in any way. Lady Kudanganya asserts her authority over the duchesses of Carnivoria the same way Carmanor does with the dukes.*

Carnivoria was divided into four duchies with the seat of power in the middle of the continent. We had traveled to the duchies in the south and west where Carmanor had challenged the dukes, their nobility and top guards to physical combat to prove they were fit to keep their positions. Lady Kudanganya had done the same thing with the duchesses in the north and east. Carmanor was ruthless when he fought and according to the reports from Bernie and Aileene, Kudanganya was equally as vicious. Neither ruler took the life of anyone they fought but there were times it took Aileene, Hillaes and Bernie working together to put a shifter back together again.

Alister also had to open a pinhole gate to Middle Earth a few times to allow magic to flood in to give him the boost he needed to heal. Even though we were thousands of miles apart, the swell of magic affected everyone almost at once. If Carmanor's intention in separating us from the rest of our party was to keep us from communicating, he hadn't been successful. Alister had added an extra boost to the thought-medallions so we could talk to each other across Carnivoria.

Except for his vicious fighting techniques, Carmanor had been an affable host for our group but there was something about the way he looked at Alister behind his back that set my teeth on edge. I know Alister can take care of himself, but I felt like danger was breathing down our necks. Alister had continued to have his nightly dream and that wasn't helping my feeling of unease, either.

I'm going to see if Joshua will be willing to give me a hint about what'll happen when we reach the capital.

Sounds good. I'd better pay attention, Carmanor is telling me another story about a time he was victorious in a fight, Alister sent and closed the connection.

Joshua and I rode in silence for about an hour while I thought about the danger looming before us. I watched guards astride hatari scouting ahead. It was amazing how quickly the huge lizards could move. Even though they were low-slung, they appeared to glide over the ground and crossed huge distances in a blink of an eye. They also displayed a cunning watchfulness and their riders had to be constantly on guard lest they become a meal for the voracious beasts.

"Shelley, can I ask you something?" Joshua whispered. I scanned his troubled face and had a surge of hope that I was about to learn something that could help us avoid further bloodshed.

Sure, I sent. *I figured it might make you more comfortable to speak mentally so we won't be overheard.*

I appreciate that. Even though he instigated the conversation it took Josh a few moments before he continued. *I've watched you and King Alister interact together and am confused because he seems to treat you as a confidant and friend. How is that possible?*

Because we are friends and have been so for as long as I can remember. In fact, I have some embarrassing stories I could tell you about Alister growing up, I laughed through our connection.

He was taken aback by my response as his eyes widened slightly and he looked around nervously. *While I'd love to hear an embarrassing story or two, I wouldn't want you to get into trouble—*

Don't worry about that, I interrupted and called back over my shoulder to Alister. "Hey, Stretch, I just wanted to give you fair warning that I'm going to tell Joshua the story about the time you tried to drink a two liter bottle of soda."

"The one where you made me laugh and the soda shot out of my nose?" Alister groaned.

"Yep, that's the one," I laughed and turned back to face the front. The look on Joshua's face made me laugh.

He allows you to make fun of him.

We make fun of each other all the time, we're kind of like brothers that way. Alister says it helps him stay grounded and reminds him that at the end of the day he's just a regular person with a lot of power and responsibility. Believe it or not, he needs me and Bernie to help him remember where he came from and he doesn't have to bear the entire burden of protecting everyone on his own.

What do you mean by protecting everyone?

You know the most important creed for the High Kings and Queens is Protect the Weak? When Joshua nodded, I continued. *Since Alister and Aileene are the most powerful shifters on the planet, everyone else is weaker than they are. That means that together they believe it's their duty to protect everyone from those who would take advantage of their positions of power to oppress others. It's what they did in Marsupia when they found out that Lord and Lady Farhana were oppressing their people.*

We heard rumors about that but Lord Carmanor told us the report must have been exaggerated and commanded us not to bring it up.

Interesting, I sent, then switched mental channels so I could let Alister know this information. He let me know he would broach the subject with the ruler of Carnivoria since he hadn't asked about it in the time we'd been here.

Joshua was looking expectantly at me so I realized I must have missed a comment or question.

I'm sorry I had a bit of a brain fart, could you please repeat that?

Joshua laughed, *I will but only if you explain what a brain fart is.* Once I explained the term from Earth, he repeated his statement. *According to Lord Carmanor and Lady Kudanganya only women and children can show any type of weakness and the strong rise to the top. We must use our strength to stay in power and that is the way we* Protect the Weak.

We rode in thoughtful silence so I could formulate my thoughts. *But you're beginning to doubt that teaching, aren't you?* I could feel his surprise through our connection.

How did you know?

It would be difficult to spend so much time around the King and not be affected by how he treats others.

He could look down on everyone on the planet, but he seems to even care about the servants who wait on us every night.

Lord Carmanor had thirty shifters travelling in our caravan who would set up camp for us and then tear the camp down again after we left. They also prepared breakfast and dinner for us and served it in the luxurious tent Carmanor stayed in each night. As usual, Alister spent time with each person and knew everyone by name.

If you haven't noticed it already, the King believes it is his role to serve everyone in his kingdom. This isn't something he's written on his coat of arms, it's the way he chooses to live his life. Consequently, it's the same way we live.

Joshua stared pensively at the road for so long I decided to take a nap. I got into a comfortable position and was beginning to dream when Joshua spoke up.

Do you think King Alister would allow me to go with you when you return to Theria?

You waited until I was asleep, didn't you? I grumbled.

He laughed, *of course I did. If I've learned one thing about you during our time together it's that you appreciate a good joke.*

I would have appreciated it more if it was a joke on someone else. Sitting up, I rubbed my hand across my face and yawned. *I can ask Alister, of course, but I know he's going to want to know two things. First, have you talked to Lord Carmanor about this already. Secondly, he'll want to know why you want to go.*

I haven't spoken with Lord Carmanor yet, but plan to after the festival. Since you're not leaving for Sirenea for a few more days, I figure I still have time. As far as the reason I want to go, I would like the opportunity to be part of the King's guard and use my skills to better all the people of Theria and not just those in a certain segment of Carnivoria.

I will talk to King Alister on your behalf, but I want you to know that he'll want to talk to you about this as well. You'll also be examined by the Einhorns, to check your reasons and motives. It's not that I don't believe you, but the King is careful about those he lets join the royal guard.

I can see Jumba la Dhahabu not too far ahead, Erich the Eagle called from his position above us. He'd been silent for so long, I'd almost forgotten he was flying above us keeping an eye out for potential enemies.

Thanks, Erich. Just to be clear, what does 'not too far ahead' mean to you? I asked.

About fifty miles, give or take, he laughed.

Great, another two hours I grumbled. *My butt's falling asleep riding in this carriage for hundreds of miles every day.*

Try flying, he shot back.

Yeah, yeah, if I know you, you've been soaring more than you've been flapping, I chuckled.

Guilty as charged, Erich quipped and closed our mental connection.

I sighed and Joshua looked at me sideways. Alister didn't want us to let anyone know how far our thought-speech travelled so I just waved off his curious look and answered, "I'm looking forward to stretching my legs; I'm tired of riding. Even though this is a comfortable seat, my butts's getting flat from all the sitting."

"Did you say your butt's getting fat from all the sitting?" Joshua snickered.

"Ha-ha, you're as funny as Alister—and that's not funny at all," I grinned. "How much longer do you think until we get to the capital?"

Joshua leaned forward and looked at the landscape. To me, the savannah looked the same, but he must have seen something he recognized because he soon settled back and said, "less than two hours."

"What can we expect when we get to the capital?"

"Tonight, we'll have a celebratory feast where the minstrels will extol the fighting prowess of both Lord Carmanor and Lady Kudanganya, followed by songs and dances native to the various duchies in Metatheria performed in the King's honor. We'll actually retire early tonight so we can prepare for the Challenge of Champions tournament tomorrow morning."

"What is the Challenge of Champions?" I asked curiously.

"That's when members of your Inner Circle face off against their counterparts in Carnivoria in feats of strength and battle," Joshua smiled at me.

"So, you're saying that the men of the King's Inner Circle will fight—"

"No, no," Joshua laughed, interrupting me. "Both the men and women will fight male or female warriors from Carnivoria. Don't worry, it's only for exhibition purposes, no weapons and everyone will fight in human form. The highlight of the festival will be Lord Carmanor and King Alister fighting one-on-one before a crowd of onlookers."

"Well, I guess that's something to look forward to then," I muttered and began sharing what I had learned with Alister and the rest of the Inner Circle.

CHAPTER ELEVEN

*A*lister

    "Is it always this hot?" Shelley asked.

"No, sometimes it's hotter," Joshua laughed and Lord Carmanor shot him a look which wiped the smile off his face.

"Sir Arktos seems a bit soft to me, it will do him good to face off against my Captain of the Guard in the ring," Carmanor sneered.

He'd become increasingly hostile as the exhibition matches continued especially after my people won. We'd been sitting under his pavilion watching the fights since early this morning. The matches so far had been physical, but not more so than how we normally trained. Carmanor would brag whenever one of his people won and grumble when one of ours did. I wasn't sure what was going on but could feel the tension rising in my companion as the day wore on. Perhaps he was anticipating the last match of the day, which would be ours.

The first time I saw the crack in the veneer of his hospitality was when Mkali was challenged by a woman who was older and more muscular than she was.

"I'm not sure this will be a fair fight," I said lightly as I watched the woman approach the young squire.

Carmanor spread his arms wide and said mockingly, "If she is old enough to be a squire to one of your knights, then she is old enough to fight."

Rather than correct his misunderstanding on what I was trying to say, I nodded to Mkali and said, "Make Bernie proud."

She nodded solemnly then bowed to her opponent. The woman sneered at the young girl standing in the circle with her and lunged at Mkali when Carmanor shouted for them to begin. Mkali ducked under the woman's arms as she lunged towards Mkali and tried to grab her. As the woman's momentum carried her past my young squire, Mkali swung her arms like she was swinging a baseball bat and hit her on her left side under her ribs. When the woman staggered from the blow Mkali clambered on the woman's back and locked her ankles around the woman's torso while she locked her arms around her neck, cutting off her oxygen.

Mkali's sudden move caught the woman off guard and she fell face down into the dirt. Mkali only got off her back when the woman passed out. Mkali stood, bowed low and smiled and waved at our people who were celebrating her victory. Carmanor was so enraged, I was afraid for the woman's safety. I sent a mental command for our healers to carry her off the field of battle to treat her wounds.

"Perhaps I underestimated your squire, that's a mistake I won't make again," Carmanor smiled darkly.

"Mkali takes her responsibilities very seriously, she is a fierce warrior and spends hours each day training with her father as well as other members of my guard, both male and female."

"What would you have done if she'd lost?" Carmanor asked.

I shrugged, "Make sure she was okay then give her pointers on what she could have done differently."

Even though my people didn't win every bout, they were still respectful towards their opponents and did their best. Sometimes they were bested because their opponents were better than they were and sometimes they were overcome with the unbearable heat in the ring. I was proud of my people and cheered for them whether they won or lost. Most of the Carnivorian combatants were good sports whether they won or lost but occasionally, they would take things too far and my people were hurt even though this should have been an exhibition tournament.

Each time this would happen, Carmanor would offer a backhanded apology like, 'I'm sorry your warrior wasn't as skilled as mine,' but I could tell he was pleased any time we lost a bout. When it came time for Bernie's match, she was pitted against a male shifter who was part of Carmanor's personal guard. He had bragged about these elite fighters almost constantly while we journeyed through Carnivoria.

Joshua was evidently upset about Carmanor's choice of opponent for Bernie, "Lord Carmanor, Hasira is supposed to be paired with Sir Einhorn. Vita is still under discipline."

"Hasira wasn't available and we don't have time to find a suitable female replacement," Carmanor said with a smile that didn't reach his eyes then raised his voice to call out to Bernie. "Sir Einhorn, do you wish to forfeit this match?"

Bernie sized up her opponent who was almost a foot taller and at least fifty pounds heavier than she was. "Sire, I'd prefer not to forfeit but I'll leave the decision up to you," Bernie's lips twitched in a semblance of a smile.

Are you sure about this?

Yes, I have this, trust me. Do me a favor and calm Shelley down. I'm afraid of what he'll do to this guy if he hurts me.

You got it, make Mkali proud.

Bernie laughed aloud and faced her opponent. While she waited for Carmanor to start the match, I was able to send Shelley a sense of calm through my connection with him.

Alister, if he hurts our friend, I'm going to rip him apart, Aileene sent. I should have sent some soothing thoughts her way as well.

Bernie will be okay. Even if she loses, it shouldn't be any worse than when she trains with you.

"Fight," Carmanor roared and Bernie and Vita slowly circled one another in the fight ring. Vita kept taunting Bernie, but I could tell she was ignoring his words while studying his movements, looking for an opening.

"Are we going to fight, or would you rather dance?" Bernie mocked after a minute of circling.

Vita roared and charged Bernie. Before he could grab her, she spun out of his way and shoved him in the back; he stumbled but didn't go down. Bernie didn't move away quickly enough, and Vita managed to backhand her and snap her head back. Before Vita could take advantage of his hit, Bernie did three backflips, so she was once again out of his range.

"I'll give that one to you," Bernie smiled then wiped the blood from her smashed lips, "but that's the last hit you get."

As Bernie ran towards Vita, I heard Shelley chuckle and say to Joshua, "I'm not sure what Vita said in thought-speech to make Bernie mad but I'm pretty sure he'll finish the rest of his discipline duty in the infirmary."

Bernie's fist was cocked back and when she feinted towards Vita's head, he held up his arms to protect his face. Instead of hitting him in the face, Bernie used the momentum from her run as well as the strength behind her punch to hit Vita in the groin. This was completely unexpected, and the air exploded from his lungs and he dropped his hands. Before he could protect himself, Bernie hit him under the chin with her forearm. Since she jumped into the hit, he was struck with her full body weight. He was unconscious before he hit the ground on his back and lay still.

Bernie rounded on Carmanor and with fire blazing in her eyes addressed the ruler of Carnivoria. "He's lucky I didn't kill him for the things he said to me as he bragged about assaulting women." She turned to me. "Sire, I ask that you open an investigation into his behavior." Since she had made the request to me as High King, Carmanor didn't have legal standing to refuse me, even though I could tell he wasn't happy.

"Very well, if he has done as you say, he deserves punishment. Take him away," Carmanor ordered.

A contingent of my guard carried Vita out of the fighting ring while the next combatants prepared for their bout.

Well done, Sir Einhorn, I sent to Bernie, Shelley, Mkali and Aileene. The rest of our friends gave her congratulations as well.

When it came time for Shelley and Joshua to fight, they were still dealing with Vita so Carmanor decided to skip their match in favor of the one between Aileene and Lady Kudanganya.

"I hope you don't mind some scars on your lady. I can't promise Kudanganya won't lose her temper. I've tried to teach her to be cold in battle, but she lets her emotions run away with her at times. Oh well, women, what can you do?" Carmanor chuckled but I didn't find any humor in his statement.

"Aileene, you know what to do," I said aloud.

Kudanganya was a vicious fighter but not as talented as she thought she was. Most people were more afraid of her husband's wrath than her. Aileene had told me about what she had done to her opponents when we were apart, and I didn't like the way she treated the people she was supposed to protect. She was a bit of a bully and there would be a reckoning for her behavior before we left Carnivoria but for now, I was going to let Aileene give her a taste of her own medicine.

The two female shifters entered the fighting ring and stood about twenty feet apart. Both wore light armor made of hardened leather. Kudanganya was wearing the colors of Carnivoria and Aileene wore something patterned after the uniform worn by Wonder Woman in the latest movie, but modified to match our livery. She stood in the circle, her auburn hair up in a fighting braid with the sun glinting off the gold of her uniform, looking every inch the warrior she was. When Aileene asked permission to design a new uniform for our female guards I didn't know what she was planning; I'm glad I said yes.

Lord Carmanor motioned to the combatants and when they stood side-by-side he stood and addressed them. "The rules of this contest are simple; you may not shift entirely into your natural form and you may not intentionally kill or permanently disable your opponent." There was a murmur from the crowd because of what he'd announced as well as what he left out of the rules. He raised his hand to quiet the crowd, then continued when they were silent, "Please remember that this is an exhibition fight for entertainment purposes only."

Aileene turned towards Kudanganya to offer her hand in respect at the same moment Carmanor dropped his hand. Kudanganya grabbed a heavy wooden baton from her belt and lashed out at Aileene as quickly as a striking cobra. Aileene threw up her arm so the blow landed on her forearm rather than her temple where Kudanganya was aiming. While Kudanganya was recovering from the force of her swing, Aileene delivered a front kick to her chest which sent her flying backward.

Before I could object, Carmanor smiled wickedly and muttered, "I seem to have forgotten to mention the rule about no weapons." Even though I felt like ripping his head off, I didn't because I'd already decided to let this farce play through, and I trusted Aileene enough to know she could best her opponent.

Kudanganya hit the dirt and rolled backward and sprang to her feet. When Aileene closed the distance, Kudanganya threw dirt in her eyes and once again lashed out with the baton. Aileene jumped backward to avoid the first blow, ducked to avoid the second and stopped the baton with her hand when Kudanganya tried to smash her head with the third blow.

Aileene ripped the baton out of her hand and used another front kick to send her opponent flying. She snapped the baton with her hands and threw the broken pieces away. Kudanganya snarled in feline rage and sprang at Aileene while shifting to her half form.

Carmanor half-heartedly chided his wife, "No Anya, you have to fight in human form," but it was too late by that time because she was using her claws to attack Aileene's chest, but the armor deflected the deadly blows.

Aileene's eyes blazed molten and I could tell she was finished with this sham of an exhibition fight. Kudanganya slashed at Aileene's exposed throat with her clawed right hand and Aileene grabbed it with her left hand and held it in place. When Kudanganya attempted to punch Aileene in the face with her left hand, Aileene caught her hand and I could hear the distinctive sound of bones breaking when Aileene squeezed.

Kudanganya screamed with rage and Aileene pulled the other woman's arms apart and smashed her forehead into the nose of the lion shifter. As Kudanganya staggered back, Aileene let go of her left arm and bent the other woman's arm behind her body and Aileene wrapped her right arm around her opponent's neck, cutting off her air and lifting her off the ground. Kudanganya continued to struggle for a moment until she was unconscious and Aileene dropped her on the ground where she lay in a heap at her feet.

Aileene dragged the unconscious woman over to where we were standing and used one hand to toss her to Carmanor. He caught his unconscious wife without effort but took a step back when Aileene turned her enraged gaze towards the now frightened ruler of Carnivoria.

"You and your wife are lucky Alister asked me to show restraint when she chose to cheat." She stepped closer and lowered her voice so only the three of us could hear what she said. "But if you follow your wife's example and ignore the rules you set forth, then you will have a very angry dragon to deal with; do I make myself clear?" She growled and smoke curled from her nostrils. Even from where I was standing, I could feel the heat pouring off her, so I knew how angry she really was.

"Be assured, Lady Aileene, Lady Kudanganya will be reprimanded for her lack of judgement." Carmanor dropped his head while he still held his wife in his arms.

"Since our match is the last of the day, I suggest we take an hour recess before commencing," I suggested as I hopped down to stand next to Aileene and walked away without a backward glance.

Aileene

I was still furious as Alister led me to the tent Carmanor had set up for us and it was only his arm around me that kept me from going back and ripping out the throat of our enemy.

When Alister chuckled, I realized I'd said that last part out loud. His love for me came through our mate-connection and soothed the fire burning inside me; it was as refreshing as jumping into a cool pool on a hot day and I was grateful for him.

"We're not completely sure he's our enemy, although evidence is mounting against him," Alister said as he ushered me out of the sun and into the shade of the tent. Thankfully, we were alone so we could talk about Alister's upcoming fight.

"You know Carmanor is going to do everything short of cheating to defeat you?"

"I put that together after he told me he couldn't wait to show me what pain felt like," Alister laughed.

"Is he insane?" I blurted and watched Alister wiggle his hand back and forth and shrug.

"I'm not ruling that out, but I believe he's more conceited and self-absorbed than insane. He is immensely proud of his physical prowess and made sure to show me how powerful he was over the past two months," Alister said.

There was a roar from the crowd outside that signaled another bout was going to start.

What's going on? I sent to Bernie.

Shelley and Joshua are about to fight. I guess Carmanor decided he didn't want to make the crowd wait for his match with Alister.

Do you want us to come out there?

No, Shelley says Joshua is honorable and out of all the matches today, I think this will be what it's supposed to be; a friendly exhibition of strength, physical ability and fighting prowess.

The crowd roared louder, and Bernie spoke again, *they're demonstrating wrestling techniques and are grappling in the middle of the ring. Unless you need me, I'm going to watch this man of mine in action.*

Have fun, I laughed and explained to Alister what we'd been talking about. After sharing a smile, I sobered and expressed my concerns. "While we were together Kudanganya told me stories every night about different times Carmanor defeated his opponents in training battles and some of them have never been the same. I'm worried for you."

Alister wrapped me in his arms and kissed me on the forehead. It was such a tender gesture, I felt tears gather in my eyes.

"Hey, I'll be okay," he said, as he wiped a tear away with his thumb and gave me the grin that melted me a bit each time he brought it out. "I figure Carmanor has a trick or two up his sleeve, so I'll be extra careful."

I snorted and looked at him disbelievingly. He held up his hands and laughed. "I'll be as careful as I can while fighting an eight-foot behemoth. I'm quite sure you scared him straight with the threat of your dragon. You even made me shudder."

"I'm serious, Alister. I have a really bad feeling about today, don't take any unnecessary chances and take him down quickly." I frowned and crossed my arms over my chest.

He rubbed his hands up and down my biceps then touched the gem on my necklace. "I promise," he said seriously and looked me in the eyes. "Now, let's get something to drink before I have to meet Carmanor in a friendly battle."

"I don't think he knows what that means," I muttered and poured both of us some water.

Someone blocked the sunlight and I looked up and saw Kudanganya standing in front of me with a vulnerable expression on her face, she nervously licked her lips before she spoke.

"Lady Aileene, may I join you?"

"Sure, after all, they're your grandstands," I said and scooted over to make room for her.

She sat with her head bowed, her unbraided hair hiding her face and spoke so softly I had trouble hearing her. "I'm sorry for earlier, my behavior was inexcusable."

I wanted to lash out at her, not only for how she acted when she fought with me earlier but also for how she treated the others throughout Carnivoria she fought with during our tour, but I knew

Alister wouldn't want me to do that, instead, I put my arm around the visibly nervous woman and asked gently.

"Why did you do what you did? And please don't give me any excuse about losing yourself in the heat of battle. Every one of your actions was planned and carefully executed." She stiffened at my accusation and I didn't need Bernie to tell me I'd arrived at the truth.

"As my future queen, I owe my fealty to you, but I will answer honestly for the mercy you showed me earlier. I know you could have demanded my head for my using a weapon or transforming, but you didn't. You didn't even transform into your dragon. You are an honorable woman and I lost what little honor I had left in the ring today."

She took a deep breath. "My husband wanted to provoke a response from King Alister so he could discredit him publicly for violating the tournament rules. He doesn't have a reason to object to King Phillip and Queen Beatrice's abdication, but he always looks for ways to paint himself in a more favorable light."

"What are his plans for the fight with Alister?" I asked.

"He plans to humiliate him before the crowd. He views Alister as an untested young boy and wants to weaken his position as High King. He believes that by doing so, his own prestige will rise, and the King will choose him to be part of his Inner Circle."

"Doesn't he know Alister was in his human form when he defeated Dimitri, who had transformed?" I asked.

She nodded, "Yes, but he believes it isn't possible and just propaganda coming from Theria to prop up the boy king, his words not mine."

"He's in for a surprise then," I chuckled darkly.

"Is he really that powerful?" she asked in wonder.

I turned to her and searched her earnest face; she told me a lot, but I knew there was much she wasn't sharing. I noticed her right cheek was red and starting to bruise and knew that wound didn't come from me. I wondered if Carmanor hit her and when she flinched as I reached out to gently touch her cheek, my suspicions were confirmed. As I touched her cheek, I whispered the *Sanos* spell and healed her. When she took a relieved breath, I realized Carmanor hadn't bothered to have her healed after our fight.

I contacted Alister and told him what I'd learned, and he assured me by the time he was finished with Carmanor he would regret hitting his wife. I sent love and appreciation back to Alister through our connection. I loved how he took his responsibility to *Protect the Weak* so seriously and how quickly he would show grace and mercy to those who were willing to change their ways. I sat back against the cushions and smiled to myself because I was really going to enjoy this exhibition battle.

Alister

Lord Carmanor and I stood side-by-side in the fighting ring as Fritz went over the rules of combat. Once again, the rules were simple; we couldn't purposefully kill each other, and we couldn't shift in any way or we would forfeit the fight. Once we agreed to the rules, I thanked Fritz and then waited until he left the ring before turning towards Aileene and giving her a wink and a cheeky grin. Aileene sat with Bernie on one side of her and Kudanganya on the other. Shelley and Joshua were standing on opposite sides of each other, just outside of the ring, acting as witnesses for our bout.

"King Alister, Lord Carmanor, please turn and face each other," Fritz called from his position in the grandstand, "begin."

I'd watched Carmanor fight enough times over the past two months, so I knew his tactics well. He would rush his opponents and use his tremendous size and strength to overwhelm their defenses. While he was a foot taller than I and probably outweighed me by seventy-five pounds or more, he wasn't used to sparring with a dragon like I was. The light of battle was in his eyes and he had a manic grin on his face as he rushed me. I crouched, spread my arms wide and waited for him to come. When he was within striking range, I punched him in the solar plexus, grabbed his upper arms, allowing our momentum to carry us to the ground and then flipped him over my head using my legs.

He landed heavily but was soon on his feet and we were once again facing each other.

"Not bad, little princeling, not bad. But it will take more than fancy tricks to defeat me," Carmanor said and came at me with his fists raised. He feinted with his right fist and then threw dirt in my eyes with his left when I fell for it. Momentary blinded, I raised my arms to protect my face as he inflicted punishing blows to my ribs. I blinked enough dirt out of my eyes so I could see again and hit him in the nose. He backpedaled as his eyes began to water so I had a moment to finish clearing my eyes.

By the time I started advancing again, he had his hands up and was ready for me. We circled one another again, looking for an opening. He threw jabs with his left hand which I blocked then tried to hit me with an uppercut. He'd slightly dipped his right shoulder before the blow, so I was prepared. I sidestepped the punch to avoid his swing and pounded him hard above his heart, which caused him to stagger. I grew too confident and stepped forward to finish him off, but he used a move to toss me over his hip and I hit the ground hard.

I rolled out of the way as he landed where my head had been and if I'd been a little slower that crippling blow would have ended the fight. I scrambled to my feet and we stood toe-to-toe and pummeled each other. Carmanor was favoring the ribs on his right side so that's where I kept hitting him, trying to wear him down. He tried to punch my nose, so I lowered my head and his fist connected with my forehead instead and he yowled in pain. Before I could move my head back, he tried to gouge out my eye but only succeeded in cutting my forehead open with his sharpened fingernails. Even though he hadn't transformed his hands into claws, his nails were sharpened into points and the blood dripped down into my eyes.

I had to back up again to clear my eyes but Carmanor kept moving forward, aiming blows to my body. I covered my face and head with my hands and tried to protect my sides with my elbows as he rained punishing blows to my ribs. If I didn't go back on the offensive soon, I would be in trouble. I saw my opening and trapped his right arm with my left and stepped close enough to him he couldn't hit me effectively.

I twisted my body when he tried to knee me in the groin and wrapped my right foot around his ankle and rode him to the ground using a technique I had seen in an MMA fight. I landed on his chest with my full weight and I both heard and felt the air whoosh from his lungs. I scrambled up his body and pinned his arms with my knees while I sat on his chest.

"Yield," I ground out and he bent his body and kneed me in the back in response. This caused me to pitch forward and gave him enough leverage that my knee slipped off his right arm. He reached out and tried to grab my throat, but I lowered my chin and he missed his chance to choke me. Grabbing his right hand, I twisted the wrist down and around as I got off his chest and stood behind him. He was only able to get to his knees because of the angle of his arm so I added pressure and once again commanded him to yield.

"Never, and you don't have the guts to finish me off," he screamed through the pain.

Rather than waste any more time I decided to prove him wrong and used my left foot to kick him in the temple. I felt his shoulder dislocate from the weight of his body when he went limp. I released his arm, he lay face down in the dirt. I leaned over him to check the pulse in his neck and when I was satisfied he was still alive, I stood and held my arms above my head in victory. The crowd roared their approval as I transformed into my dragon and launched into the sky, roaring my victory and shooting flames into the air. My aches and pains were instantly healed, and I left Carmanor where he lay so he could be tended to by his healers.

Where are you going? Shelley asked me as I started to fly away.

I need to hunt something, or I'll give into my temptation to tear Carmanor apart.

Oh, came Shelley's small reply, *then you'd better go. We'll hold the victory ceremony when you get back.*

That would be best, I growled and flew away.

Aileene

Alister was gone for two hours but we had been in communication the whole time and I agreed it was best if he was by himself for a bit. I could feel his churning emotions and even though he won the fight, his dragon was calling for blood. I'd never seen Alister so close to losing control before, so I kept sending soothing thoughts to him while he was away. I also described the scene of Carmanor being carted off the field of battle on a stretcher and Alister laughed through our connection.

We were currently sitting at the high table by ourselves, because Lord Carmanor was handing out prizes to the victors and Kudanganya had been informed she no longer had a place at the Lord's table when she tried to join us. Apparently Carmanor was expressing his displeasure with her by removing her from her position as his wife.

I wish you would have ripped him apart after instead of flying away, I sent to Alister.

So do I, but I've already made my decision that Carmanor will be stepping down as ruler of Carnivoria before we head to Sirenea. He's proven unworthy of the trust father gave him. We'll let him have his moment of glory today then explain the changes tomorrow. He squeezed my knee under the table, and I felt a little better. Carmanor had been droning on and on but my attention sharpened when I heard Alister's name.

"When I was informed that King Phillip and Queen Beatrice had abdicated their thrones and their son Alister had already claimed kingship, I was understandably upset and frankly wondered how a boy could be strong enough to rule. I might have voiced my displeasure to one or two of you," he paused while many of his subjects laughed weakly while his booming laughter echoed throughout the hall. "Okay, I was terribly upset and decided I would use the tournament today to show that he wasn't physically fit to be king. Rather than that happening, I was defeated. I may not say this very often, but I admit I was wrong."

"I don't think you've ever admitted that before," someone called out from the crowd and a flash of anger passed over Carmanor's face. He nodded tersely to the stewards who began to distribute goblets to the guests gathered in the banquet hall with instructions to wait to drink until the toast.

"Please stand and raise your glasses to the future of Theria," we all stood, and I beamed at Alister as Carmanor officially recognized what he should have known all along. Alister was the future of Theria and I was grateful we would be walking into that future together.

"Change is coming to Theria and this change is symbolized by the drakka juice we have in our cups. It takes years of careful planning and tending of the trees to produce enough fruit to make one glass of this rare juice. Today we all drink it together to toast Alister, High King of all Theria." Carmanor raised his glass and said, "To Alister," and drained his goblet. The rest of us said, "To Alister," in unison and did the same.

The moment I swallowed the juice I knew something was wrong. My throat was freezing and on fire at the same time. The goblet slipped from my nerveless fingers and clattered to the ground. Carmanor looked triumphant as he stared in our direction and I watched Alister slump to the floor. I wanted to reach out to rip Carmanor apart and his eyes widened in alarm when I managed to take two steps toward him, but in the end my effort didn't matter. The world tipped around me and I realized I was falling. There was burning at my throat as my sight dimmed and I slipped into oblivion.

CHAPTER TWELVE

*A*lister

Aileene's anguished scream echoed in my mind as I lay with my eyes closed. Moments before it felt like an electric current had rushed through my body and left me weakened and drained. My throat felt like I had been gargling with shards of glass and I was certain Shelley was sitting on my head—again. Someone was laughing nearby but I don't think I understood the joke. I could hear footsteps coming towards me and I knew there was something important I was supposed to do.

Be strong, An'Ceann's voice whispered and everything became clear; Aileene and I had been poisoned by Carmanor. I quickly cast the *Adamantem* spell over Aileene and myself and began absorbing the magic pouring into Theria through the pinhole gate to Middle Earth I had opened before the start of the banquet. While I connected to my people to make sure they were okay, I filled my magical reservoir. I heard a scuffle and the unmistakable sound of flesh hitting flesh was accompanied by the sound of someone getting stabbed and the smell of blood.

I sent a pulse of magical energy and healing through the conduit I had connecting myself to the rest of my team and I got an infusion of energy from them as well. I opened my eyes in time to see Carmanor attempting to plunge a bloody dragon bone dagger into my chest, thankfully the spell deflected the blow. I grabbed Carmanor by the throat and stood, holding him off the ground with one hand. He continued to try to stab me with the dagger but was unsuccessful due to the shield that surrounded me.

I continued to cut off the blood and oxygen supply to his brain until he passed out and I looked around the room. After I saw Aileene was beginning to stir, I noticed Joshua lying on the ground, a pool of blood spreading from the stab wounds in his stomach. Tearing the dagger out of Carmanor's hand, I carelessly tossed his unconscious body across the room where he landed in a heap against the wall. I rushed to Joshua's side and began pouring healing energy into his body.

Aileene joined me and put her hand on my shoulder and I could feel the grief and rage pouring through our connection. "Are our people—" she began then stopped as though saying the words would bring the worst to pass.

"They're all alive, but it will take them some time to fully recover. Once I've finished healing Joshua, I'll pour more healing energy into them," I said as I watched the color return to my patient's face.

"And everyone else?" Aileene asked sadly and I saw the tears streaming down her face. She already knew the answer to her question, but I shook my head anyway and she sobbed. I looked around the room and only half of the people were stirring, all the citizens of Carnivoria were dead and lying where they had fallen after drinking the poison Carmanor had given them. I gathered Aileene in my arms while she sobbed for the loss of the men, women and children who were scattered around the banquet hall.

"Please make sure Carmanor isn't able to escape. He will answer for what he's done and pay for his crimes," I said with steel in my voice.

Aileene let me hold her a few minutes then straightened her spine and looked me in the eye, nodded, then stalked away to where

Carmanor had fallen. I turned back to face Joshua and the rest of my people who were recovering; I had work to do.

"You mean to tell me the only thing that saved my life was the fact I hate drakka juice?" Joshua asked in a dull voice.

Even though we'd checked every Carnivorian in the banquet hall in case I'd been wrong, Joshua was the only survivor. Even Lady Kudanganya had been killed by her murderous husband.

"Yes," Shelley said from the chair next to his friend's bed. "But you almost died when Carmanor stabbed you as you tried to protect the King."

"And for that, I'm grateful," Aileene said as she bent over and kissed the rhino shifter on the forehead.

"I know you have a lot of questions, but you're still healing and need your rest. King Alister did a marvelous job in saving your life, but you'd almost bled out before he got to you," Bernie said as she ran her glowing hands up and down his body to speed his healing.

"Please, I need to know two things before I sleep." At Bernie's nod he continued. "How were you able to avoid the poison and what's going to happen with the traitor?"

I looked intently at Joshua as I mentally consulted with my Inner Circle. Bernie had informed us that while she and Frieda worked on Joshua earlier, they had questioned him extensively and were certain he hadn't known about Carmanor's plans and wasn't part of the conspiracy. She affirmed what I had already known; he is an honorable man and wants what is best for Carnivoria and Theria as a whole.

"Joshua, I'll explain how I protected my people from the poison later when we have the conference call with my father. As for what will happen to Carmanor, for now he has been healed and is in chains and under guard. He will be questioned by the Einhorns to find out who else is involved in the conspiracy. Even he won't be able to withstand three unicorns interrogating him at once. Tomorrow we will travel to the four duchies in Carnivoria to show them Carmanor in chains and announce what he's done. You will come with us to stand as witness to his crimes."

Joshua looked confused, "Of course, I'd be honored to accompany you but why me?"

Aileene looked at me and at my nod took Joshua's hand and finished explaining. "First of all, you are the only Carnivorian witness left alive who can describe the horrors wrought by Carmanor. More importantly you will be coming as the new ruler of Carnivoria."

Joshua's mouth dropped open in surprise but before he could respond Aileene continued.

"You have my eternal gratitude for your willingness to sacrifice your life to save Alister's but we decided you would be the best ruler for this land because you truly care for its people and will use your gifts and talents to build and heal rather than destroy."

"And An'Ceann told you to," Shelley coughed in his hand.

Aileene shot him a fond look and grinned at an even more flabbergasted Joshua then responded, "And An'Ceann told us to."

"But, why would he do that? I'm—" Joshua began but was interrupted by a new presence in the room.

"The fact you don't think you're worthy is exactly the reason I chose you," An'Ceann said as he moved to the bed, pushing me out of the way.

"I'll just get out of your way, shall I?" I laughed.

"I figured you'd get the hint," he smiled and pressed his nose on Joshua's forehead. "Joshua Vifaru, do you promise to follow my ways for the rest of your life and pledge your fealty to High King Alister? Do you promise to uphold the laws of Theria and serve your people? Do you promise to *Protect the Weak* until your dying breath?"

Joshua said yes to each question.

"Then by my own authority, I name you Lord Vifaru, ruler of Carnivoria. May your rule heal this land and help King Alister reunite all Theria under his banner." An'Ceann exuded a sense of peace and wellbeing then disappeared before I could ask him any questions.

Spoilers, he laughed in my mind and I had to grin at his predictable response.

"Did that just really happen?" Joshua asked in awe.

"Yes, it did, and I think you'll find you're quite ready to get out of bed now," Bernie answered for all of us.

Joshua stood and Shelley laughed. "You might want to put some clothes on before the conference call."

Joshua looked down and noticed he was naked. "Don't worry about it," I said and clapped him on the shoulder. "You burst out of your clothes when you partially transformed to protect me. I have something I'll give you later that will help with that."

Shelley threw him a towel which he wrapped around his waist.

"I'll join my parents so we can question Carmanor and will meet you later for the conversation with King Phillip," Bernie said.

"I'm coming, too. Hopefully Carmanor will give you trouble, and you'll need my help persuading him to talk," Aileene said as she joined arms with Bernie, and they left the room.

"Well, we have some things to talk about before the conference and I think the least Lord Vifaru can do is feed us; something with a little less poison would be nice," Shelley said and put his arm around Joshua's shoulder and led him out of the room.

"You're looking well, Son, any lasting effects from the poison?" my father asked from the screen on the wall. Carmanor never installed the equipment as I'd ordered but my technicians were able to take care of it before our scheduled meeting. I guess since he thought I'd be dead he wouldn't have to do what I told him to do.

"None, except for a few headaches when people woke up, the spell worked as planned and everyone was protected."

My Father laughed when Joshua raised his hand. "Lord Vifaru you don't have to stand on ceremony around us, if you have a question just ask. And if you haven't figured it out already the King prefers it if you call him by his first name in informal settings."

"Yes sir, thank you sir," Joshua stammered and blushed. "My

question has to do with the spell King Alister mentioned, what is that about?"

Joshua was the only person in the room who wasn't a member of my Inner Circle and based on An'Ceann's recommendation I knew I could trust him. However, I cast the *Indicens* spell to make sure we weren't overheard outside of the room.

"How much do you know about magic and how it is used on Theria?"

Joshua looked thoughtful for a moment then answered, "Certain shifters, like unicorns can use magic to heal and discern the truth in others. The High King or Queen can use magic to open gates between worlds and can also use magic to heal, and that's about all I know."

Hillaes jumped in. "I come from another dimension from a planet very much like this one that we call Claw—"

"Middle Earth," Shelley interrupted.

Hillaes rolled her eyes. "The residents of the planet call it Claw, the members of the King's Inner Circle call it Middle Earth, and before you ask, I'm not going to tell you why because it would take too long to explain."

"Don't worry about it dude, I'll explain it to you later complete with visuals and an awesome soundtrack," Shelley whispered loud enough for everyone to hear, including both sets of my parents who were at the Royal Palace in Theria.

"Moving along," Hillaes added. "Magic is more abundant on my planet and there are some of us from there who have chosen to study magic and explored the various ways to create spells and use magic in many useful ways. I have been studying my entire life and am considered a sorceress and the most powerful magic user among my people. The problem with most spells is the caster can't harness enough magical energy to power them so there is a limit to how much they can carry out.

"But I found a way to create a magical reservoir using a crystal found on my home planet, so I've been more successful than others with creating new spells. Please understand I'm not bragging when I say that I am the best on my planet but I look like a first year student compared to what King Alister can do."

"Something happened to me when I healed my parents from the same poison that killed so many people today. I opened a gate to Middle Earth and let so much magic pass through my body I created a natural reservoir that can contain a vast amount of magic for me to use when needed," I explained.

"But it's not only that," Hillaes interjected excitedly. "You're also able to create complex spells in a way I've never seen before with seemingly little effort. The poison detection and cure spell you combined was brilliant and even though we weren't a hundred percent sure it would work, it did, and everyone was saved."

"Woah, wait a minute, if you weren't a hundred percent sure, what percent sure were you?" Shelley asked me.

"I felt seventy-five percent sure it would work," I answered lamely.

"I'm just glad you didn't tell me the odds before I relied on this to save me," Shelley muttered and held up the necklace with the large crystal I'd given him.

"Um, King Alister, can you pretend I don't know what you're talking about and explain how you used magic to save everyone?" Joshua asked.

"Sure," I laughed and tossed my crystal necklace to him. "This is one of the crystals Hillaes and Wu brought back from their honeymoon on her home planet. As she mentioned earlier, she discovered these could be used as a magical battery and store the energy until it was needed for a spell. I was able to infuse each crystal with a spell to detect and cure the poison used on my parents once the wearer encountered it. In this case, the person had to ingest the poison before the protection was triggered. I only wish I was able to save everyone but by the time I'd finished dealing with your former ruler, everyone else was gone."

"I still can't believe that Carmanor was willing to poison everyone just to kill the two of you," Joshua said sadly. "How could I have missed the depth of his evil?"

"When we have time, I'd love to tell you how I completely missed the hatred a member of my Inner Circle had for me that led to him poisoning my wife and me," my father said and nodded for me to continue.

"Carmanor let his jealousy grow until it consumed him, and he was able to justify his actions as long as he came out on top," I said.

"You also said earlier that we would be traveling to the four duchies to announce Carmanor's crimes. How will we be able to get to each one in a day?" Joshua asked.

"Not only can I open gates between worlds, I can also open gates to anywhere I've been before. One of the reasons I've travelled to every duchy in every kingdom is so I could easily open gates there again if necessary. I'll be opening gates to each duchy and we'll take Carmanor with us to present the evidence to each duke and duchess."

"But we only went to two of the four duchies, how will we gate to the other two?" Joshua asked.

Aileene jumped in to help me explain that part. "Since we are true mates and are always connected, Alister can also open a gate to wherever I am. He and Shelley visited us in each duchy we stayed in."

"Even with full chaperones it was totally worth sneaking out to see our future mates," Shelley grinned smugly and I'm sure my expression mirrored his.

"Back to the matter at hand," Father brought us back to order. "King Alister, shall I get the rulers who are loyal to you from the other kingdoms on the conference call?"

"You just like playing with the new system, don't you?" I teased.

He grinned like a kid at Christmas, "I don't know why I didn't think of using this technology years ago, it would have saved so much time on travel."

"It's because you're an old dragon and don't love change," Mother lovingly teased.

"We're the same age," my father groused.

"True, but I'm quicker than you are to embrace change," she patted his hand and picked up a remote control and muttered to herself as she pointed it towards us, and her finger hovered over the buttons. She must have finally figured out the correct one to push because she grinned triumphantly and the view on our screen changed. The screen, which was as large as the wall, split into six sections and a ruler from each of the kingdoms appeared with their name and kingdom they represented written under their image. When it seemed like everyone was ready, I began.

"Thank you for meeting with me on such short notice, for some of you it's either quite late or too early. As you can tell, the person standing next to me isn't Mfalmi Carmanor, but rather Lord Joshua Vifaru; he is the new ruler of Carnivoria." I held up my hand to forestall any questions. "I promise to explain everything in good order. There have also been some changes to the rulers of two of the other kingdoms, so I want to introduce these new rulers to you as well. First, I'd like to present Lady Falenas Omalen and Brooklyn, Queen of the Pixies. They are leading a coalition government in Marsupia after Lord Elandorr was deposed, which is also something I'll explain later. Lady Morwenna is the new ruler of Metatheria after Lady Lynx abdicated to spend more time with her children and grandchildren."

"That will just give her more time to meddle in our lives," Lady Morwenna smiled fondly and everyone laughed with her.

"Lord Moss of Eutheria and Lady Zhaleh of Oceania are still ruling their kingdoms and have also pledged their loyalty to me as High King." After the rulers exchanged pleasantries, I brought everyone up to speed on the main things that happened on our journey across Theria. I could see the anger growing on their faces as I related the incidents in Carnivoria, and everyone was visibly shaken when I told them about Carmanor killing his own people using poison in an attempt to kill Aileene and me.

"Forgive me for stating the obvious, but I notice Lady Baolong isn't with us, I assume she is part of the rebellion?" Lady Zhaleh asked.

I mentally asked Bernie to make her report.

"My lords and ladies, my parents and I questioned Carmanor extensively and discovered that both he and Lady Baolong were working together to overthrow the High King. They successfully recruited Dimitri to their purpose shortly after the birth of King Alister."

Shouldn't you say after King Alister hatched? Shelley mentally asked Bernie, Aileene and me. Aileene growled softly and Shelley mimed zipping his lips. I smiled and shook my head.

"Are we missing something?" Lady Omalen asked.

"If I had to guess, Sir Arktos said something inappropriate to the others and they're trying not to laugh," Mother said resignedly.

"Sorry," Shelley muttered but by the smirk on his face, he wasn't sorry at all.

"Anyway," Bernie said with great restraint, "Baolong and Carmanor figured if they poisoned the High King and Queen, they could try to control the young Alister or kill him outright. Either way they figured Dimitri was the perfect scapegoat and was just a tool in their hands. They didn't expect the magical barrier or the rest of us escaping to Earth.

"When King Alister killed Dimitri and destroyed the barrier, Carmanor and Baolong resumed their long-term plans and prepared to kill all of us. While Carmanor consolidated his power throughout Carnivoria, Baolong amassed an army in Sirenea and planned on deploying them once the King is dead. Carmanor doesn't know how large the army is, but from what we've already seen from those who attacked us, most of them have probably been coerced in some way to join her."

"This is disturbing on so many levels," Lord Moss added after everyone had digested Bernie's report, "but I'm most concerned about the weapons created of dragon bone."

"Yes, how were you able to survive Carmanor's attack with the dragon bone knife? Did he miss?" Lady Morwenna asked.

I had already explained about the magical spells held in the crystals, but I now explained about the *Adamantem* spell Hillaes and I'd created.

"Will those wearing crystals be protected from the dragon bone weapons as well?" Queen Brooklyn asked.

I shook my head. "Unfortunately, the crystals can't hold the *Adamantem* spell and the needed energy to cast it, it's just too complicated. Aileene and I are the only ones powerful enough to cast the spell on our dragons. However, she's not able to hold as much magic as I and can only cast the spell on herself. I'm able to cover a few people if they are standing right next to me but it takes a tremendous amount of power and I can only maintain the spell for a few minutes."

"Phillip," Fritz spoke into the silence following my revelation, "have you heard from Elmas Forelock and the others I sent ahead to meet with Lady Baolong?"

"No, he hasn't returned here," my father shook his head.

"I was afraid of that," Fritz said grimly. "I sent Elmas and about twenty others to update Lady Baolong when we'd arrive and if my suspicions are correct, I unwittingly sent them to their deaths."

Even though we didn't know for sure the group Fritz sent to Sirenea was dead, by the silence in the room and among the other rulers, we assumed they had been murdered. I'd seen firsthand what she did to her own soldiers, I can't imagine what she'd do to those she considered enemies

"She will pay for their deaths and the deaths of those she's murdered over the years." I was surprised to hear Bernie speak with such vehemence, but we all nodded in agreement.

"It's getting late and tomorrow we're taking Carmanor to each duchy here to present his crimes to the dukes and duchesses. Even though Carmanor believes he was working with Baolong alone, we'll also get an opportunity to question each leader to make sure that's accurate. Let's plan to meet tomorrow at the same time to continue working through our plans—"

"If I may, Sire," Stavros interrupted and continued when I asked him to. "I suggest you allow me to work with the military leaders of each kingdom to come up with the best strategy for our confrontation with Baolong."

"That's a good suggestion," Lord Moss interjected, "I know General McIntyre would appreciate the chance to work with you again."

"That's settled then," I said and stood. "General Stavros will serve as the Supreme Commander and speaks with my authority on this matter. Thank you for your time, I wish these were better circumstances but An'Ceann has chosen each of us at this time to reunite Theria. I pledge to you I will do everything in my power to bring Baolong to justice and stop her plans to destroy Theria." I finished with *"Protect the Weak"* and cut the connection once the other rulers responded.

Ceitain 16, 10,258

"Happy birthday, Aileene and Alister, happy birthday to you," Bernie and Shelley sang, badly and Aileene and I blew out the candles on our cake.

"You do know our twentieth birthday isn't until tomorrow, right?" Aileene asked while she made 'gimme' motions with her hand until Bernie handed her a slice of cake.

"Yeah, we know, but thought we might be too busy to celebrate tomorrow, what with fighting a war and all," Shelley said sarcastically.

"Doesn't Alister know how to give me the best birthday presents," Aileene said with a smile and took a bite of her cake.

"Most people wouldn't think fighting a battle would be a present," Shelley said.

"But then again, Aileene isn't most people," Bernie teased.

I laughed with my friends and it felt good to be together, especially on the eve of what could prove to be deadly for all of us. We'd had so much to do over the past two plus weeks we hadn't had much time for the four of us to be together. The trip around Carnivoria with Carmanor took less than a day. Every duke and duchess handed down the verdict of death after they'd been presented with the evidence of Carmanor's crimes against his own people as well as his part in the rebellion. Carmanor didn't show any remorse but instead continued to issue threats at each place we visited. He spewed his verbal abuse up to the moment when Shelley executed him by using a sword to separate his head from his body; a more merciful death than he deserved.

We also made plans for the Siege of Sirenea, as Shelley was calling it. So far, he was the only one. Plans, contingency plans and then more plans when everything went wrong and we had to adjust on the run. I'd also done a few things to tip the scales in our favor. When I first started dreaming about the valley of death, I described the landscape to Elle the phoenix, an amazing artist who was able to create the setting for me. Once we knew Lady Baolong was our enemy, I had Josef use his resources on Earth to see if they could find the place in Asia; they did.

Shelley and I gated to Phoenix, Arizona on Earth, then used the Rex Industries corporate jet to fly to Guilin, China. We were met by a Rex Industries employee named Gracie. Gracie was a panda shapeshifter and new member of Tionchar. Gracie and her family had been assigned to China to replace the woman who had been murdered by Alex Farrel. Gracie was enthusiastic about her adopted country and told us about the people and culture of the area while our driver took us to the valley in the painting.

We made our way to Moon Hill and got out of the van. A shudder ran through me as I saw the valley from my dream. The landscape was undeniably dramatic and beautiful as limestone peaks rose from the valley like green, tree and shrub covered dragon's teeth. Except for the tourists surrounding us, it was serene and peaceful, but my vision was clouded by the scene of horrors I had seen each night for months. This would be the place of the final battle with Baolong and her army.

Shelley sensed my mood so he did what he always does and made a joke. "I can't believe we're standing where the Siege of Sirenea will take place."

"What's the Siege of Sirenea, I haven't heard about that," Gracie asked, and I laughed.

"I'm sure Shelley will tell you all about it on the way to the hotel," I said and headed back to the van.

"That's it?" I heard Gracie ask. "The King wanted to come all this way and is only going to stay for a few minutes?"

"We'll be back later, when there aren't so many people around," Shelley explained as he walked back to the van with Gracie.

And he was right. Now that I'd been here, I'd be able to gate here any time and then open a gate to Sirenea from here. Lady Baolong wouldn't know about it until it was too late, but I planned on opening gates from each of the kingdoms on Theria and bringing our own army to face hers.

"More cake?" Aileene asked me, breaking me out of my memories.

"Please," I said absently and looked down at my plate which still held my untouched first piece. Grabbing it, I shoved the whole thing in my mouth and grinned as she added the second piece to my plate.

"Hey, Stretch, I'm not sure I want to know the answer to this but, has the dream changed again?"

It took me a minute to finish the food in my mouth, but I nodded. "Yes, now instead of all the armies fighting against each other, everyone is fighting against Baolong's army."

"That's true enough, love, but don't leave out the most important part," Aileene looked at me intently.

"Well, even though we win the battle there are a lot of casualties on both sides, but it still comes down to whether or not I survive whatever is waiting for me. Even though Aileene is protected from the dragon bone missile, if I die in the dream, she burns the Kingdom of Sirenea to the ground, is overwhelmed by her grief and eventually destroys Theria and everyone on it."

"Well, aren't you the overachiever," Shelley quipped and took another bite of his cake.

"Shelley this isn't funny," I fumed, "if I'm killed tomorrow everything is lost and everyone I care about is destroyed."

Aileene and Bernie held their breath as they looked between Shelley and me. I'd never been so angry with my friend before, but I needed him to take this seriously and it seemed like this didn't bother him at all.

He opened his mouth to speak but instead put another bit of cake in his mouth and chewed slowly. When he'd swallowed and took a long drink of water, he wiped his mouth with his sleeve and stared at me intently. "You want me to be serious Stretch, here goes. I seriously want this cake for my birthday next week. And do you know why I'm so confident that we'll be around for my birthday? Because you'll do everything in your power, and then some to keep the rest of us safe. If you knew the only way to keep us safe was to sacrifice yourself, you'd do it in a second. Well, this time I believe An'Ceann is using the dream to remind you that it's important for you to live. I'm not sure what weapon Baolong has reserved for you but I know you, Alister, and I know you'll win tomorrow because you don't have any other choice."

"And you can't deprive Shelley of his cake," Bernie added.

"This is seriously good cake," Shelley grinned.

"Alister," Aileene said quietly, "I would be devastated if something happened to you tomorrow, and will probably want to do exactly what the dream describes, but I also promise you I will do everything in my power as well to protect our friends and the people of Theria. The warnings in the dream have already helped us create ways to nullify the poison and dragon bone weapons and we'll be victorious over Baolong and her army as well. I need you to focus on fighting whatever you face and let us take care of the rest. If one thing has been made clear, the weight of the battle rests on your shoulders and I know you'll be able to handle it."

We were silent for a few moments, as I thought about what my friends had said. I took a deep breath and let it out slowly. "Thank you. I know people will die tomorrow and I'm powerless to stop it. If we left Baolong alone she would continue to oppress her own people. We saw what she was willing to do to her own soldiers as she blew them apart or poisoned them rather than let them be captured. If we don't stop her tomorrow, her evil will continue to grow like a cancer until it affects all Theria. She must be stopped, and the only way to do that is by fighting her.

"As much as I hate it, we have to hit her hard tomorrow and destroy her army before she can cause more death and destruction."

"Each person in our army has volunteered for the opportunity to wipe out this evil and are willing to put their lives on the line to protect others. We can hope that Baolong's forces are being coerced in some way which will make it easier to defeat them. We will spare anyone who surrenders but we must be decisive in our victory tomorrow to spare more lives in the long run," Shelley said seriously.

Aileene lay her head on my shoulder and I put my arm around her.

"I know," I said and kissed the top of her head. "I swear to you I will do whatever I can to ensure we all make it through tomorrow alive."

"We already knew that, Stretch, but just in case, I don't want this little beauty to go to waste," Shelley said grimly as he reached for another slice of cake.

CHAPTER THIRTEEN

eitain 17, 10,258
        Sirenea

I stood on a cliff looking down at a valley filled with early morning mist. On one side of the valley there were hundreds of tents each flying the Sirenean flag, a red Long Dragon on a field of yellow. I shivered at the image that had haunted my dreams for most of a year.

"Cold?" Aileene asked me as she slipped her arm around my waist, warming me instantly with the fire that was always burning inside her, and pulled me against her side.

"If I were, I wouldn't be any longer. I'm definitely going to keep you around, you're like my private electric blanket," I laughed grimly.

She poked me in the side, "And don't you forget it, mister."

"I'm not cold, I was just thinking of how many times I've watched everyone I love die in this beautiful valley this past year." *What if I'm not strong enough to protect everyone?*

Aileene squeezed me gently, *I hate to break it to you, love, but you're not strong enough to protect everyone—by yourself. But you're not alone, we're here with you. If you keep your focus on taking out the weapon Baolong has put so much confidence in, we'll be able to take care of the rest.*

I'm afraid, I said and turned to face her and rested my forehead on hers, *afraid of losing you or one of our friends.*

I know, and I'm afraid of the same thing, but we both know we'll do what we have to this day and hope that An'Ceann will give us the strength to stop our enemies to keep this evil from spreading. Besides, we both know the Adamantem *spell is going to mess with Baolong's plans. I hope I get to see her face when she realizes one of her weapons has been nullified.*

I laughed at the expression on Aileene's face; it was the same look she had when she saw her presents piled under the Christmas tree. She may share my fears about the outcome of the battle, but she was also eager to tear into our enemies.

"It seems like Baolong got your message," Shelley said sleepily, rubbing the sleep out of his eyes as he walked up to us.

"It looks like it," I said dryly. Two weeks before I'd connected to all the shifters in Sirenea and mentally broadcast Baolong's crimes and had challenged her to battle on this day, at this location.

"I hate to complain, but next time we have to camp can we find somewhere less rocky?" Bernie groused.

"If you'd just sleep in your unicorn form, this wouldn't be a problem," Aileene teased her friend.

'Whatever," Bernie added, "it's too early."

"This view is breathtaking, it's a great day for a battle," Mkali added enthusiastically as she handed out breakfast sandwiches.

I laughed at the absurdity of this conversation and was overwhelmed with the realization that even though I was still concerned for my friends, we would emerge victorious today because moments like these were too precious to me and I refused to let Baolong steal anything else from us.

Aileene and I landed in front of our gathered forces, about a quarter mile from the enemy line. The thousand soldiers in our army stood in their natural forms, the Royal Standard proudly displayed in the ranks.

Shortly after sunrise Baolong began to muster her troops and they stood in formation upon the grass. There were at least ten thousand enemy soldiers and the small army I'd gathered were outnumbered at least ten to one.

I connected to the opposing troops and broadcast to them, *Lady Baolong of Sirenea is accused of high treason against the Throne, has conspired to incite rebellion and has murdered her own people. Her life is forfeit but yours can be spared if you surrender now. There is no need for the shedding of more Therian blood.*

A pretty speech, King Alister, but as you can see none of my people are willing to bend their knees to you; they are completely loyal to me, Lady Baolong said contemptuously. She was in the form of her Long Dragon and wove sinuously through her troops as she spoke. *We reject your authority over us and by the look of your puny army it won't take us long to destroy you.*

Good people of Sirenea, I implore you to abandon this futile battle and surrender. If you stay on the field of battle, you will be destroyed. I broadcast letting them feel my sincerity through our connection, unfortunately no one moved, but I wasn't surprised.

Lady Baolong, if you care for your people at all, release them from your service and face your punishment alone.

You talk of punishment and crimes but instead you should spend your time saying goodbye to those you love. I reject you as king, I reject your authority over this land, and today you will lie dead at my feet.

So be it, I responded to Baolong and asked Aileene, *are you ready my love?*

Let's do this, she responded enthusiastically.

I chuckled then mentally shouted the command to *Attack.* Our army surged forward, each of them wearing the armor made for them over the past two weeks. I also opened the gates I'd prepared earlier, and thousands of troops poured in from each of the kingdoms loyal to me.

General, the field is yours to command, I sent to Stavros and I launched myself into the sky. Aileene quickly followed and I took a moment to connect to my Inner Circle as I searched for Baolong's secret weapon. *Fight well, stay alive and spare those who surrender.*

You too, love, Aileene sent as she searched for Baolong.

My attention was drawn to something that resembled a short circus tent that had been hidden behind the others. I could feel a sense of danger, rage and malice coming from the tent and I flew towards it.

Aileene, I see Baolong, she's in her human form and running toward the large tent behind the others. The wrongness emanating from it was so overpowering, I was surprised the air around it wasn't polluted with noxious smoke. Baolong gave a command and the tent fabric was pulled away revealing a cage filled with an enormous beast. As she transformed back into her dragon and shot into the sky, the front of the cage opened and the monstrosity crawled out. With a roar of rage, it unfurled its wings and shot fire in my direction. I was momentarily filled with panic when I realized what I was seeing and froze in place as it hurled itself towards me. Before we collided, I had a chance to broadcast a warning to my entire army.

She's got a Royal Dragon—

Shelley

This is boring, I sent to Bernie and got a laugh in response, which was what I was hoping for.

I'm sure you'll get enough excitement once Alister gives the signal to attack—be careful. Bernie sent.

You as well. I love you Bernie, watch your back.

I love you too, you big oaf, Bernie cut our mental connection.

I stood in formation with the rest of the army waiting for the battle to begin. We'd been in our position facing Baolong's army for about thirty minutes, but it felt like hours.

Look alive, the King and Lady Aileene are about to land, my dad broadcast to our troops and I watched them land on the field between our armies. I felt a sense of pride as I watched my king and soon to be queen put themselves in harm's way to protect us; unlike Carmanor,

Baolong or any of the others we'd fought who used their people as shields and treated them as things to be used.

Alister was trying to convince Baolong to surrender but I already knew it was useless. I wasn't really paying attention to what he was saying because I was listening to instructions from my dad.

Sheldon, when the King gives the command, lead your platoon up the middle to break through their line. Fight well.

Thanks, Dad, when we finish today, there's this great cake you have to try—

Attack, Alister shouted and we surged forward. I was leading fifty grizzly and polar bears and it was our job to hit the enemy hard. We were all wearing spiked armor which would give us protection that Baolong's troops didn't have and I hoped would make a difference. As we closed the distance with those rushing towards us, I had a glimpse of Joshua in his rhino form bursting through the gate from Carnivoria and mowing down the enemies before him.

And then I didn't have time to watch anyone else because I had my own battle to fight. I lowered my shoulder as I rammed into the unfortunate black bear that stood in my way. I felt the jolt when we hit but since I was almost twice the size of the Sirenean shifter he fell back from our onslaught and I raked him with my claws as I ran over him. Once we broke through the front line, we kept moving forward while the large cats rushed through the gap and started tearing into the terrified troops. Our first attack was so fierce, we gained a foothold against the enemy and we weren't going to give up any ground.

There was an ear splitting roar and I felt my stomach drop when I realized what that sound signified.

*She's got a Royal Dragon—*Alister broadcast and then his mental voice was cut off. *The King has engaged the enemy, let him do his job and we'll do ours,* I mentally shouted to our troops and we redoubled our attack.

I don't know how long I fought but the pattern was continual, engaging an enemy, avoiding the teeth, claws, sword, stinger, etc. of said enemy and keep fighting until it was incapacitated; repeat. The sounds of battle raged around me as the air was filled with roars, screams and the whooshing sound of arrows passing overhead. Countless arrows were deflected by my armor but occasionally, I felt the stabbing pain as one made it through an opening.

There was the sound of a sudden explosion to my right and I saw the body of one of my polar bears roll on the ground and lay still.

Dad, some of the soldiers have been rigged to explode when they're killed, I sent and was hit in the side and knocked over by an enemy tiger that had barreled into me. I rolled to my feet and ducked the clawed paw aiming for my head. Thankfully, the claws were deflected by my armor and the tiger screamed in rage. Rather than wait for him to attack again, I lunged forward and struck my enemy in the head with my clawed right paw. *Surrender,* I shouted at the tiger, but he took advantage of my momentary distraction to lunge for my neck to rip out my throat. I was again grateful for my armor as he got a mouthful of metal instead of my skin, but I was thrown off balance by the hit.

I narrowly avoided his snapping teeth as I raked my claws down his side, tearing him open. *Surrender,* I shouted again but he continued to attack, although he was much slower due to pain and blood loss. As he lunged again, I rose on my hind legs, brought my weight down on his back and turned so I could grab the back of his neck in my jaws. As I shook my head to break his neck, I saw the blinking red light on the backpack I'd just noticed he was wearing. I tossed him away just seconds before the backpack exploded and I felt myself being engulfed in flame and tossed backwards. *I hate getting blown up,* I thought as I hit the ground and lay there gasping for breath. *I'm sorry Bernie,* I sent as my sight dimmed.

Bernie

The rest of the healers and I were standing behind our army with the centaur archers. Mkali stood next to me and the fierce expression on her face reflected her determination to serve well. Part of me wanted to protect her from the war but since her parents were standing on the other side of her, she wouldn't appreciate it. There were times I still thought of her as a little girl, but in the centaur world she was a warrior and wouldn't like to be coddled.

This is boring, Shelley sent, and I laughed.

I'm sure you'll get enough excitement once Alister gives the signal to attack—be careful, I replied.

You as well. I love you Bernie, watch your back, Shelley responded.

Even though we stood on a field of battle waiting for the signal to attack, butterflies filled my stomach at those powerful words.

I love you too, you big oaf, I smiled and cut our mental connection.

Even though I hated being separated from my friends, I knew my duty and trusted in our battle plans.

Look alive, the King and Lady Aileene are about to land, Stavros broadcast to the army.

I trotted out of formation and raced up and down our line making sure our people were ready. I was in my unicorn form along with half of the unicorn shifters. The others were in human form and would ride their shifted partner to find wounded and either treat them where they lay or bring them behind our line for treatment. Each of us wore armbands or banners on our flanks signifying we were healers. Even though this was war, healers from either side were to be left alone so they could care for the wounded of both allies and enemies alike.

Attack, Alister shouted and the sky was suddenly filled with arrows flying towards the enemy. *I guess Baolong wasn't willing to surrender,* I thought to myself and ran back to my place so Gwayne could hop on my back.

May your arrows fly true, I sent to Mkali as I bounded away to look for wounded shifters.

There was an ear splitting roar followed by Alister's booming voice sounding in my head *She's got a Royal Dragon*—then nothing from him again. I wanted to rush to where I'd seen him last but knew that was futile, I was no match for a Royal Dragon. I would have to trust that Alister could handle this. I heard Aileene roar and saw a flash of her scales above me as she looked for Baolong.

"Sir Einhorn, twenty yards ahead at two o'clock," Gwayne called to me and I raced over to the downed bear. He was wearing the colors of Sirenea and he was barely breathing. Gwayne jumped down to help him and began to use his healing magic on his body.

Leave me, the shifter sent weakly, *I don't deserve your healing. Please tell the King I am sorry*—his mental voice trailed off and I looked at Gwayne.

"I've rendered him unconscious; he'll be okay. I've already stabilized him. Call the marshals and let them know we have a prisoner," Gwayne said as he turned him over to bind his arms with zip ties, something Alister brought back from his most recent trip to Earth.

Gwayne jumped back into the saddle and we quickly moved from one wounded shifter to the next. I was startled by an explosion and saw the body of a polar bear roll on the ground about twenty yards to my left. As I turned to race towards the downed body, I heard a cry from Gwayne and was knocked to the ground as he was ripped from my back. Transforming swiftly, I turned my momentum into a roll and sprang to my feet, my sword held in front of my body and confronted the werewolf who was holding Gwayne's headless body.

He carelessly tossed what was left of the healer to the side and sniffed the air and stalked towards me. "Unicorn," he growled, "I'm so hungry, you'll make a tasty treat." He opened his slavering jaws and let out a howl as he prepared to leap at me. I didn't waste any time and plunged my sword into his heart, killing him instantly.

"You talk too much," I said as I wiped my sword on his fur. *Baolong's fighters don't recognize medics as neutrals, watch yourselves,* I warned as I heard another explosion and felt agonizing pain through the mate bond I shared with Shelley. I staggered as if I'd been hit physically as Shelley's weak voice sounded in my mind, *I'm sorry, Bernie*—then nothing.

You will not die on me today I mentally shouted and followed our weakening connection. Shifters fought all around me as I raced to where I knew I'd find Shelley and I lashed out with my sword at anyone who came close to me while I filled Stavros in on what I knew.

Watch yourself Bernie, Baolong has wired her soldiers to explode when they die, Stavros sent back.

Rally to me, I shouted to our soldiers as I got closer to Shelley, *Sir Arktos needs our help.*

I felt the color drain from my face when I saw Shelley's bear lying on the ground. He had dozens of arrows sticking out of his body and his fur was burnt and bloody. I slid to the ground near his head, trusting in our troops to keep us safe. I reached out with my healing magic and could feel his life force draining from his body. Without thinking, I reached for the magic pouring through the baseball-sized gate from Middle Earth and channeled it through my body into Shelley's.

One time when I was little, I grabbed an electric fence because Shelley and Alister had dared me to do it. The jolt of electricity I felt that day was nothing compared to being struck by lightning like I was right now. I screamed in pain and terror but couldn't release my hold on Shelley. I could smell burning flesh as I collapsed on top of Shelley, and my last conscious thought was how much my hands hurt.

Aileene

Alister was going over some last minute instructions with Stavros but I was ready to engage the enemy. I had already transformed and was perched on the cliff looking down at the opposing armies. Ours seemed so small compared to Baolong's but I knew there were fifty thousand troops each from Eutheria, Metatheria, Cetacea, Marsupia, Carnivoria and the Kingdom of Theria ready to come to our aid when Alister opened the gates.

There wasn't a scenario where Baolong made it through the day alive although we were hoping to spare as many of her troops as possible. I was looking for the traitor when Alister walked up and rubbed his hand along my jaw. For fun, I nudged him with my snout, and he landed on his butt.

'I can tell you're ready to go," he laughed, and I chuffed in response.

Are you finally ready? I sent.

"Yes, everything's set. Let's not keep Baolong waiting any longer," he said and dove off the cliff. I watched him fall, then transform into his dragon and I growled in appreciation and followed him. We glided down and landed between the two armies. I kept my eyes trained on Baolong as she snaked her way through her troops. Her dragon really was beautiful with yellow scales on her belly and bright red everywhere else; it's too bad she was so evil and I'd have to destroy her.

My role in the battle was simple, I was supposed to fly around until Baolong shot her dragon bone missile at me, then I was to call for backup and kill Baolong. I had to promise Alister that I would stick to that plan so he could concentrate on dealing with Baolong's other secret weapon. We still didn't know what that was but felt it was up to Alister to deal with it.

Are you ready my love? Alister sent.

Let's do this, I responded enthusiastically.

Attack, Alister shouted then opened the gates he'd prepared. I felt the rush of magic as the baseball-sized gate was opened to Middle Earth and I cast the *Adamantem* spell upon myself. When Alister launched himself into the sky, I followed and began to fly over the battlefield trying to locate Baolong. How hard could it be to find a bright red Long Dragon, I thought to myself.

Alister broke through my musings, which was good because I was about to strafe the enemy troops with my fire, *Aileene, I see Baolong, she's in her human form and running toward the large tent behind the others.*

I turned my attention to the tent and saw Baolong scurrying towards it. She did something and the fabric was pulled away, but my eyes were on her as she transformed into her dragon and shot back into the sky. I beat the air with my powerful wings and rushed after her. I was about to let loose with a burst of flame when Alister broadcast *She has a Royal Dragon—* and his sending was cut off. I could sense the dismay and fear from Alister come through our connection and I was tempted to turn back to help him. There was a tremendous crash and I knew it was the sound of two Royal Dragon bodies impacting one another.

There was a flash of red ahead of me and my attention was drawn back to the fleeing Long Dragon. I had to trust Alister to take care of the Royal Dragon, just as he trusted me to take care of our enemy. I roared my rage and shot towards Baolong again. She seemed to be waiting for me to get to her and I realized it was a trap. At the same moment I put that together I was struck in the chest, I'd been shot with the dragon bone missile. I'd been so intent on killing Baolong, I'd momentarily forgotten about the bigger threat.

I waited for the pain, but instead saw the missile disintegrate on impact and all that remained was a cloud of bone dust. Unfortunately, I could also tell my *Adamantem* shield had dissipated upon impact. Rather than take a chance that Baolong only had one missile I tried to cast the spell again but before I could do that, I felt a searing pain down my side. I screamed in pain and looked around to see Baolong twisting in mid-air coming to attack me again.

I shied away from the swipe of her other claw and put some distance between the two of us. The air stung my open wound as I flew and tried to work out how she managed to hurt me so badly. There were flashes of light from the battlefield and I heard explosions. I watched in horror as members of Baolong's army exploded, killing our shifters in the process.

Captain Jormis flew past me as I soared above the carnage, shooting shards of ice at Baolong who was once again on my tail. He managed to get her to veer off course so she didn't hit me again, but she was close enough that I got a good look at her claws and teeth; they were covered in dragon bone. Even though she was dangerous, I was now confident she didn't have another missile, so I called in my backup.

Captain Jormis, stay out of reach of her teeth and claws but can you and the other flyers keep her off me?

Yes, Lady Aileene, how long do you need?

A minute?

We're on it. He sent and I watched as Captain Jormis, Dad and Uncle James attacked Baolong to keep her away from me while I did what I had to do.

Father, Mother, the missile has been destroyed and some members of Baolong's army are rigged to explode as we feared.

Thank you, we're on our way, Mother sent, and I watched her fly through the gate from Theria.

Stavros have your troops fall back while Beatrice and I take care of this, Father commanded as he flew after Mother.

I knew they would do whatever they could to convince Baolong's soldiers to surrender but they would rain fire down on those who wouldn't. They weren't willing to lose any more of our fighters to treachery. I was tempted to see how Alister was doing in his fight, but I didn't want to distract either one of us and I had a traitor to put down.

Baolong, I'm coming for you, I roared and quickly found my prey.

If you come close, I'll kill you with my teeth and claws. I don't know how you survived my missile, but I know I cut you open when I hit you.

I had her in my sights now and gained on her as she tried to fly away.

Oh, you hurt me when you sliced me with those dragon bone claws but you've lost the element of surprise and you've forgotten something.

The panic coming from Baolong was palpable and only intensified as I drew closer to her.

You may have pieces of a Royal Dragon that can hurt me, but everything about me can hurt you. I matched her pace and flew above and slightly behind her now.

Mercy, she cried when she knew she couldn't get away from me no matter how many twists and turns she tried.

The only mercy you'll receive from me will be a swift death, you should never have murdered the people you were sworn to protect, and you shouldn't have tried to kill my mate.

With that I let loose a blast of inferno fire and Baolong was blasted into oblivion so quickly she didn't even have time to cry out. As my fire turned her to ash, there was a blinding flash of light and I knew the dragon bone had been destroyed as well. Satisfied that I had done what I promised Alister I would, I turned back toward the battlefield so I could help my mate defeat his foe.

Alister

Time slowed as the enormous onyx dragon drew closer, I could see rage in his eyes as our chests collided. As we fell, we used our teeth and back claws to rend and tear into one another. My claws tore through his scales like they were made of tissue paper, but his claws were doing the same thing to me. He opened his mouth wide and tried to tear out my throat, but I jerked to the left and he latched onto my right shoulder instead.

We were thrown apart when we hit the ground, so I had a momentary reprieve from the attack and was able to cast the *Adamantem* and *Sanos* spells at the same time. Since my magical reservoir was filled, I healed instantly. As tempting as it was to take a moment to check on my friends now that I was shielded, I had to trust in their abilities and face the foe in front of me.

We circled each other and I tried to connect with him on a mental level.

I don't know what Baolong promised you, but we don't have to fight, I sent but my sending bounced back at me. The dragon used his neck to strike out at me like a snake and he grabbed my left foreleg with his teeth. He couldn't break through my shield, but he did wrench my leg when he pulled his head back and I felt the bone snap. I kept trying to mentally reach him, but it was no use, the dragon attacking me didn't have a dual nature—he was an enraged wild dragon without any humanity. The only way for me to survive this encounter was to kill the unfortunate creature before me.

As I was about to strike out, I felt Aileene's pain through our connection and I faltered. That was enough to give my enemy a chance to hit me with his flame. My shield held but I could feel my reservoir draining to support the integrity of the spell. If I stayed where I was the flame would overwhelm me and I would be too injured to continue the fight. I transformed into my human form; grateful I had enough magic left to protect my body and ran towards the enraged dragon. My broken left arm throbbed as I ran but my sudden change was enough to confuse him so I could run under his belly and transform into my dragon.

My sudden shift had the desired effect as my spikes punched through his belly and the sudden expansion of my body threw him off me as the *Adamantem* spell completely failed. He screamed in rage and pain and I propeled myself into the sky to put some distance between us. Even though he was wounded he was still incredibly fast and latched onto my tail and dragged me back to the ground. The impact didn't hurt but I landed on my side and was vulnerable to his teeth and claws.

As he tore into my flank, I snaked my head around and blasted him on the left side of his face with my plasma torch. He roared again and scrambled away from the deadly fire as I slowly got to my feet. Enough magic had filled my reservoir for me to cast *Sanos* again and my pain vanished and the bleeding stopped. When I spread my wings wide and roared in challenge my enemy backed away with his head lowered, hissing like a snake.

Growling, I stalked forward as the mighty dragon cowered before me. As I took in a breath to finish this battle, he lunged forward and as I jumped out of the way of his attack, he took to the sky trying to escape. If he were a normal shifter, I could accept his surrender but wasn't able to show mercy to this deadly animal who could decimate the entire continent if left to roam free.

My heart was heavy as I followed this unfortunate creature. He was only acting according to his nature and was defending his territory against another male dragon, but I couldn't let that sway me from what I had to do. As I climbed, I kept the dragon in my sight as he flew away from the battle. We were about five miles out when I decided we'd flown far enough. He was to my right and about a quarter mile below me and I dove towards his exposed neck.

Since his left eye was useless on the severely burned side, he never saw me coming as I landed on his back, my claws digging in while I bit down on the back of his neck in the space between two of the protective spikes. He thrashed as we fell but I held on viciously shaking my head and continued to dig into his neck until I severed his spine. We were about a hundred feet from the ground when I leapt from his back and unfurled my wings to hover while his lifeless body impacted on the rocks below.

The dragon is dead and once I destroy the body I'll come back, I mentally broadcast to Stavros because I didn't want to distract anyone else if they were fighting for their lives.

No need, Sire, we have things well in hand here. Those who haven't surrendered are dead, your parents took care of that while Lady Aileene destroyed Baolong.

Alister, we're coming to you, Aileene shouted so I lay down to wait for their arrival. As I looked at the dead dragon before me, I was overwhelmed with grief as I thought of the death and destruction Baolong, Carmanor and Dimitri caused in their rebellion against the High Kingdom.

I felt Aileene before I saw her and looked to the west to see her flying rapidly towards me. My parents were flying side-by-side behind her and they all sped up when they saw me.

Are you bleeding? I asked Aileene when she landed.

Baolong had her claws and teeth tipped with dragon bone and I got careless, she sounded embarrassed.

I transformed and placed my hand on her side and healed her as my parents landed. Aileene shifted when I was finished, and we stood looking at the dead dragon.

"Where did he come from?" Father asked in wonder.

"Hopefully, we'll find some explanation in Baolong's palace," I answered. "I don't know what she did, but he was a wild dragon, he only acted on animal instincts."

Aileene put her arm around my waist and put her head on my chest because she could feel my emotions and the pain I was in because I had to put the dragon down.

"You did what you had to do, we all did," she said, and I silently thanked her.

"We can't leave this carcass here," Mother said, "we need to burn the body with our hottest flames."

"Let's do what we did to Dimitri's castle," Aileene suggested and we moved to the four cardinal points so we could shift and immolate the body. Even though I was saddened so many had died, I was relieved we had stopped Baolong and could now rebuild Sirenea and finally reunite all the kingdoms under my rule. I looked at these three people I loved so much and was filled with gratitude that we were in this together. As I was about to shift, a thought struck me, so I asked, "Where are Shelley and Bernie?"

CHAPTER FOURTEEN

e waded through the carnage as we toured the battlefield. Tattered banners stirred listlessly in the slight breeze that blew acrid smoke from the fires, which stung my eyes. Healers were huddled over the wounded, valiantly striving to save those who still had a spark of life. Lifeless bodies lay where they'd collapsed, a silent testimony to all that had been lost. Yes, we'd defeated Baolong and prevented future death and destruction, but we had paid an astounding price.

Aileene slipped her hand in mine in silent support. I had to stop postponing the inevitable, so I walked to where my two best friends had fallen. Shelley was still in his bear form and Bernie in her human form, draped over his back. Mkali and a contingent of soldiers stood guard, facing outward and I could see where Mkali's tears had left clean lines through the grime on her face. The soldiers parted as we walked closer, allowing us to stand beside our friends.

I felt and heard Aileene's grief as her sobbing broke the silence; I squeezed her hand comfortingly. Bernie and Shelley looked so peaceful together that I hated to disturb them, but we couldn't leave their bodies out here to be ravaged by the carrion birds that were already circling overhead. I bent down and kissed the foreheads of first Bernie, then Shelley.

"Farewell my friends, until we meet again in An'Ceann's kingdom," I managed to choke and placed my hands on their bodies as my grief overwhelmed me.

I'm not dead yet—Shelley whispered in my mind.

"It turns out both Bernie and I were so exhausted from the healing we didn't have the energy to move and could only use thought-speech with those we were touching," Shelley said between bites as he shoveled food into his mouth.

"At least we had each other to talk to but I'll admit it was scary being frozen in place like that," Bernie continued.

Shelley picked up the story. "Well, we weren't too worried since An'Ceann met us on that cliff you've told us about and let us know it wasn't our time to cross over to his kingdom yet and we were being sent back—oh, I just thought about this. What if he meant it wasn't time right then but if you hadn't found us when you did and poured in your healing energy, it would have been time to cross over then?" He just shrugged and continued eating.

"Well, you found us so, we'll just leave it at that," Bernie added and pushed her plate away with a groan. "I'm completely stuffed but am finally starting to feel more like myself. No, go ahead," she said to Shelley when he motioned to her plate and she smiled fondly at him when he scraped the rest of the food from her plate onto his and kept eating.

"I see your near-death experience hasn't diminished your appetite," I smiled at my friend.

"Hey, it takes a lot of calories to heal from getting blown up," Shelley joked and stretched. "That's the second time I've been caught in an explosion, I'd rather never do it again."

"I'd rather you never do it again, either. I've had to see your bloody, tattered body two times and that's enough for me," Bernie said and lay her head on his chest. Even though we'd shared our parts in the battle while we ate, I could tell by Shelley's gray pallor that he was even more disturbed by their near death than he wanted to admit.

"Well, unless we've more enemies we don't know about, we should have a break for a bit. We've reunited the seven kingdoms and defeated those who were leading the rebellion. What else could go wrong?" Aileene asked.

Bernie, Shelley and I groaned and started talking over each other explaining to Aileene why it was a terrible idea to ask that question. We gave her examples from TV shows and movies about the worst that happened after someone asked something like this. She laughed at our antics as we debated the best of the examples we gave her. Even though the conversation was frivolous, it was exactly what we needed to remind us that there was life to live even though we'd seen horrible things. It was the best way to spend the rest of the night.

Ceitain 24, 10,258

Sirenea

We spent a week on the battlefield tending the wounded, burying the dead and trying the remaining members of Baolong's army. Of the ten thousand soldiers, over half had died in the battle and another thousand were willing participants in the rebellion and had enslaved and used the explosive devices on their fellow Sireneans. My father offered to preside over the trials and executions but as much as I appreciated his willingness to spare me from these events, as King I had to see them through.

We found a broken and emaciated Galen Forelock locked in Baolong's dungeon. She had forced him to interrogate those Baolong suspected of treachery and the diplomat had to witness unspeakable horrors starting with the rest of his traveling companions being fed to the dragon. Fritz and Frieda escorted him back to the Royal Palace where he would receive the best mental and physical healing available.

Alister, I'm here with your parents, are you ready for us? Aileene called to me and I stood from the desk in Baolong's former throne room where I'd been writing instructions for the new rulers of Sirenea. Even though I yawned as I stretched, I wasn't tired; I hadn't had another of my disturbing dreams since our victory. It's amazing how rejuvenating dreamless sleep can be.

Come on in, I'll send for a snack. After asking the kitchen to send enough food for four hungry dragons, I welcomed my parents and asked them to join Aileene and me on the couches in the sitting area. Mom and Aileene chatted about renovation plans in our palace while Father and I talked about the problems we were facing in choosing a new ruler for Sirenea. Once we were served and the steward withdrew from the room, I cast the *Indicens* spell to shield the room so our conversation couldn't be overheard.

"What have you discovered about the dragon egg clutch," I asked.

Rage flashed across his face before he answered, and a wisp of smoke curled from his nostril. Mother placed a calming hand on his knee and after a deep, cleansing breath he answered. "They've all been destroyed. We were able to find out about the book written by Zhèng the Merciless that Baolong bragged about and that led us to the location of the clutch. She destroyed thirty eggs in her attempt to hatch a Royal Dragon and only managed to incubate two of them. Of the two eggs that hatched, only one dragon survived into adulthood and that one was a wild dragon, as you know. The other dragon, a female, was killed by the male and her bones were used to create the weapons used against you and Aileene.

"Fortunately for us, Baolong kept copious records and every piece of bone has been accounted for and destroyed. Unless a Queen Dragon supplies eggs for a new clutch in the future, there will never be another Royal Dragon coming from Sirenea."

"I'm not so sure that's a bad thing," Mother added. "Sirenea has a bloody history when it comes to Royal Dragons. Believe it or not, Zhèng the Merciless was considered kind compared to other Sirenean Royal Dragons throughout history."

"I think it's time we change the history of Sirenea and that has to start with the new rulers we appoint," I said thoughtfully as I took a sip of my Mountain Dew. I was grateful that Josef sent regular shipments of my favorite soda through the gate so I could enjoy it whenever I wanted.

"Alister and I discussed this, and we've decided to ask if you two would be willing to be co-rulers of Sirenea. We aren't trying to get rid of you," Aileene added hastily, "but we need someone strong enough to face the challenges inherent with ruling Sirenea but also completely loyal to the High King and invested in the welfare of all Theria."

"We don't expect an answer right away—"

"Yes," Mother interrupted me, and I laughed. "C'mon Phillip, you've enjoyed acting as Regent as much as I have in Alister's absence and we'll be bored to death if we spend all our time on the beach. We'll be able to gate home to see the kids any time we want, or they can visit us and with the new technology our son is insisting each kingdom uses it'll be even easier to stay connected."

Father laughed at Mother's enthusiasm. "You don't have to talk me into this, I was going to say yes as well, but you beat me to it. Are you sure, Son? We don't want to step on your toes," Father finished lamely, and I stood.

"By the power and authority vested in me as High King of all Theria by An'Ceann, I hereby appoint you, Lord Phillip and you, Lady Beatrice, to the office as co-rulers over Sirenea until either death take you or you are released from your duties by the High King or Queen of Theria. Do you accept?"

It was humbling when my parents each took a knee and agreed to serve the Crown faithfully and we took turns hugging each other in joy at this turn of events. I knew there was a lot of work to be done to heal Sirenea, but I also knew my parents were up to the task.

The four of us discussed our future plans for Sirenea over an intimate meal. They planned to ask Fritz, Frieda, Stavros and Miriam to stay on to help until they could select Sirenean natives who would choose to put the needs of the people over their own. For the first time since I left Theria on this around-the-world journey, I felt like the seven kingdoms were truly reunited and I was filled with joy.

Ceitain 25, 10,258
    Theria
    Royal Palace

Aileene and I stood on the roof of the Royal Palace watching the meteor shower in the night sky. We'd enjoyed a sumptuous feast created by the chefs we'd brought from every kingdom on Theria and watched a movie with Bernie, Shelley and Mkali but had stolen away for some time to ourselves; sort of.

"Hey Shelley, if you and Bernie are going to stand guard for us, even when I expressly told you we wanted to be by ourselves, could you please try to be less gassy?"

"Hey, it's not my fault. Those chimichangas from Metatheria give me indigestion," Shelley complained.

"It is your fault because you ate a dozen of them," Bernie grumbled. "Oh, switch sides with me, Sir Fartsalot so I'm not downwind from you. I swear if I hadn't seen you turn into a bear, I'd think you were a pig shifter."

"Anyway—my point is, Aileene and I are trying to have a moment to ourselves. We don't need you two providing comic relief," I laughed.

"I don't know, I think they are kind of funny," Aileene mock whispered.

"And that's why you're my favorite, oof—" Shelley said before Bernie smacked him in the stomach.

"All I wanted was some time with just you," I grumbled to Aileene and she leaned in and gave me a quick kiss.

"You'll have plenty of time to spend together," An'Ceann said as we were suddenly standing before him in a field of flowers, "centuries, in fact."

Aileene squealed in delight and flung her arms around his neck and buried her face in his mane. I'd like to say I was statelier in my reaction but except for the squeal, I did the same as Aileene. An'Ceann rolled on his side and we found ourselves lying on top of him, the sun shining brightly about us.

"Why are we here?" Aileene asked.

"I wanted to let you know how proud I am of you and to thank you for reuniting Theria. You acted with courage and resolve and saved millions of lives."

"Thank you," I whispered, "it wasn't easy."

"Nothing good ever is," he said, "but you'll find it's always worth the effort in the end."

"I was afraid you were going to tell us to get ready for another battle already," Aileene admitted.

An'Ceann laughed, "Not yet, there are more wrongs to right but for now, you get to rest and enjoy your new life as High King and soon to be High Queen of Theria. You may not see me for a while, but I want you to know I'm always with you—I'm just not always under you," he said and disappeared.

We were instantly back on the roof of the palace and in a heap on the ground.

"He loves doing that," I laughed and helped Aileene to her feet, his laughter echoing around us.

Aileene put her arms around me and said, "Well, we might not have any battles to fight for a bit, but I know that each day with you will be an adventure and that's the way I like it."

"Me, too," I said and kissed her, suddenly nervous as I felt the weight of the ring in my pocket. I broke off the kiss and held her at arm's length. She gave me a puzzled expression but I was determined to continue.

"Hey you two reprobates, since you insist on intruding on our private moment, I want you to bear witness," I called out to Bernie and Shelley. They approached quietly, with eyes full of expectations for what was about to happen.

"Aileene, even though we know we're made for each other and are destined to be mates, I want to make this official," I said and pulled the ring from my pocket as I knelt before her on bended knee. Aileene smiled widely and I heard a squeal of delight from Bernie.

"My love, will you agree to be my wife and marry me on the morning of my coronation?"

Aileene nodded her head while tears of joy streamed down her face. *Nothing would make me happier, Alister. I will be yours now and forever,* she broadcast and pulled me to my feet after I slipped the ring onto her finger.

With Bernie and Shelley standing beside us, arm in arm, I kissed the woman who would soon be my wife and High Queen of Theria. Suddenly, a meteor shower painted the starry sky with a brilliant display of light that was reflected in Aileene's watery eyes. I couldn't help but feel this was An'Ceann's way of blessing our formal engagement.

EPILOGUE

I sat in the conference room and Lady Omalen and Queen Brooklyn were on the screen. They were evidently nervous as they kept looking side to side and flinching at things going on in Marsupia. Even though they were trying to tell me something, I couldn't hear their voices. I realized this was a dream because I had no recollection of how I arrived or why I was in my pajamas. It had been quite a while since I'd had one of these dreams so I was curious to see how it would play out.

The co-rulers on the screen jerked their heads to the right and their eyes widened in fright. The camera on their end was obscured by a sudden blizzard and when it cleared, the room was blanketed in snow. Omalen and Brooklyn were encased in ice, expressions of terror frozen on their faces. A woman swept into view and carelessly shoved Omalen out of her chair, as her body fell to the floor it shattered like a glass dropped onto rocks.

The woman settled herself into the recently vacated chair and smiled, showing her pointed teeth. Her ethereal beauty took my breath away. Her skin was unblemished and the same color as newly fallen snow and she wore a midnight-blue gown lined with fur. Her black eyes were ancient, and she wore a crown that seemed to be made of icicles. Her power was palpable even from thousands of miles away and when she spoke, her voice was a rich contralto that made me shiver.

"I am Mab, Queen of the Winter Court and I have come to take back what is mine."

AFTERWORD

Thank you for reading *Rebellion*. I love authoring these stories and would appreciate it if you'd take a few minutes to leave a review so I can learn what you think about *Rebellion*, as well as the previous books. As an independent author, reviews help my books get noticed and help me grow as a writer.

Rebellion wraps up the first story arc for Alister and his friends. Alister will return in *Winter-Dragonborn Book Five* at some point but he needs a bit of a break. I've put him through a lot since he learned he was a Royal Dragon. But don't worry, I'm going to write more stories in the Dragonborn Universe and have two new series planned so far.

Tionchar Tales is an Urban Fantasy series geared more for an adult audience. This series will deal with some darker themes as the shifters on Earth confront human evil in its many guises. You'll get a chance to see how Cyndi, Brian, Wayne and Josef use their powers to *Protect the Weak*.

Therian Shapeshifter Academy is a series geared for children and set on Theria. The main protagonist is ten-year-old Mkali, and the series reveals how she grows into her role as a squire as well as learning how to connect with other shifters her age. Of course, they will have lots of adventures and interact with Bernie, Shelley, Aileene and Alister.

I started *Rebellion* on April 13, 2020 and finished on July 23, 2020. What a crazy three-month journey that was. Not only were we dealing with COVOD-19, racial and social injustice, but my wife was also diagnosed with Breast Cancer. We're grateful the doctor was able to remove the cancer through DMX surgery and she is 98-99% cured but not everyone with Breast Cancer is so lucky. I pledge to donate a portion of each *Rebellion* book sold to the Dr. Susan Love Research Foundation. For more information about the good work they do feel free to check out drsusanloveresearch.org.

I'm grateful for your support as an author and love hearing from you. My contact information is on my website. Visit www.bretthumphreyauthor.com for cool stuff and updates on what's next in this series, and beyond. While you're there, I invite you to join my text notification service and sign up for my email distribution list for announcements, random stuff and weekly dragon jokes. Just follow the **Stay in Touch** link on the menu. I look forward to hearing from you.

I hope Alister and his friends inspire you to make a positive impact in the life of someone you connect with every day.

Brett Humphrey

August 2020

Protect the Weak!

SHIFTER GLOSSARY AND PRONUNCIATION GUIDE

Earth and Therian Month Crosswalk:
  January: Faollich (Fowl-itch)
  February: Garwan (Gar-one)s
  March: Mart (Mart)
  April: An'Ceann (Awn-Sheen)
  May: Giplane (Gee-plane)
  June: Ceitain (She-tain)
  July: Lunsdail (Luns-dale)
  August: Athas (At-tas)
  September: Síocháin (Show-chain)
  October: Damlar (Dam-lar)
  November: Suttain (Sut-tane)
  December: Dóchas (Doe-Chaz)

Adamantem: (Adam-ant-em) Magic spell which can be used to make skin hard enough to turn aside Royal Dragon bone

Cecaelia: (See-say-ee-lya) Octopus person with the head, arms and torso of a human and, from the lower torso down the tentacles of an octopus.

Hatari: (Ha-tar-ee) Beast of burden found in Carnivoria. Can be ridden like a horse or connected to a harness to pull wagons. It resembles a large monitor lizard, is vicious and can capture its prey using its long tongue like a frog.

Ice Dragon: Dragon capable of shooting ice from its mouth rather than fire, able to freeze anything in its path. Can also shoot out ice spikes.

Indicens: (In-dice-ens) Magic spell to create a shield of silence so sounds cannot get in or out of it.

Kingdom of Carnivoria: (Car-ni-vor-eeya)

Kingdom of Cetacea: (Set-a-see-a)

Kingdom of Eutheria: (Eww-there-eeya)

Kingdom of Marsupia: (Mar-soup-eeya)

Kingdom of Metatheria: (Met-a-there-eeya)

Kingdom of Sirenea: (Siren-eeya)

Kingdom of Theria: (There-eeya)

Kraken: (Crack-in) Enormous squid-like creature able to destroy ships with its tentacles and huge maw of razor sharp teeth. Has the ability to change colors to blend into its environment.

Lady Baolong: (Bow-long) Ruler of Sirenea.

Lady Falenas Omalen: (Fa-lean-as Oma-len) Part of the coalition government in Marsupia.

Lady Kudanganya: (Cu-dang-ann-ya) Married to Lord Carmanor.

Lady Morwenna: (More-wenna) Ruler of Metatheria

Lady Zhaleh: (Za-le) Ruler of Cetacea

Lord Carmanor: (Car-man-ore) Ruler of Carnivoria

Lord Joshua Vefiru: (Vef-i-roo) Ruler of Carnivoria

Ngiri: (Na-gee-ree) Warthog-like creature found in Carnivoria.

Pixie: (Picks-ee) Small, winged-fairy found in the forest. Usually peace-loving but can be fierce if provoked. Only the most powerful can transform to the size of an adult human.

Plesiosaur: (Plee-see-uh-sor) Creature resembling the extinct marine reptile found on Earth. It has a long torpedo-shaped body, long tail and four flippers instead of legs. It also has a long serpentine neck.

Stark: (Stark) Magic spell to create a beam of energy from the caster's hand which pushes any object away at high speed.

Visus Magicae: (Vee-sus Magi-kay) Magic sight-allows the caster to see magical workings.